No More Trumpets

No More Trumpets

AND OTHER STORIES

BY

George Milburn

Short Story Index Reprint Series

BOOKS FOR LIBRARIES PRESS
FREEPORT, NEW YORK

Reprinted 1970 by arrangement with Mrs. George Milburn
and her literary agents, Paul R. Reynolds, Inc.

INTERNATIONAL STANDARD BOOK NUMBER:
0-8369-3699-X

LIBRARY OF CONGRESS CATALOG CARD NUMBER:
79-134968

PRINTED IN THE UNITED STATES OF AMERICA

TO DR. GEORGE H. SEMKEN

Grateful acknowledgments are hereby made to the publications in which these stories first appeared: the American Mercury, Folk-Say, Harper's Magazine, *the* New Yorker, Real America, Scribner's Magazine, *the* Southwest Review, *and* Story. *Some of these stories also were reprinted in* Evening Standard (*London*), Der Uhu (*Berlin*), *and in the* 1931, 1932, *and* 1933 *volumes of O'Brien's* Best Short Stories.

CONTENTS

[redacted] [redacted]

I

THE VISIT TO UNCLE JAKE'S

MY GRANDFATHER BEALS was a slow-talking man. His talk was that of the Virginia hills, and I suppose that the whining Arkansas share-croppers and the drawling Texans thought him a little queer on account of it. They could understand why their farm neighbors from Kansas and Iowa and other Yankees and foreigners had strange accents, but a man whose talk was Southern and yet unlike their own was unaccountable. They used to mimic the old man when he wasn't around.

His way of talking slowly and gently gave him an innocent air that was a good help to him in his cotton business. While he had a name for honesty and pride, his methods, perhaps, were as sharp as the next cotton-buyer's. Lots of times the farmers, misled by those guileless accents, would be bested in a deal at the very moment they felt that they were skinning the simple old man.

Although his dialect got him a reputation for eccentricity, the only surprising thing I ever heard of his doing was buying a Ford touring-car. During the War he made money with cotton, and after the War he was able to retire, well fixed. He was about sixty-five then, tall and dignified, with a fine head of white hair. The first thing he did, after he sold the good-will of his cotton business, was buy a flivver.

That was extraordinary, because he had done without a car in his cotton business, where he had had a real need for one. Year after year he had driven about the country, sizing up the cotton crop, in a ramshackle old phaëton hitched to a team of roans. The automobile agents had been after him for years, but he had put them off. Then, when he was an old man and out of business, he up and bought an automobile for his own pleasure.

I say for his own pleasure, because my Grandmother Beals refused, from the day he came driving up with the salesman, to ride with him in his automobile. There was wisdom in her decision, too. My Grandfather Beals never did get to be a very good driver. He had the most trouble with the foot-pedals which that model Ford had for gear shifts, and he was apt to step on the reverse instead of the brake and go wheeling backward to the detriment of whatever was behind him. Another thing that made riding with my Grandfather Beals a dubious pleasure was his habitual neglect of the steering-wheel. Driving his roans in the old days he got used to letting the reins fall idle across the dashboard while he pointed and gestured toward the fields along the way. When he began driving the Ford he was likely to let go the wheel completely while he motioned toward a fine stand of cotton.

It was a wonder that he didn't kill himself and others too. He didn't, though. He plowed through barbed wire, he backed off into deep ditches, he knocked a row of cast-iron palings off the neighbor's ornamental fence, and once he broke out one end of the converted stable in which he kept the car. The new flivver got woefully scratched and battered, but my grandfather always came through unscathed. That is, excepting the acid comments of my grandmother. They must have wounded him.

But he was a headstrong man, and my grandmother's ridicule served only to make him more determined. He practiced driving on country dirt roads, and he cut a droll figure, jouncing over the ruts with his legs akimbo, crooked up on each side of the steering-wheel. He escaped having any serious accident, and in a few months he was getting the gully-jumper up around twenty-five miles an hour regularly.

II

It was about this time that presages of the post-war business depression were beginning to appear. The first was a lowering of prices on Fords. My Grandfather Beals saw then that he could have saved fifty dollars had he waited two or three months to buy his car. He took this as a personal grievance against Henry Ford. The manufacturer had got the best of him in a business deal. At the time he had bought his car from him, Ford had known that prices were going to be lowered shortly, and he had taken my grandfather to a cleaning. Other price-cutting followed and hard times were at hand. My Grandfather Beals blamed Henry Ford for everything.

"That man Fohd," he would say in opening his remarks on the subject, "that man Fohd ought to be took out and hanged on the highest tree in the land."

His resentment was so strong that he could no longer get any pleasure out of driving his automobile. He would have sold it, but it was so bent and torn, it would have brought scarcely any price at all, even if the market had not been falling. So he drove the Ford touring-car into the stable, where he had cut out the stalls and mangers to make a garage, and there it stayed for several years, gray and dejected under its coating of silt and straw and dust.

There was only one thing, perhaps, that could have made my grandfather forget his grudge and set those narrow-tired, mud-crusted wheels in motion again. That came one morning in the fourth June of his retirement. It was word from his brother Jacob.

He hadn't seen or heard from Jacob in more than fifty years. There had been eight brothers in that family. As each of them had come of age, the father had given him a horse, saddle and bridle, a jug of brandy and twenty dollars in cash and had told him to light out. Some of them had ridden west, some of them had ridden south, and one of them had ridden over the hill to marry a moonshiner's daughter.

Jacob was the oldest, so he was the first to go. His going made a strong impression on my grandfather, a boy of fifteen, and he carried the memory of it through the years. He had stood in the yard with the rest of the family that morning watching Jacob mount up. Better than half a century had passed since he had stood gazing after Jacob galloping away from the hills, the jug of liquor bouncing at the saddle-side and the twenty silver dollars clanking in time.

In later years Jacob's destiny was my grandfather's favorite topic for surmise. He would spend futile hours making guesses about what had become of his oldest brother. Out of fictitious circumstance he would build up possible careers for Jacob, and then, at the end, he would reject all of them.

He had kept up with all the others. His brother Charlie, he knew, had a good thing of it with a melon farm in Colorado. Lacey had frozen to death in the Yukon, Web had a homestead in Idaho, Dick was a tobacco farmer back East, and so on down the line. But Jacob interested him more than all the others put together, and of Jacob he knew nothing.

Then one morning the letter came bearing word of my grandfather's oldest brother. It had an Arkansas postmark, and it was written by Jacob's second wife.

She explained that they had been married three years. She had been a widow and he had been a widower and both of them had families grown and gone away. She called Jacob "daddy," and I thought that was out of keeping when I read the letter. Daddy had often wondered about his brothers and sisters, but he had never made any attempt to get in touch with them. At last she had written to the cross-roads postmaster near the old home back in the Virginia hills, and from him she had obtained the addresses of various members of the family. Daddy was getting old, she wrote, and she thought it would be nice if he could hear from his favorite brother before he passed on.

My grandfather was not a demonstrative man, but the letter put him in a transport of joy. He was triumphant. It was as if he, unaided, had worried through to the solution of a problem that had puzzled everyone for ages. He wore the letter to a limp, ink-stained frazzle, rereading it, studying it, speculating on ambiguous phrases, trying to read more than was in the writing.

The woman wrote a fine Spencerian hand, making her first esses like f's and finishing off words with slight curlicues. That was a good sign. Jacob's second wife was an educated woman. My grandfather said, "Well, Jake's got him a good woman, as old as he is, so he must have got to be somebody." But the handwriting was wavering, and that showed that the woman was old.

My Grandfather Beals got a road-map of Arkansas and began hunting for the town of the postmark. It was a hard search. But finally, deep among the hachures of the Ozarks, dense as a handful of eyebrows, he located the name in print so fine it was barely legible. The discovery delighted him almost as much as the letter had, and he was in a fever of excitement.

That same day he backed the old Ford out of the stable. It was the first time he had laid hand on it in three years. He washed it carefully. What black enamel there was left on the scarred, dented sides was peeling, so he made a quick job of repainting the body. He used some paint he had around the barn. When this turned out to be a peculiar shade of green, my grandfather insisted that it was "ginger blue," a good color and the very one he was after.

He made his preparations quickly, and when he announced one night that he was going on a trip over into the Arkansas hills the next day, and that my brother Ed and I were going along, he took everyone so completely by surprise, no one opposed him. At least that is the only explanation I can make for our ever going with him on that wild trip. As I remember it, no one raised any objection at the time. All I remember is that my grandfather told me and Ed the evening before we started that we'd have to get to bed early, because we were going to start for Arkansas the next morning before day.

"It's three hundud mile, a right smaht piece," my Grandfather Beals said, "and we ah goin' to staht in the mawnin' befo' day."

III

The cold engine banged and started all the roosters in the neighborhood crowing before their time. A spasm shook the old car and it shivered and clanked as my grandfather twisted the wheel around and the flivver lights cut a broad arc. We rolled out of the abandoned barnyard, halting for Ed to get out and close the gate. Ed ran back and got up in the front seat. I sat in the back drowsing and running my tongue over my front teeth, feeling the place where the breakfast coffee had scalded it.

We rattled out of town and went wheeling eastward at a great speed. The lights let a dim, quivering swath ahead on the dirt road, turning the cool, dewy dust to talcum. My grandfather pulled the gas-lever down and the powdered road went slithering out from under us. Ed and I held on for dear life. Through the dark we could make out the grim set of Grandfather Beals's jaw.

It was getting light and the foot-hills had appeared out of the dusk before us when he finally pushed the throttle back up to its usual notch. As the speed slackened and the engine quieted, he turned to Ed.

"I alluhs like to staht in like I can hold out," he said, smiling softly.

These were the first words spoken, and Ed took advantage of the opening to ask, "How long are we going to stay over in Arkansas, grandpa?"

"Oh, we'll talk about that when we get thah. Me and brothah Jake ah goin' to have lots to talk about."

He had put the treeless prairies behind us and we were in the shaded hills when the sun, like a bloody thumb, came poking up through the mist wreaths.

As day broadened and we were rolling along at a more leisurely rate, my Grandfather Beals began to take notice of the surrounding landscape. We were climbing a mountain road, where a slight jog to the right would have meant plunging over the bluff into the creek-bottom, hundreds of feet below. My grandfather let go the wheel and threw out both his hands with a Delsartian gesture toward the smoky valley.

"Now, look ye thah!" he exclaimed. "Ain't that a mästuh sight?"

"Watch it, grandpa, watch it!" said Ed, snatching at the wheel.

Grandfather Beals resumed the wheel coolly and held it until, a short distance on, a vineyard marching up over a hill-top attracted his attention.

"See thah, you boys. You-all ain't nevah seen nothin' like that. That just like back East. You-all ain't nevah known what it is to live in the hill country."

And he was forgetful of the steering-wheel again.

Occasionally we would stop to consult the road-map, or to question ruminative mountaineers.

"Just keep right on follerin' this main-traveled road, and it'll get you whurever you're goin'," they always said.

The road led through summer-resort towns with their concrete, wire-fenced bathing-pools, past tall-stacked canning factories, along the base of high, sheer stone bluffs, with Bible texts, sets of gums and teeth advertising dental parlors, and short Holy Roller exhortations stenciled on the rock. By noon, however, these encroachments vanished. We were deep in the hill country. We came to the town of the postmark.

The postmaster let his tilted chair thump down on the store-porch floor. "They's a Jake Beals that gets his mail out on the Goshen Road," the postmaster said, rubbing his thighs, "but most possible he lives off back of the road a ways."

All along the Goshen Road, an engine-racking mountain trail, we stopped to look at mail-boxes. Finally we found one, almost hidden by tall weeds, with "Jake Beals" scrawled on it in black paint. There was no sign of a house, but a narrow, rock-strewn lane wound off from the road.

After we turned off on this lane, I remember thinking that it was all very much like one of those Irish stories in which the heroes are always stepping over into the land of youth. Grandfather Beals had hurtled us back through fifty years of time with his quaking flivver, let alone over a hundred miles of high road and low road.

When I got out to inquire at a cabin, I noticed a hand-wrought grubbing-hoe in the yard and the ax sticking in the chopping-block had a whittled handle. A stately, red-haired woman chewing a snuff-twig said, "Uncle Jake Beals? Why him and his woman lives up the lane a piece, over on Seven Mile Crik. Won't you-all git out and come in?"

IV

But we drove on, and just as the lane was petering out we reached a log house on a knoll. A barrel-stave hammock was stretched between two trees in the yard, and lying in it was a small, white-haired man dressed in faded blue overalls. As my grandfather stopped the Ford and shut off the engine, the little man sat up in the swing, blinking.

"Howdy do, suh?" said my Grandfather Beals.

"Quite well, thank you, suh. How ah you, suh?" said the little old man. He got to his feet and sauntered out to the car.

A faint smile quivered on my Grandfather Beals's lips. "We're lookin' foh a man by the name of Jones that lives around in this country somewhuh," he said.

"Jones?" said the old man of the hammock. "Well, now it appeahs to me like thah is a family of Joneses livin' on down the crik a ways, but I 'low you'll have to go back around by the big road to get thah. Won't you-all light and rest yo'-se'ves a while?"

My Grandfather Beals was close to tears. His eyes glistened. This was the meeting he had tried to envisage untold times during the fifty years they had been separated. It was sad that he should recognize Jacob without Jacob's knowing him.

"Don't you know me, Jake?" he said softly.

The old man stepped back, startled. He put his hand up to his frowsy white head, scratched, and peered suspiciously at the man in the automobile.

"Why, no, stranguh, I can't say as I do."

"It's Jawn," said my grandfather in a voice so low it was almost a whisper.

"How was that?"

My grandfather cleared his throat. "It's yo' brothah Jawn," he said.

The transformation was immediate. The gnomish little man jumped and pranced.

"Jawn! Jawn!" he shouted, scrabbling up on the running-board. "Get out o' thah and let me see you!" He jumped back down and made off toward the house to bring up short and bawl, "Mahthy, come out o' thah! Brothah Jawn's hyah!" Then he came charging back.

My Grandfather Beals descended stiffly from the car. This was not the tender reunion he had dreamed about. His dignity, alongside the joyous unrestraint of his older brother, made him seem pompous and a little ridiculous.

He was straight and well fed, whereas Jacob was stooped and scrawny. The inactivity of his retirement had let my grandfather develop a paunch.

When he stepped to the ground Jacob ran up to him with a rigid forefinger. "Lawdy, what a belly!" he shouted. "Jawnnie! Jawnnie! Lawdy, what a belly!"

My Grandfather Beals colored and chuckled uncomfortably. His older brother ran circles around him, as delighted as a puppy.

A woman came out from the cabin. She wore a dingy Mother Hubbard. Her yellowish-white hair flew in strings about her face, and her eyes were pink and weak.

"Mahthy," cried Jacob, "this is my brothah Jawn you heered me talk about."

Martha batted her eyes and smiled a toothless smile and shook hands. "And whose younguns air them?" she asked pleasantly, turning to Ed and me. It was the first time we'd been noticed.

"These ah Cayoline's boys," my grandfather said, "Eddie and Dave."

"Cay'line's boys?" said Jacob. "Who's Cay'line? That yo' old woman?"

"No, Cayrie's my oldest daughtah."

"Law, law, got a grown daughtah and grandchilduns!" shouted Jacob. "Little Jawnnie! And lawdy! what a belly! Little old Jawnnie!"

He capered up to the Ford and ran his hand over the green-enameled sides. "Little Jawnnie," he murmured proudly, "come drivin' up hyah in a cah, just as big as you please. Jawnnie sho' has got ahead in the wohld."

He spoke with genuine respect, but my grandfather was more embarrassed than he had been when Jacob had poked at his stomach.

Jacob turned away from caressing the Ford. He said, "Well, I guess you-all is right duhty from yo' trip. Come on down to the branch and we'll bathe while the old woman stuhs us up a snack."

We went trooping down the other side of the knoll, the four of us. My Grandfather Beals had been so important to Ed and me during the trip. He had kept his plans mysterious and had evaded our questions. But he seemed out of it now, trying to regulate his steps to keep them with the spry little skips and curvets of Jacob.

Ed and I had our clothes all unbuttoned by the time we had crossed the slope and reached the creek, a sluicing mountain stream, polka-dotted with sunlight. Jacob began pulling off his overalls, too.

My Grandfather Beals had on his Sunday suit, so he spread out his handkerchief before he sat down on the creek bank.

"Jawnnie Jawnnie! Ain't you goin' to bathe?" said Jacob, unstrapping his truss and placing it carefully in the crotch of a tree. He walked mincingly over to the stream and felt the water with a knotty toe. "That watuh's just right—not too wahm and not too chilly."

Ed nudged me and we giggled. The idea of Grandfather Beals stripping off naked and going in swimming was funny.

But he answered Jacob's question as if it were the usual thing for him to swim in the creek. "No, Jake," he said, "I've been having rheumatism pains hyah lately, and I guess I bettuh not go in today."

Jacob dived off a log and swam as gracefully as a water animal. He came to the surface, treading water, shaking the drops from his grizzled eyebrows.

"Pshaw!" he whooped. "Crik watuh won't make it no wuss, will it, boys?" And he dived again and pinched my ankle.

My grandfather sat on the bank in his Sunday suit, watching us. Once or twice he skipped some stones across the water, but he looked out of place even doing that.

The sun was going down by the time we got our clothes back on. We came stringing up the rise toward the house. Martha had supper ready, and the oil-lamp was lighted in the kitchen.

We were hungry, after the long trip and the cold bath, but the food, cooked by the decrepit, weak-eyed old woman, was more than we could stomach. It was greasy and slightly soured. And the coffee was worse than the food. My grandfather scarcely touched his plate. Jacob, however, ate with relish.

Martha stood up at the head of the table, minding off the swarms of flies with a big turkey-wing fan.

"This hyah ain't much eatin'," said Jacob, blowing on the coffee in his saucer, "but tomorrow I'll make us a ketch of fish. And when we have a mess of trout, I wouldn't set down to eat with President Coolridge. No, suh!"

We left the old woman to clear off the dishes and we sat out in the front yard under the trees. My Grandfather Beals gazed off through the twilight.

By and by he said, in a sad, far-away voice, "You know, Jake, the way that stream bends around down yondah just puts me in the mind of the way ouah old stream cut around back in Vuhginia."

Jacob slapped his leg. "Yes, suh! don't it now! Can't you just hyah them old foxhounds bellering now? Old Nig and Coon and Josie away off in the chinkapin thicket. Recollect what mästuh fox-hunts we used to have back yondah, Jawnnie? And what was that we called that big lead hound we had?"

"Old Blanche," said my grandfather softly.

"Old Blanche," said Jacob. "Yes, suh, Old Blanche."

Bedtime came and Jacob showed us the big feather bed where we were to sleep. Martha was putting a quilt pallet down for them. My grandfather had asthma, so he slept on the outside. We all sank down into the great, soft bed. My grandfather had a hard time getting his breath that night.

The last thing that night I heard him wheezing. And then someone came pattering across the board floor, barefooted. There was a poking on the outside of the bedclothes and then I heard Jacob chuckle under his breath and mutter, "Jawnnie! Jawnnie! Lawdy, what a belly!"

V

The next morning, long before breakfast, my Grandfather Beals was out in the yard puttering around the car. He filled the radiator from the well, he measured the gasoline with a stick, and he pumped up a back tire. It was evident that he was getting ready to travel.

Jacob was incredulous. "Jawn, you ain't leavin' a'ready? I allowed from what you said when you come that you was aimin' to stop with us a spell."

Then my Grandfather Beals told a lie.

"No, Jake," he said. "You see, I've got a business, and I have to be thah to attend to it. I hate to leave so quick, and I wish I could stay longuh, but I have to get back. But I know the way to come now, and next time I come I'll be in a fix to stay longuh."

Grandfather Beals knew then that there never would be a next time. But business had an important sound, and Jacob didn't try to argue it down. He said in a dull voice, "Well, Jawn, it grieves me pow'ful to have you go off sudden like this. I had a heap of things I wanted to say to you, and I'm sho' goin' to miss you."

All the liveliness he had shown the day before had suddenly gone out of him. He and Martha stood in the yard while Ed cranked the Ford. The quiet hills echoed with the engine's explosions. We pulled out, trailing a haze of blue smoke. Ed waved back at the forlorn old couple and they waved until we lost sight of them.

In the town of the postmark we stopped to have the gasoline-tank filled and my grandfather bought cheese and crackers. We ate as we rode, washing the food down with strawberry soda pop.

My grandfather drove fast and it seemed that we would be out of the hills before the morning was gone. We were coming along a level stretch of mountain road at a good clip. He caught a glimpse of the prairies spread out beyond the hills, far below us, and he let go the steering-wheel to point. But before he could get words out of his mouth the front wheels of the car struck a soft spot in the road, and the car headed for the bluff, a deep, sheer drop.

"Wup! Wup! Wup!" my grandfather exclaimed, grabbing at the wheel and twisting the car back into the road. He cut the wheels too short and the car reeled, teetered and went crashing over, bottom side up in the road.

The air went yelling out of me as I struck the ground. "This is the way it feels to be dead," I kept telling myself. No one moved for hours, it seemed. Then I could feel the acid from the storage-battery dripping down on my back. I began squirming around, and my Grandfather Beals came to, and, groaning, worked his way out from under the wreckage. Ed and I crawled out after him.

A few minutes before the road had been deserted, but now the car was surrounded by mountaineers and more were coming. They helped us turn the Ford right side up.

The wind-shield was shattered, the top was a mass of splinters and torn cloth, and the steering-wheel was held on by a single spoke. Strangely, none of us was badly hurt. All three of us were bleeding from small cuts and skinned places, and my Grandfather Beals complained that his side was paining him, but when we looked down into the purple depths of the valley, we forgot our slight hurts.

Ed cranked the engine again, Grandfather Beals

grasped the splintered steering-wheel, and we drove away without thanking the gaping hill people.

Ed said nervously, "Grandpa, I bet you're tired. Don't you want me to drive?"

"No, son," said my Grandfather Beals with a bland smile; "you can't tuhn it ovah as slick as I can."

On the steep declines going out of the mountains it became apparent that our brakes were no longer working. The air was acrid with scorching oil and rubber. But my grandfather had a substitute for brakes. He started braking with the reverse gear.

"Now you see, Eddie," he said suavely, "thah's mo' ways of killing a dog without chokin' him to death with buttah!"

That was the last time he spoke on the trip. We whirled down out of the hills at a terrific speed. Grandfather Beals drove like a man possessed, his face wooden, grasping that one sound spoke of the steering-wheel and craning his neck forward.

It seems to me now that all of us must have had a touch of the heat that day. There was no glass to protect us from the furnace-blast that struck us when we reached the treeless plain. We had left the wreckage of the top back on the mountain road and we were exposed to a cruel white sun. We split the flickering heat-waves, rolling up long columns of dust, and our faces were like masks. The prairies danced to the slow, giddy pulse of the sun-rays. But my Grandfather Beals checked the speed not a whit until he reached home.

As we neared town we met Amos Pridgeon, a Negro cotton farmer whom we knew well, homeward bound with his mule team and wagon. He shouted and waved at us, but my grandfather gave no sign of recognition. Amos Pridgeon was the only person who saw us drive in.

At the outskirts of town my grandfather began to cut around back ways, taking corners on two wheels. He drove the car into his barnyard and on into the garage. When the car was inside we all crawled out. My Grandfather Beals staggered a little, but he came outside and closed the garage doors and snapped the padlock on its hasp.

He turned to Ed and me. "Now, boys," he said, "if you-all won't say nothing to anyone about this, I'll give you both a piece of money. I want to see how long you-all can keep anything to yo'se'ves."

He pulled out a canvas pouch, unwound the string, and handed each of us a silver dollar.

VI

Ed and I took the money and left him cooling his hands and face at the horse-trough. We came along down Main Street. At the drug-store, Ed said, "Let's go in and get a coke."

In the drug-store, at one of the soda tables, there was a bunch of men crowded around watching a checker game.

"Hey, do you-all want to know something?" Ed said loudly.

Some of the men turned around and looked at us. Our clothes were torn, our faces were sunburned to a sausage red, and Ed had a cake of dried blood in his hair.

"Sure, we want to know something," one of the men said.

"Well, Grandpa Beals turned over his Ford today and smashed it all up and nearly killed us all," Ed said.

"He sure wrecked it for good this time," I said importantly.

Until his dying day my Grandfather Beals was bitter against Amos Pridgeon, the nigger cotton-raiser.

2

HEEL, TOE, AND A 1, 2, 3, 4

ONE NIGHT Joe had been staring at the white paper in his typewriter so long that he thought he would go snow-blind. Finally he let his tilted chair down and began writing.

The types did a tap dance on the platen and words marched across the page: "*Wife:* Henry, have you got everything shut up for the night?"

Joe double-spaced and wrote: "*Hubby:*" but, before he could finish the line with the good one he had thought up for *Hubby* to say back to *Wife* he heard a scratching on the iron grille of the basement window. He turned around in his chair and saw two hands gripping the bars and a twisted monkey-face squeezed between them.

"What do you want?" he asked.

"Say, buddy, how do you get down to the Lake from here?" the monkey-face said without moving its lips.

Joe got up and went over to the open window to see how anyone could talk without moving his lips. He said, "You follow this street right on, and it'll take you to the Lake. It's only three blocks on over."

"What street is this, buddy?"

"This is Superior Street,—East Superior Street," Joe said.

The stranger took his hands away from the window bars and sat down on the basement steps so that his head was level with the sidewalk and the window. Joe could see now that when he talked his lips did move a little. They jerked down on one side like those of a man rolling a cigar in the corner of his mouth.

He didn't make any move to go. Instead he began explaining, apologetically, "Well, I know Chi' pretty good, but I ain't never been down to the Lake. I thought I would go down to the Lake tonight. Reckon is there any benches a man could sleep on down there at the beach?"

"Sure, you can find plenty of benches if you'll walk on up the shore a ways, up about Oak Street."

Joe turned around and went back over to his typewriter again. But the bum kept on sitting there, hunched up on the basement steps. It annoyed Joe to have him sitting there looking in, and he was about to tell him to move on, when the bum said, "What're you doing, buddy? You writing a story book?"

"No, I'm writing two-line jokes," Joe said. "I make my living writing two-line jokes." Joe was proud of making his living by writing jokes.

The bum commenced talking again without paying any attention to what Joe had said. "Listen, buddy, you let me come in there, and I'll tell you some good stories you can write."

"What kind of stories?"

"Oh, all kinds of stories. Any kind of story you want to hear."

Joe got up and walked out into the hall and turned

back the snap-lock on the basement door. The bum had moved quickly, because he was there at the bottom of the steps waiting when Joe opened the door. When he stepped inside he put his foot down on some plaster that had fallen and it made a loud gritting noise on the concrete floor.

"Sh-h-h!" Joe said. "Don't make so much noise. The landlady lives right back there, and if she caught me letting you in she'd throw me and you both out in the street."

The visitor, stepping high, walked on past quickly and stood in Joe's room under the electric light, blinking. When Joe saw him in the light he knew that there wasn't any danger. The bum was a kid about sixteen years old. He looked tough, but not hard to handle. His back was twisted and he held his elbows out from his sides as if he had boils in both his armpits. His marmoset's face was broad and pleasant, but one of his eyelids drooped halfway shut. His other eye was as black and lively as a beetle.

II

"Start in," said Joe, sitting down in his chair.

"Well, what kind of a story would you want to hear?" the little bum asked, seating himself nervously on the edge of the cot.

"Just use your own judgment," Joe said. "You were the one that suggested this."

"Well, I can tell you about when I was handling greyhounds for the races out in Tia Juana and one day Roman Queen broke her leg and they give her to me to shoot. So I took her and set her leg and fixed it up and cured her. That dog sure did love me and I sure did love that dog. So one day Mr. Rambo, that was my boss, seen that Queenie was up and getting around again without much of a limp, and nothing would do him but he should run her. Well, she wasn't much account for running, the bone in her leg wasn't good and knit yet, but Mr. Rambo took Queen and shot her full of dope, and that day she run and win the race and Old Man Rambo win six grand. I sure did love that dog. But that last race tore her leg loose again and the dope and all was too much for her and I had to shoot her after all. How is that for a story? Is that the kind you like?"

"That's all right," Joe said. "Go slower and talk so as I can understand what you're saying."

"Well, I've been all around. All over this country, Canada, and Mexico. I've been to Havana and Bonus Airs. I've just got out of a turpentine camp down in Florida. When the boom bust down there me and another kid was riding out in a Studie that was hot—that we had stole. We was almost to the line when the law caught us, and the judge shipped us off to this turpentine camp. They used to whup us regular, whether we'd done anything or not. But that turpentine gets into your hide and it gets so they can't hurt you so much when they cut you up with a cat-tail whip. I've got a back like a washboard. Here, let me show you something."

The little bum unbuttoned his coat and slipped his arms out of it gingerly. He bent his naked back over under the light bulb. The close, narrow welts on his back made it look like a piece of tan corduroy.

"Just feel that," the kid said. "Go on, just feel it."

Joe ran his finger tips along the leather colored welts.

"That's what them cat-tail whips they use on you in a turpentine camp does to you," the boy said proudly.

"Well, me and this other kid was in there, and this kid was a wop kid from Chi'. He said that if ever he could get back to Chi' ever'thing would be jake for him and me both, because he could get me a job driving a beer truck for fifty bucks a week. He was a good kid all right. I sure did like him. So after a while he gets out and comes back to Chi' and before long he sends the money to get me out and sends me an address to come to here in Chi'. I didn't lose no time.

"I was riding the blinds out of Atlanta when a railroad dick come climbing down over the tender. She was hitting around seventy. I steps around on that little ledge out of sight, and when this yard dick sticks his beezer around trying to see where I had went, I lets him have it, and he goes over, squealing like a stuck pig.

"I got into Chi' this afternoon late, and I went around to this tobacco store on North Clark Street, this address this buddy of mine had give me. When I got there they told me that this dago buddy of mine had been put on the spot day before yesterday and they had a big funeral for him yesterday. I sure liked that kid. Kid by the name of Liberatore. Old Vic Liberatore.

"Well, here I am now. That's the breaks. The next

time you see me I might be wearing a silk shirt and smoking a two-bit cigar. That's the breaks. That's what they call the lawr of averages. I've had it to work out for me before. I've had the bucks before this, plenty, and I spent 'em, too. Say, buddy, you ain't got another hump there, have you?"

Joe pulled a paper of cigarettes out of his shirt pocket and handed them over to the little bum. The kid took one, lighted it, and sent a gray veil eddying up around the electric light. He stood there, naked to the waist. Joe was looking at the bum's arms. From wrist to elbow they were splotched with livid scars. Some of the places were unhealed and they were open wounds.

"How did you burn your arms like that?" Joe asked.

"Them blisters? Buddy, if I told you how I got them, I'd have to tell you about Heavy Henderson. I don't know if I can tell you about Heavy, exactly. I ain't right in my head yet about Heavy. You see how I walk? Sort of on my heels? Some thinks I'm punch-drunk, but I ain't punch-drunk. I never have talked to anybody about this before, but I'll try and tell you about it.

III

"I wasn't more'n ten years old when I first started on the road. My old folks used to live in a little town in Missouri. I guess they still do if they ain't dead. That's been six or seven years ago. My old man always said that if ever I run off, I could just keep on a-running, because he never would send after me. So I run off.

"Well, I hadn't been out long before I met up with Heavy Henderson. It was in the jungles near Boise, Idaho. I had been having a plenty tough time of it, and I sure was needing somebody who was big enough to stand up for me.

"Heavy was a big, fine-looking man, and he was looking to get a good punk to do his moochin' for him. So when I come along Heavy and me joined up. Heavy was a good guy at heart; they don't make them no better than Heavy was. He'd 'a' done anything in the world for me, but I have to admit that Heavy did have a mean temper. Part of it was my fault, though. I was always kind of headstrong, and that made it hard for him to keep me in line. So Heavy used to have to put the bug on me pretty often. That's what made them burns."

Joe said, "Oh, I see!"

"You know what the bug is, don't you?"

"Well, it seems to me like I do, but I'm not quite sure," Joe said. "What is it?"

"The bug is what they call blister beetle, a sort of a little bug. The juice of it on you blisters to beat hell. Heavy nearly always used some kind of acid on me, but he called it the bug just the same. Ever'time I got so I wouldn't do like he said, or when I helt out something on him, Heavy would catch me and take and blister my arms. That worked two ways. For one thing, it hurt me a whole lot more than a whupping, and for another thing, the next day when I went into town to batter backdoors, why I could show the woman that opened the door the sores on my arms and tell her I had got scalded in an accident and that I was trying to get back to my folks. That always worked, and sometimes it paid off in money, too.

"I used to try to fight Heavy off, but that didn't do no good. That was one strong man. He had a big heart, and I bet that'd he 'a' gone through Hell for me, but, like I say, he did have a quick temper. When he got mad, he'd just burn the hell out of my arms. I guess I needed it sometimes. But Heavy sort of overdone it. Some of them sores ain't never healed up yet, and that turpentine I been working in is a quick healer.

"But I never could find it in my heart to anything else but respect Heavy. I sure did like him. He was as good a jocker as any kid could want. Wasn't scared of nobody, and I seen him mash a bird's face in for just grabbing me by the neck. I sure did like Heavy, but I never did know how much I liked him until after it was too late.

"The way it was, one night Heavy tanked up on white mule out in a place in Dakota. Man, talk about your raw liquor, that stuff was *raw*. I seen one guy take a snort of it, and an hour later he was having a hem'-rhage. But stuff like that didn't bother Heavy. He was a *man*. He had a set of cast-iron guts. We was waiting for a train, and Heavy was feeling good.

"I remember just as well. It was moonlight, and we was laying around a water-tank waiting for the flyer. The drip from the tank made a funny sound where it splashed in the white gravel down below. The moon made ever'thing look kind of like silver, except in the shadows. Old Heavy was propped up again' one of them water-tank posts singing just as loud as he could sing. He was singing a song he knew about a bum that was one hell of a liar, and one day while he was setting there telling these lies a fly crawls up him and tickles him to death. It's a kind of a dirty song in places.

"Pretty soon we could hear a train working steam away off down the track. I don't know if you know how it is out there on the prairies, but the first thing you see is this long white light come shaking down the rails. It don't make no noise at all, just white and still. It sure is pretty. It puts me in the mind of one of them stories my old woman used to read out of the Bible. Then after awhile you begin to hear the drivers, away off acrost the plains. Pretty soon, when it gets nearer, it seems like the dark is just alive and beating with that sound.

"Well, this here was a manifest coming, a hot-shot freight. Heavy and me was passenger stiffs and we never did ride nothing slower than a fruit express. It was two hours yet before the flyer was due, but Heavy took it into his head that he was going to ride this rattler. Nothing would do him but we had to ride that manifest freight out. He got stubborn spells like that when he had been drinking.

"I thought he was too lousy drunk to even get on, and I tried to talk him out of it. But he slapped my jaws, and nothing else would do him, so we walked on down the track a ways, and when she stopped for water, I got Heavy on.

"After we was on, Heavy took a notion that he would ride the bumpers. You know how the bumpers is on a box car: there's a block where the coupling pin is fastened on, and it sticks out far enough for you to set on it. Heavy was riding down there between two cars, setting on the bumpers with his feet propped up over the coupling pins.

"I was riding the tops right above him, where I could keep my eye on him, like I aimed to do. I guess I must of drowsed off, though. I never will get through blaming myself for what happened anyway. Pretty soon something woke me up. It was old Heavy screaming. I climbed down to where he was. He had went to sleep and let his foot slip down between the coupling pins. The cars had jostled and the coupling pins had jammed together and it had smashed Heavy's heel off. I felt of it, and it was all bloody and mushy there in his shoe.

"God, I was scared! I knew that I had to get that train stopped. Old Heavy was just like a daddy to me. I was so scared that I didn't want to think about what had happened.

"I climbed back up on top, and I begin to run over the tops toward the engine. It was funny, but you know something popped into my head about that time, and I can't get shut of it yet.

IV

"How I happened to run off from home: the Spring I run off they was learning us kids at school a dance for some kind of a doings they was having. I mean they *tried* to make me learn it along with the others, but I never did like any sissy business like that, and I wouldn't learn it. So they whupped me. My old man always said that if ever I got a whupping at school I'd get one twicet as hard when I got home. And when my old man set out to whup me, he would just about half kill me. So I just didn't go home that night. I left out of there.

"Well, of all the crazy things, this tune they tried to learn me to dance to back in the fourth grade at school popped into my head, and it kept running in my head all the time I was high-tailing it down toward the engine acrost them box cars.

" 'Heel, toe, and a one-two-three-four,' it went. 'Heel, toe, and a one-two-three-four!' I got so I could make it come out even, and when I got to the 'four' I would be at the end of a car and I would have to jump acrost to the next one and begin all over again, 'Heel, toe, and a one-two-three-four!'

"That seemed to me like the longest rattler ever I rode, and I thought I never was going to reach that engine cab. Finally I did, and I crawled up over the coal and jumped down into the cab, screaming and bawling and carrying on. They couldn't make out what I was saying, but they stopped the train. The head-end shack got off and run down the track with me, and finally we found the car where Heavy was, cussing and groaning. Ever'time old Heavy groaned, it was just like someone had slit me with a shiv. We got him off of there, and they carried him back to the caboose. I plugged along behind the con and the shack that was carrying him, and every time I took a step one of them words,—heel, toe, and a one-two-three-four—would snap into my head. It just kept running through my head.

"And when the train started up again, it seemed like the wheels was clicking, 'Heel, toe, and a one-two-three-four!'

"They put us off at a little town about fifteen miles up the line so as I could get Heavy to a doc. I don't know how I ever did get that croaker out of bed that night, because I must have been crazy in my mind. Anyhow, the one I got must of been a horse doc, because he just looked at Heavy's smashed heel once and says, 'Um-mmm. Iron rust in it. I'll have to cut it off.'

"He fixed up a little frame over Heavy's face, and he showed me how to drop the ether. I let the drops fall, and as they dropped this 'Heel, toe, and a one-two-three-four' jerked through my head in time to the drops.

"After a while the croaker started sawing. I could see the bone show white where he had laid open the flaps of raw meat. Zup! that saw would go acrost, and I would think, 'Heel!' and Zup! it would come back, and I would think, 'Toe!'; and then it would go zup-zup-zup-zup, and I would count, one-two-three-four.

"Pretty soon I passed out myself. I was awful sick that night, but I went to sleep there in the croaker's office on a couch he had there, and when I woke up the next day the doc told me that Heavy was dead. They claimed he died of lock-jaw. I don't know.

"I didn't cry or anything. All I done was lay there with that crazy dance tune running through my head.

"They buried Heavy that same day. They had him a coffin made out of a goods-box and they loaded that in an old wagon and hauled him out to the graveyard. I walked along behind the wagon. I remember how the dust let my feet go down in it easy like I was walking on clouds. And the wagon wheels was warped and they clocked back and forth, making a kind of a hollow sound in a regular beat, and that 'Heel, toe, and a one-two-three-four' kept time to that beat the wheel hubs made.

"I sure did hate to see old Heavy go. Nothing never has meant anything to me since then. I didn't take on or nothing, but I don't have no memory of what happened at the grave or how I ever got away from there. I get that way ever onct in a while now. I'll be walking along and that 'Heel, toe, and a one-two-three-four' will start up in my head and I take to walking in time to it. Some thinks I'm punch-drunk, walking like that, but I ain't punch-drunk.

"And sometimes I have dreams at night. I drempt that I was running along the tops of a long string of box cars that seems like it hasn't got no end, and the cars is swinging and swaying and I'm screaming and screaming, but the engine whistle up ahead is blowing so loud I can't hear what I'm screaming. Only I know what I'm screaming. It's that 'Heel, toe, and a one-two-three-four!' "

V

The little bum stopped talking and peered at Joe with one bright black eye. "You think I'm as full of nuts as a peach-orchard boar, don't you? Crazy as hell, ain't I?"

He stood up. "Well, I guess I'll try and see if I can't get on down to the Lake," he said briskly.

Joe said, "No, you don't need to do that. You can sleep here tonight if you want to. I've got me a shower bath fixed up back there. You go in and take a good bath, and you can sleep here."

The little bum said, "No, I'll find me a bench down on the beach somewheres. You don't want me sleeping here. I'm crazy in the head."

Joe stood watching him get into his coat. The kid slipped his arms tenderly into the sleeves. When he had reached the door, Joe called, "Well, so long, then!"

"So long, buddy. Did I give you any ideas you could use for stories?"

"Sure, you gave me some swell ideas," Joe said. "I can get a whole batch of stories out of what you told me. Much obliged!"

"Well, so long then, buddy. You're O.K."

The basement door slammed. Joe heard a footstep on the bottom step. There was a pause. One on the second. Another pause. Then, in quick succession, four that brought his departing visitor to the sidewalk level.

Joe walked over to the typewriter and ripped out the sheet that had his half-finished married-life joke on it. He crumpled the paper and threw the wad on the floor. Then he sat down, fed in a fresh sheet, and gave the space bar two or three nervous taps.

He started writing rapidly, "*Kind Old Lady:* My poor man, what brought you to this miserable state?"

Joe double-spaced and wrote "*Hobo.*" He paused to phrase a snappy comeback for *Hobo.*

Off down the silent, lamp-lit street he could hear the footclicks growing faint.

3

THE APOSTATE

HARRY, you been jacking me up about how I been neglecting Rotary here lately, so I'm just going to break down and tell you something. Now I don't want you to take this personal, Harry, because it's not meant personal at all. No, siree! Not *a*-tall! But, just between you and I, Harry, I'm not going to be coming out to Rotary lunches any more. I mean I'm quitting Rotary! . . .

Now whoa there! Whoa! Whoa just a minute and let me get in a word edgeways. Just let me finish my little say.

Don't you never take it into your head that I haven't been wrestling with this thing plenty. I mean I've argued it all out with myself. Now I'm going to tell you the whyfor and the whereof and the howcome about this, Harry, but kindly don't let what I say go no further. Please keep it strictly on the Q.T. Because I guess the rest of the boys would suspicion that I was turning highbrow on them. But you've always been a buddy to me, Harry, you mangy old son of a hoss thief, you, so what I'm telling you is the straight dope.

II

Harry, like you no doubt remember, up till a few months ago Rotary was about "the most fondest thing I is of," as the nigger says. There wasn't nothing that stood higher for me than Rotary.

Well, here about a year ago last fall I took a trip down to the university to visit my son and go to a football game. You know Hubert Junior, my boy. Sure. Well, this is his second year down at the university. Yes, sir, that boy is getting a college education. I mean, I'm all for youth having a college education.

Of course I think there is such a thing as too much education working a detriment. Take, for instance, some of these longhairs running around knocking the country right now. But what I mean is, a good, sound, substantial college education. I don't mean a string of letters a yard long for a man to write after his John Henry. I just mean that I want my boy to have his sheepskin, they call it, before he starts out in the world. Like the fellow says, I want him to get his A.B. degree, and then he can go out and get his J.O.B.

Now, Harry, I always felt like a father has got certain responsibilities to his son. That's just good Rotary. That's all that is. You know that that's just good Rotary yourself, Harry. Well, I always wanted Hubert to think about me just like I was a pal to him, or say an older brother, maybe. I don't know that him and I ever was that way in the fullest sense of the word, but God knows I've tried to make things like that between us.

I mean I've always wanted to be just a big buddy to Hubert.

I'm not saying that I haven't made a pretty poor out of it sometimes. But anyhow that's the spirit I've tried to get into our relationships ever since he was a little tike. Too many parents never actually get acquainted with their boys, see, Harry? I always encouraged Hubert to come to me and talk things over just like it was man to man. I will admit that since Hubert got older I would sometimes find out about things that he had been keeping from me, especially after he got girl crazy. But however, as I say, Harry, Hubert always knew that all he had to do was come to me, and I would act like a big buddy to him, irregardless.

III

Well, like I was telling you, Harry, I started Hubert in to the university last year, and after he had been there about two months, I thought I would run down and see how he was getting along and go to a football game. So I and Mrs. T. drove over one Friday. We didn't know the town very well, so we stopped at a filling station, and I give Hubert a ring, and he come right on down to where we was to show us the way. Just as soon as he come up, I could see right then that he had something on his mind bothering him.

He called me aside and took me into the filling-station rest-room, and says: "For the love of God, Dad, take that Rotary button out of your coat lapel," he says to me.

Harry, that come as a plenty big surprise to me, and

I don't mind telling you that it just about took the wind out of my sails. But I wasn't going to let on to him, so I rared back on my dignity, and says: "Why, what do you mean, take that Rotary button out of my lapel, young man?" I says to him.

"Dad," Hubert says to me, serious, "any frat house has always got a few cynics in it. If you was to wear that Rotary button in your lapel out to the frat house, just as soon as you got out of sight, some of those boys at the house would razz the life out of me," he says.

"Hubert," I says, "there's not a thing that this lapel badge represents that any decent, moral person could afford to make fun of. If that's the kind of Reds you got out at your fraternity, the kind that would razz a what you might call sacred thing—yes, sir, a sacred thing—like Rotary, well, I and your mamma can just go somewheres else and put up. I don't guess the hotels have quit running," I says to him.

By now I was on my high horse right, see?

"Now, Dad," Hubert says, "it's not that. I mean, person'ly I'm awful proud of you. It's just that I haven't been pledged to this fraternity long, see, and when some of those older members found out you was a Rotarian they would deal me a lot of misery, and I couldn't say nothing. Person'ly I think Rotary is all right," he says to me.

"Well, you better, son," I says, "or I'm going to begin to think that you're sick in the head."

The way he explained it, though, Harry, that made it a horse of a different tail, as the saying goes, so I give in and took off my Rotary button right there. Stuck it in my pocket, see? So we went on out and visited at Hubert's fraternity house, and do you know that those boys just got around there and treated we folks like we was princes of the blood. I mean you would of thought that I was an old ex-graduate of that university. And we saw the big pigskin tussle the next day, fourteen to aught, favor us, and we had such a scrumptious time all around, I forgot all about what Hubert had said.

Ever'thing would of been all right, except for what happened later. I guess some of those older boys at the frat house begin using their form of psychology on Hubert. I mean they finely got his mind set against Rotary, because when he come home for the summer vacation that was about the size of things.

IV

I mean all last summer I thought Hubert never would let up. He just kept it up, making sarcastic remarks about Rotary, see? Even when we was on our vacation trip.

You know we drove out to California and back last summer, Harry. Come back with the same air in the tires we started out with. Well, I thought it would be kind of nice to drop in and eat with the Hollywood Rotary—you know, just to be able to say I had. So I contacted them and had ever'thing all fixed. Well, do you know that that boy Hubert made so much fun of the idea I just had to give it up?

That was the way it was the whole trip. He got his mother around on his side, too. Just to be frank with you, I never got so sick and tired of anything in all my born days.

Well, Harry, I had my dander up there for a while, and all the bickering in the world couldn't of shook me from my stand. But finely Hubert went back to college in September, and I thought I would have a little peace. Then I just got to thinking about it, and it all come over me. "Look here, Mister Man," I says to myself, "your faith and loyalty to Rotary may be a fine thing, and all that, but it's just costing you the fellowship of your own son." Now a man can't practice Rotary in the higher sense, and yet at the same time be letting his own son's fellowship get loose from him. So there it was. Blood's thicker than water, Harry. You'll have to admit that.

Right along in there, Harry, was the first time I begin to attending meetings irregular. I'll tell you—you might not think so—but it was a pretty tough struggle for me. I remember one Monday noon, Rotary meeting day, I happened to walk past the Hotel Beckman just at lunchtime. The windows of the Venetian Room was open, and I could hear you boys singing a Rotary song. You know that one we sing set to the tune of "Last Night on the Back Porch." It goes:

> I love the Lions in the morning,
> The Exchange Club at night,
> I love the Y's men in the evening,
> And Kiwanis are all right . . .

Well, I couldn't carry a tune if I had it in a sack, but anyway that's the way it goes. So I just stopped in my tracks and stood there listening to that song coming out of the Hotel Beckman dining-room. And when the boys come to the last verse,

I love the Optimists in the springtime,
The Ad Club in the fall,
But each day—and in every way—
I love Rotary best of all . . .

I tell you, Harry, that just got me. I had a lump in my throat big enough to choke a cow. The tears begin coming up in my eyes, and it might sound ridiculous to hear me tell it now, but I could of broke down and bawled right there on the street. I got a grip on myself and walked on off, but right then I says to myself: "The hell with Hubert and his highbrow college-fraternity ideas; I'm going back to Rotary next week."

V

Well, I did go back the next week, and what happened decided me on taking the step I decided on. Here's what decided me. You know, I never got very well acquainted with Gay Harrison, the new secretary. I mean, of course, I know him all right, but he hasn't been in Rotary only but about a year. Well, on that particular day, I just happened to let my tongue slip and called him Mister Harrison, instead of by his nickname. Well, of course, the boys slapped a dollar fine on me right then and there. I haven't got no kick to make about that, but the point is, I had a letter from Hubert in my pocket right then, telling me that he had run short of money. So I just couldn't help but be struck by the idea "I wish I was giving Hubert this dollar." So that's what decided me on devoting my time and finances to another kind of fellowship, Harry.

I get down to the university to see Hubert more frequent now. I make it a point to. And the boys come to me, and I been helping them a little on their frat building fund. There's a fine spirit of fellowship in an organization like that. Some boys from the best families of the State are members, too. You might think from what I said that they'd be uppish, but they're not. No, siree. Not a bit of it. I been down there enough for them to know me, now, and they all pound me on the back and call me H.T., just like I was one of them. And I do them, too. And I notice that when they sit down to a meal, they have some songs they sing just as lively and jolly as any we had at Rotary. Of course, like Hubert said, a few of them might have some wild-haired ideas about Rotary, but they're young yet. And as far as I can see there's not a knocker nor a sourbelly among them. Absolutely democratic.

It puts me in mind of a little incidence that happened last month when the frat threw a big Dad's Day banquet for us down there. All the fathers of the boys from all over the State was there. Well, to promote the spirit of fellowship between dad and son, the fraternity boys all agreed to call their dads by their first name, just treating the dads like big buddies. So at the table Hubert happened to forget for a minute, and says to me "Dad" something. Well, sir, the president of the frat flashed right out: "All right, Hubie, we heard you call H.T. 'Dad.' So that'll just cost you a dollar for the ice-cream fund." Ever'body had a good laugh at Hubert getting caught like that, but do you know, that boy of mine just forked right over without making a kick. That shows the stuff, don't it, Harry? Nothing wrong with a boy like that.

And the whole bunch is like that, ever' one of them. I'll tell you, Harry, the boys at that frat of Hubert's are the builders in the coming generation. Any man of vision can see that.

Well, that's that. Now what was you going to say?

4

THE FIGHT AT HENDRYX'S

THE BLIZZARD struck on a Saturday morning. None of the storekeepers was expecting to do enough business to say grace over, but Herschal Gunther, the grocery clerk at Herzog's Bargain Depot, had a good fire going in the big stove. The flames mumbled in the throat of the chimney and tiny points of light began flickering over the great dull-red paunch of the cast-iron heater.

Even that early a few loafers were sitting around the stove. The small ring widened as they pegged back on the legs of their tilted chairs to escape the hide-parching glow. They inclined their faces only to spout toward the stained, quid-strewn sawdust that filled the square frame around the base of the big stove. The loafers, drowsy with heat and lulled by the soft roar of the fire, chewed in meditative silence, but sometimes their tobacco juice would strike the blazing iron belly and sizzle off quickly in little balls of steam.

Up in the woven-wire enclosure at the front of the store Abe Herzog was working at his rolltop desk, moving papers and barking occasionally with a hard cough. He was making up his February accounts. Every few minutes he would get up and come back to the circle of warmth, chafing his pudgy fingers and rubbing himself under the lower points of his broad vest. He would bask himself before and behind. Then he would go on back to his desk without having said a word. On a counter fifteen feet away from the stove the drinking-water keg was freezing solid.

Thin white diagonals of sleet rustled against the frosted plate-glass windows. The gale came whooping down across the prairie. Out in front the wooden awning creaked and swayed and a loose piece of sheet iron on the north wall of the store banged without let-up. Herschal Gunther, weighing up two-bit pokes of sugar, scraped the scoop against the sides of the tin sugar tub. He grunted every time the scales balanced and stopped to take a drag off his cigarette. Nobody said a word.

A man wearing only a mule-skin jacket for an overcoat and an ear-flapped fur cap clicked the latch on the north side-door, opened the door slowly, and stood on the threshold stamping the sleet off his boots. A bitter gust swooped in, setting all the clusters of bandanas, mittens and work sox hanging from the ceiling into violent twirls. Abe Herzog grabbed for his scattered papers. All the dozing loafers let down their chairs quickly and cried as one, "Shet that door!"

The man in the leather coat turned and closed the door deliberately and walked over toward the stove. He worked his stubbled face stiffly. He fingered his whiskers, breaking away the little beads of ice. They saw that it was Old Man Luther Peck from the Verdigris bottoms. All the elements put together couldn't have kept Old Man Peck from hitching up and coming to town on Saturday.

He joined the circle at the stove, prancing slowly with the pain in his fingers. He unbuttoned his outer coat and his vest, and left them hanging open while he stood with his back to the stove, holding the black-creased palms of his thick, stubby hands outspread toward the blistering heat. He stood facing the grocery counter, and Herschal Gunther called out to him brightly.

"Well, Mr. Peck, this here is Winter, ain't it?"

"This here is Winter!" the old man repeated solemnly and with finality.

"Is it cold enough for you today?"

"I've seed it colder," said Old Man Peck grimly.

"Not here in Oklyhomy you ain't!" one of the loafers said in a pert voice.

"Yes, sir, right here in Oklyhomy, too," the old man said flatly, unruffled. He did not even trouble to glance at the upstart.

Old Man Peck had a theory that the Winters were getting milder, and he fitted all temperatures to it. No matter if the thermometer showed ten below zero, he would be unshaken in his belief that he had gone through colder weather back in the early days. He was, nevertheless, an earnest, truthful man, given neither to heated arguments nor to tall tales. No greater insult than "Liar" could have been offered Old Man Peck, and he was unaccustomed to being doubted. He was too positive and impassive to debate his theory. His reputation for honesty was secure, and he never went to any great pains to convince anybody.

"Well, this here is plenty cold anyhow, Mr. Peck," said Abe Herzog, who had come back to the stove. "It was six below when I come to open up this morning."

"Oh, yes, this here is right smart cold," the old man admitted generously. "But I been out in it when it was a heap colder, right here in this country. We used to get a still, quiet cold like you don't see no more in this country. These winds we have fools you and it ain't actually as cold as it appears like it is. That wind cuts like a razor, but that still cold we used to have, it bit deeper."

The challenging loafer leered his disbelief. "Just name a time," he said with cruel persistence, "when you seen it colder outside than it is right now."

Old Man Peck gave the loafer a pitying look. It seemed for a long moment that he would not condescend to reply, but he broke silence by saying, "All right. I'll name you a time: it was a January, 1903. It was the time they had the fight at Hendryx's."

The old man peeled off his leather coat and looked around for an empty chair. He dragged one up and took his place in the circle around the stove. Old Man Peck was stolid and humorless. If he had not expected to be believed he would not have spoken in the first place.

II

"I mind that time they had the fight at Hendryx's, Abe," he said, ignoring the loafers and addressing the storekeeper with whom he had been trading for twenty years. Abe Herzog knew that Peck's word was unimpeachable. He settled himself in a tilted chair.

"That was as cold a time as ever I seen in this country," the old man went on. "It was so cold that the horns on the steers all froze up and bust wide open. It was so cold that the snot froze on the ends of the young-uns' noses. You'd see the sparrers set out to fly and they'd just drap down out of mid-air, froze stiff. Alongside of that there big freeze, this here blizzard is just a little cold snap.

"It was so cold folks couldn't do nothing only just set around the stove toasting their shins, dreading for the time when they would have to git up and go out back and git to theirselfs, and everybody was mighty t'ard of setting and was ready for a little ex-cite-*ment.*

"The cold spell had been set in for nigh on to a week when Old Man Hendryx sont word around that he was going to th'ow him a dance over at his place. By that time even the Hardshell Baptists was anxious to fix up and git ready and start out and go to a dance. This country wa'n't settled up as close then as it is now, but the news got norated around, and that there dance at Hendryx's turned out to be quite a gethering. Quite a gethering."

Old Man Peck had his pipe out and he searched through the pockets of his vest until he found a dingy sack of Old Hillside smoking tobacco. He filled his pipe and lighted it. Then he went on talking as if Abe Herzog were the only one there. He knew Abe would take his word. He was the oldest customer Abe had.

"Hendryx had him a house out on the bald prairie north of here. I guess you know about whur it set, Abe —up above that little draw ten mile west of Muddy Flat schoolhouse? Well, it was just a two-roomed house and before noon come that day Hendryx's place was so crowded that you couldn't cuss the cat without getting hairs in your teeth. Old Man Hendryx and his two oldest boys was taking turn about doing the fiddling, and a cow-hand by the name of Boyles was calling the sets.

"So it look like everybody was proud to be there at Hendryx's dance and was in for a high old time so long as the grub and liquor didn't give out.

"Well, along there in the middle of the afternoon a feller name Russell Hayes and a man, Merryweather, he called hisself, took to scrapping out in the yard. The two Hayes brothers, Russell and Monroe, was there at Hendryx's dance, and they was always pretty tough customers. The Hayes boys was mean scrappers, and neither one of them didn't like nothing better than a good scrap. But they each of them did their own scrapping.

"This here Merryweather, he was a new man in the country. No one had ever heered tell of him before. He just showed up there at Hendryx's that morning when the dance commenced.

"Well, Merryweather he was a good match for Russ Hayes. They was matched even. They would stand up and fight along awhile, slugging one another, and then they would stop and take a sort of breathing spell and go over to the woodpile whur they had their whiskey hid and h'ist the jug together. Then they would come back to the house yard and begin their fighting again.

"The way they done, it was just like at one of these here prize-fights. I ain't never been to one of them yit, but the way Hayes and Merryweather took spells, from all I've heered about one of these here prize-fights, I reckon them two boys done the same way. They would fight along there for about a half hour, then lay out about five minutes to take on a few slugs of liquor, and then they would git back to their scrapping again.

"When people got t'ard of dancing, they would come out of the house to watch the fight a while. But it was too danged cold for them to stay out in it long. They was always some of them dancing and some of them out there watching the fight. Everybody done a little of both and people kept coming and going, in and out of the house. Hayes and Merryweather, they had the chill stove off with their flailing and their liquor, and they just stayed out there in the cold, as bad cold as this country ever seen, fighting along. They never did come back in the house."

"What was they fighting about, Mr. Peck?" Abe Herzog put in politcly.

"What was they fighting *about?* Oh, I don't know what they was fighting about, Abe. I don't know as they was fighting *about* anything. They was just fighting. Some folks claimed that it was over Flossie Greet, the U. S. marshal's daughter. Flossie was a single womern, and she was there at the dance trying to git her a man. Russ Hayes had been sparking her pret' nigh a year. The word was out that they was aiming to git spliced. But seems like Flossie Greet was more intrusted in marrying than Russ Hayes was.

"So this here feller Merryweather, he was a new man in the country, and he come to Hendryx's dance and took a shine to Flossie right off. He begin dragging his wings around her, and I reckon that she figured that if she would give Merryweather a run it would git Russ Hayes as intrusted in marrying as she was. I heered it said that Merryweather thought he had Russ Hayes already cut out, so he got Flossie off in the corner and named a dirty question to her. So she got mad and went to Russ Hayes and told him that Merryweather was pestering her. Then him and Merryweather took to fighting.

"That was what folks had out, anyhow. I wouldn't take no oath on how true that was. It appeared to me like there at first they was just scrapping along friendly-like without no hard feelings on neither side. You find the usual thing is, a man don't fall out over a womern nohow. He might make his brags he is, just to git on the good side of the gal, but most times a man just scraps because he wants to see how another man's crooked nose would look set around the other way, or because he likes that good feeling a jolt on another man's jaw gives you.

"Anyhow, Russ Hayes and Merryweather hammered on one another all that afternoon, and it look like neither one could git the best of the other. They would stop and take a few drinks and then start right in again. Supper-time come and they stopped and et and, without much more'n giving their victuals time to settle, they got back to their scrap.

"They was both getting consid'able battered up, but it appeared like the both of them was going just as strong as they had been when they first begin about three P.M. that afternoon. Both was good scrappers and neither one could git the edge on the other.

"When it commenced to git dark, they moved around by one of the winders whur the light was coming th'ough and kept right on, going at it just as hard as ever. Some of the men folks carried up bresh and made a bon-f'ar so as to keep warm by when they come out from the dance to watch the fight. That bon-f'ar give off a good light, too.

"Well, it come midnight and Hendryx's dance was going full blast, of course. Hayes and Merryweather was too. But a little after midnight they run out of liquor. They had dreened that gallon jug between 'em. So they both got on Merryweather's horse and went loping off with their arms th'owed around one another, riding two in the saddle, to Collins's store over to Muddy Flat, ten mile away, to buy some more drinkin' liquor."

"How come they both rode the same horse, Mr. Peck?" Herschal Gunther asked.

"Why, son, they had to ride double, because it was too cold that night for a man to ride single. They would of froze riding single. Besides, that's what I say, it never look to me like there was any real, sure-enough hard feelings between Russ and Merryweather. Not there at first, nohow. I never heered it named till later that they'd had a falling out over Flossie Greet, the U. S. marshal's daughter. I know one thing: I know Flossie was having a hard enough time getting one beau, let alone two.

"Anyway, a bunch of us got on horses, riding two in

the saddle, and we went along with them to watch the scrap. We would ride a mile, then we'd all pile off, and Russ Hayes and this Merryweather would have a set-to. Then we'd git back on and ride another mile, and so on till we got to Collins's store and got the liquor jugs filled up.

"Same way coming back to Hendryx's place. We'd unmount, Hayes and Merryweather would drink first, and then they'd fight while we passed the jugs around and watched the fight. Finely we got back to Hendryx's. The rest of us went inside to warm and dance, and left Hayes and Merryweather out in the yard to go to it some more.

III

"Well, they kept right on scrapping till it was commencing to git day. Seem like neither one of them was ever going to give in and say he was whupped. But some of the boys watching it the closest come in and claimed that they was both beginning to act oneasy and sort of cranky with one another.

"The dance was still going strong. It got so danged cold along in the morning that the most of them, the women folks in particular, had all quit watching the fight. They was all in the house. Well, it was just gitting light when Russ Hayes, he sort of turned his ankle or something and fell down. They was just a few of us out there, but I was right there and I seen him when he done it. I'd take oath on it that Merryweather didn't best Russ, nor knock him down, nor nothing like that. The way it was, Russ Hayes swang at Merryweather, and he just sort of slipped and fell down hard. But anyhow, it appeared like that hard fall kind of made Russ lose holt on his temper. He was laying spraddled out there on his stomach and he retch out with one hand and got him a rock and th'owed it at Merryweather just as hard as he could.

"Merryweather ducked down and the rock missed him, but it seem like he just went crazy-mad when Russ Hayes started acting thataway, th'owing rocks and all. Merryweather whupped out a long knife and he jumped over on Russ Hayes and flopped him over on his back and started stobbing him in the chest and th'oat.

"After a little he quit and got up and stood back wiping his knife on his britches lag. Russ Hayes sort of struggled up with the blood gurgling in his lights and he staggered into the house to whur they was dancing. Course the fiddling stopped and the women all commenced to screaming when they seen Russ Hayes come in spoutin' blood like that. Monroe Hayes quit dancing and come running over to his brother.

"Russ grabbed holt on the mantelpiece on the f'arplace and kind of wheezed, 'Monroe, go out there and git the knife-totin' son of a bitch. He's done kilt me.' Then Russ slipped down on the floor and the blood on his chest quit bubblin' and he jerked around there a little and died.

"Well, Monroe, he didn't even stop to git on his coat and hat. He run out without no weepon nor nothing, aiming to git the man that had stobbed his brother. Everybody come out of the house to watch it.

"Meantime, this here Merryweather, seem like he had smelt the blood or something and he had just went crazy-mad. He was going around in circles like a horse with the blind-staggers, frothing at the mouth and pawing up the ground and waving his knife in his hand.

"As soon as he seen Monroe Hayes come out the door, why he lit right out after him with his knife. Monroe, he didn't have no weepon handy. So natcherly there wa'n't nothing for him to do but h'ist tail and run. He took out acrost the corn field, right up a corn row, with Merryweather after him brandishing that long knife and bellering like a bull in a hailstorm.

"It seem like Monroe Hayes, he could outrun Merryweather. This here Merryweather, it look like, was a man use to going everwhur a-horseback. He was sort of bench-lagged, and he wa'n't no great hand at sprintin' acrost a corn field. So Monroe Hayes was outdistancing him right along. Monroe charged on up the field to whur they was an old, broke-down cultivator standing out there. Monroe stopped and yanked him off one of the single-trees off'n this here cultivator and turned around.

"Merryweather was almost up on him with his knife, but he seen right away that Monroe Hayes could outreach him with this here heavy single-tree and could cave in his head with it. Up again' that there single-tree he didn't have no use for a knife. So when he seen Monroe Hayes come at him with the single-tree in hand, Merryweather switched around without ever stopping and come tearing back down the field to'ards the house, running for sweet life.

"Monroe Hayes was right in after him with the

single-tree, gaining on him ever' jump. We seen him when he caught up with Merryweather, and we kept looking for him to club his brains out with the single-tree. But he never even made a pass at him with the single-tree and we was all wondering how come he helt off mashing in Merryweather's head.

"They come on down the field to'ards the house, up to whur we could hear them panting. Then we seen that Monroe Hayes had managed to git his own knife out somehow, and he was trying to git it open with his teeth. About that time he finely did git the blade open. They was still running when he just retch around over this Merryweather's shoulder and cut his th'oat clean acrost from ear to ear.

"Well, sir, I swan, you'd be surprised to see how much a big stout man like that there Merryweather would bleed. He slounched down there in his tracks and the blood run down that corn row for twenty steps or more.

"After the ruckus was over, Old Man Hendryx got everybody to come on back into the house and start with the dancing again. Old Man Hendryx kept saying, no use to let a little murderin' like that bust up a good time. They danced a few more sets. But a few of the women got sort of twittery and they begin putting on their wraps.

"The main trouble was, it seem like they couldn't git this here Flossie Greet to hursh up. She kept running around the place squalling and saying over and over, 'Oh, they've kilt him, they've kilt him! They've kilt my darling man! My darling sweetheart is dead!'

"She never did call him by name, just keep whooping, 'They've kilt my darling man!' like that and nobody could git her to shut up. They tried th'owing cold water on her and ever'thing, but they couldn't git her quiet. Nobody's nerves was much good nohow. Before long they was all tired and wore out with hearing her and was anxious to git on home. So folks started kind of slipping off, and by nine o'clock that morning ever'body was gone. The way that Flossie Greet carried on just busted up Hendryx's dance.

IV

"Well, about a week later the cold spell was still on. If anything, it had got colder. I was riding past Hendryx's place and Old Man Hendryx come out of the house and hailed me. He says, ''Light and hitch your horse and come on in a while, Luther.'

"I told him, no, that it was late and I'd ort to be gitting on home to he'p my womern with the milkin', but Hendryx says, 'Well, just come in for a minute. I got something I want to ast you.' So I rode up and hitched and went on into Hendryx's place.

" 'What was it you wanted to ast me?' I says just as soon as I put my foot in the door, because I didn't want to have the sun go down on me a-horseback and it gitting colder ever' minute.

" 'Luther,' Old Man Hendryx says to me, 'what am I going to do with that there son of a bitch?"

" 'What son of a bitch?' I says.

" 'Why, you know, that there Merryweather fellow that got his th'oat cut over here at my dance last week.'

" 'God A'mighty!' I says. 'Is he still here?'

" 'Still here!—how was he going to git away?' Old Man Hendryx says. 'I got him setting up out there in the mule shed, and he's froze stiffer 'n a poker. Now what do you reckon I'd ort to do with him? Monroe Hayes hauled off his brother's corp' that same morning, but they ain't nobody come after this Merryweather. He ain't got no relations in this part of the country, so far as I can find out. He ain't even got no friends nor acquaintances nor nothing. And I'm aiming to git shut of him.'

" 'Well,' I says, 'why don't you just take him out and bury him?'

" 'Bury him!' Old Man Hendryx said, 'bury him in ground froze harder than a marble slab? Talk sense, Luther. You know that a man cain't stick a spade in the ground with it froze like it is now. Anyway, I ain't going to try it. And I sure as hell ain't going to keep him out there in that mule shed until the thaw comes.'

" 'No, that's not right,' I says, 'you hadn't ort to keep him out there in the mule shed, Hendryx. That ain't Christian.'

" 'I know it ain't,' Hendryx says, 'and I'm bound to git shut of him somehow. I know what I'm *aiming* to do. If somebody don't come and claim him and take him off'n my hands in the next day or two, I aim to hitch the mules to him and drag him off down in the holler to the big bresh pile and set f'ar to him.' "

Old Man Luther Peck knocked the dottle out of his pipe and filled it and smoked without saying anything more. No one else spoke. After a while he looked up and said, "What price you-all got on dry salt meat today, Abe?"

"Twelve for the jowls and sixteen for the sidemeat," the storekeeper said. After a moment Abe asked, "Well, what did Hendryx finally do about getting rid of the body, Mr. Peck?"

"Oh, Old Man Hendryx? Why he done just like he said he was going to do. He waited a couple more days, and one morning he sont for me to witness it. I rode over early, though I didn't figure to take no hand in it. But I stood and watched while him and his boys done it, and I seen it burn on the big bresh pile.

"I stayed and et dinner at Hendryx's. Just about the time we was gitting up from the table, it was about one P.M., here come this Flossie Greet in a buckboard, driving hell for leather.

"She come driving up in Hendryx's yard. She was all dressed in black and she kept dabbing at her eyes, which was watering. She jumped out of the buckboard, and says in a stuffed-up voice, 'Where is he?'

" 'Where is who?' Old Man Hendryx says.

" 'Mr. Merryweather's body—my pore sweetheart's dead body,' Flossie Greet says. 'I heered you was holding him and I made haste to come after him. I aim to give him decent burial.'

"Old Man Hendryx kind of squinted at her a minute and says, speaking slow and soft, 'You sort of took your time making up your mind, didn't you, missie?' he says. 'Well, I'll tell you: if you'll go off down in the holler to whur my big bresh pile *was* and poke around in the ashes, you might be able to gether up some of your pore sweetheart's bones. But I'm skeered that the most of your sweetheart's dead body is done gone up in smoke.'

"Flossie, she wouldn't believe Hendryx at first, but when she went down there and seen the ashes at the bresh pile, she come running back just a-faunchin'. Well, sir, I wisht you could of heered the screaming and crying and taking on that Flossie Greet done. You'd 'a' thought she was a wild womern. She cussed Old Man Hendryx for everthing she could lay her tongue to. She wa'n't even polite about his kin folks. She just talked like an old rip. She even claimed that she was going to have her daddy, the U. S. marshal, put the law on to Hendryx for setting f'ar to her sweetheart's dead body."

Herschal Gunther gasped, and rolled his eyes knowingly. "Well," he said, "I guess then she wasn't as peeved when this here Merryweather first propositioned her as she let on like she was. She must of fell for him hard. If he'd just of played his cards a little different, he could of got over there. I mean she must of loved Merryweather more'n she did that Russell Hayes, making all that fuss about his dead body."

Old Man Peck looked mildly at the youth. "Loved Merryweather? Yeow, Flossie made a big fuss about Merryweather's dead body. Her pappy never had seed Merryweather. So when she seen the picture Greet got in the mail offering $500 reward for an exscaped ex-convict that had been robbing banks and had murdered a Federal man—$500 for him, dead or alive, no questions asked—she thought she had an inside-track. She seen it was Merryweather's picture, and she dang nigh busted a hame string gitting out there to git holt of the body before Hendryx found out what it was worth. It just about set Flossie crazy when she seen that Old Man Hendryx had done burnt up that $500 she thought she had cinched."

The old man lapsed into silence. After a few minutes the loafer who had challenged him in the first place perked his head and let his chair down and said peevishly, "Well, I still don't see whur you showed it was any colder that time than it is today."

5

A STUDENT IN ECONOMICS

All of the boys on the third floor of Mrs. Gooch's approved rooms for men had been posted to get Charlie Wingate up that afternoon. He had to go to see the Dean. Two or three of them forgot about it and two or three of them had other things to do, but Eddie Barbour liked waking people up. Eddie stuck his weasel face in at Charlie's door just as the alarm clock was giving one last feeble tap. The clock stood on the bottom of a tin washpan that was set upside-down on a wooden chair beside the bed. The alarm had made a terrific din. Eddie had heard it far down the hall. The hands showed two o'clock. Pale needles from a December sun were piercing the limp green window shade in a hundred places.

Eddie Barbour yelled, "Aw right, Charlie! Snap out of it!" He came into the chilly room and stood for a moment staring vaguely at the ridge of quilts on the sagged iron bed. The only sound was the long, regular sough of Charlie Wingate's breathing. He hadn't heard a thing. Eddie made a sudden grab for the top of the covers, stripped them back and began jouncing the sleeper by the shoulders. Charlie grunted every time the bed springs creaked, but he nuzzled his pillow and went on sleeping. Eddie went over to the study table where a large, white-enameled water pitcher stood and he came back to the bed with the water, breathing giggles. He tipped the water pitcher a little and a few drops fell on the back of Charlie's neck without waking him. Eddie sloshed the icy water up over the pitcher's mouth. A whole cupful splashed on Charlie's head. Charlie sat up quickly, batting his arms about, and Eddie Barbour whinnied with laughter.

"Arise, my lord, for the day is here," he said, going across and ceremoniously raising the crooked window shade. Charlie sat straight up among the rumpled quilts with his head cocked on one side, staring dully. He had slept with his clothes on. He sat up in bed all dressed, in a soldier's brown uniform, all but his shoes and roll puttees.

"You got army today?" Eddie asked, putting the pitcher down.

Charlie looked at him for a moment and blinked. Then he said in a voice stuffy with sleep, "Naw. I had army yesterday. I got army make-up today." He worked his mouth, making clopping noises.

"What time you got army make-up, Charlie? When you come in from class you said get you up because you had to go see the Dean at two-thirty."

"Yeah, I do have to go see the Dean at two-thirty. But I got army make-up too. I got to make up drill cuts from three till six." All at once he flopped back down on the bed, sound asleep again.

"Hey!" Eddie cried, jumping forward. "Come out of that! Wake up there, Charlie! You can't sleep no more if you got to see the Dean at two-thirty. You just about got time to make it." He jerked him back up in bed.

"Screw the Dean," Charlie said; "two hours' sleep ain't enough."

"Is two hours all the sleep you got last night?"

"Where you get the 'last night'? I worked all night last night. I had classes till noon. Two hours' sleep was all I got today. And darn little more yesterday or the day before. When is Sunday? Sunday's the first day I'm due to get any real sleep. Two hours' sleep is not enough sleep for a man to get."

He plumped his stockinged feet onto the cold floor and got up stiffly. He went over to the washstand, where he picked up his tooth brush and tooth paste and a bar of soap and slowly took his face towel down from beside the warped looking-glass. He came back to where his shoes lay and stood looking at the toilet articles in his hands as if he had forgotten what he meant to do with them. He dumped them on the bed, took the pan with the alarm clock on it and set it on the floor. Then he sat down on the chair and picked up one of the heavy army shoes, held it and felt it and studied it carefully before he put it on. He put on the other shoe with equal deliberation and stood up without lacing either of them. He took his things up from the bed and started off for the bathroom, his loose shoes clogging. Eddie Barbour followed him down the drafty hall.

The creosote disinfectant that Mrs. Gooch used in her bathrooms gave off a strong odor. "Dag gum bathroom smells just like a hen coop," Charlie said thickly as he stood in front of the white-specked mirror twisting his face. He wouldn't need a shave for another day. He had a fairly good-looking face, tan and thin, with ringlets of black hair tumbling down over his forehead. His large ears stuck straight out. He looked at his image with dark eyes made narrow by two purplish puffs under them, and he yawned widely.

Eddie Barbour stood leaning against the jamb of the bathroom door. He said, "You ought to try and get more sleep, Charlie."

"Are you telling *me?*" Charlie said, running water in the face bowl. Eddie Barbour was a freshman too.

II

Charlie Wingate came walking along University Boulevard toward the campus, hunched up in his army overcoat. The raw December wind whipped his face and made him feel wide awake. He passed a bunch of fraternity men pitching horseshoes in the drive beside the K.A. house. Two or three, sprucely dressed, gave him impersonal glances as he passed. They did not speak, and he walked past self-consciously, seeing them without looking toward them.

When he reached the business section opposite the campus he turned in at the white-tiled front of The Wigwam. The noon rush was over and Nick was not at the cash register. A few noon "dates" were still sitting in the booths along the wall. Charlie walked straight back along the white-tile counter and sat down on the end stool. Red Hibbert was standing by the coffee urns reading the sports section. When Charlie sat down Red folded his newspaper slowly and came over to wait on him. Charlie sat with his cheeks resting on the heels of his hands.

"How's it, Chollie, old boy, old boy?" Red Hibbert said.

"Not bad. Give me a cup of javy without and a couple of them Grandma's oatmeal cookies over there, Red. Where's Nick?"

Red scooted the plate with the cookies on it down the glassy white counter top and came along with the cup of black coffee. "This is Nick's day for Kiwanis," he said. "It looks to me like you'd stay home and get some sleep once in a while. You're dyin' on your feet."

"I am going to get some sleep Sunday, don't you never worry. I have to go see the Dean this afternoon. And I got make-up drill at three o'clock. I've got to make up some drill cuts."

"What you got to go see the Dean about?"

"I don't know what about; here's all it said." Charlie reached in his overcoat pocket and pulled out a jagged window envelope and a mimeographed postal card. He pushed the envelope across the counter along with the postal card. "I got that other in the morning mail too."

Red took the printed form from the Dean of Men's office out of the envelope and glanced at it. Then he picked up the postal card. It was headed,

FOURTH AND FINAL NOTICE

You are hereby summoned to appear before the chairman of the Student Senate Committee on Freshman Activities, Rm 204 Student Union Bldg., not later than 4 P.M., Friday afternoon. It will be to your advantage not to ignore this summons as you have three previous ones. This is positively the last opportunity you will be given to rectify your delinquency. Should you fail to appear this time, steps will be taken to bring you.

(signed) Aubrey H. Carson, Chrmn
Com. on Frshmn Actvts.

Red waggled the postal card. "What you going to do about this?"

"Tear it up like I did the others, I guess. I know what they want. They want to try and make me buy one of them damn' freshman caps."

"Take a tip from me, Charlie: I'd go see them. It won't hurt nothing, and it might be a lot easier on you in the long run."

"Hell, what can they do?"

"Plenty. They could sick the Black Hoods onto you."

"Ah! The Black Hoods, that bunch of amateur ku kluckers!"

"Call 'em amateurs if you want to, Charlie, but it wasn't only but last Friday night they took that little Jew-boy, Sol Lewis, out of the rooming house where I stay. It look to me like they did a pretty professional job on him. They used the buckle-end of a belt on him. They claim he was a stool pigeon for the University."

"Stool pigeon! Ah, you know that guy wasn't a stool pigeon, Red."

"We-ell, I'm not saying one way or the other. Anyhow, that's what you're up against when you take to fooling with that Student Committee on Freshman Activities, Charlie."

"Prexy claimed in his opening address at the first of

school that he had put a stop to these masked frats and all this hazing."

"Yeah, he said he had; but how's he going to put a stop to the Black Hoods? He can't kick out all the biggest shots in the University, can he? All the big shots on the campus are Black Hoods. Football stars and fellas like that. You won't see the President kicking guys like that out of the University."

"Maybe not, but—why, hell, that freshman cap business is nothing but a racket. That's all it is. Damn' if I let 'em scare me into paying a dollar for a little old sleazy green cloth cap!"

"O.K., Charlie; I guess you know what you want to do."

"Anyway, how could I get around to see that committee before four o'clock this afternoon, and see the Dean at two-thirty, and go to make-up drill from three till six? I'll be late to drill and get bawled out by the captain again. The captain's already about to flunk me for cuts. That's what's getting me down—Military. It's this Military that's getting me down."

"Jees, I don't know, Charlie; seems like I get a bigger kick out of army than I do any other course I got. They sure learn you more in army than they do in anything else *in* this University."

"Yeow, you learn plenty in army, all right. But what I don't like is the compulsory part. I don't think they ought to be allowed to make it compulsory for freshmen and sophomores. That's just like they had it over in Germany before they got rid of the Kaiser."

The red-haired boy gave him a startled look. He

frowned heavily. "Charlie," he exclaimed, "where are you getting all these radical ideas you been spouting around here lately?" Charlie peered at him. Red's face was set in earnestness.

"Why, that's not a radical idea," Charlie said, pushing back his empty coffee cup. "That's just a plain historical fact, that's all that is. I don't see where they got any right to make Military Training compulsory. This is supposed to be a *free* country. That compulsory stuff is what Mussle-leany and birds like that pull."

"But, Charlie, it's all for your own benefit. The University is just looking out after your own interests."

"How do you figure they're looking out for *my* interests?"

"Well, for one thing, when the next war comes we'll all be officers, us fellas that got this training in college. We'll go right into the regular army as officers. There's where we'll have the edge on guys that never did take advantage of a college education. Person'ly, when the next war comes along, I'm not hankerin' after any front-line trenches. And you know darn' well they're not going to stick their college-trained officers into front-line trenches to get shot. So there's where I figure us guys in R.O.T.C. will have a big advantage."

"Yeah, you might be right, at that, Red. But I'm not kicking about R.O.T.C. It's just the compulsory part I'm kicking against."

Red perked his head and scowled impatiently. "Charlie, they *got* to make it compulsory. If it wasn't compulsory, how many of the fellas would enroll in it?

They have to make Military compulsory in order to give the fullest benefits. What good could they do if only a few of the fellas was taking it?"

"Anyway, I know some it's not compulsory for," Charlie said stubbornly. "Last night there was a Phi Gam pledge in here bragging about how he got out of Military. He told them at the first of school he didn't want to take Military. They told him he *had* to take it —required of all able-bodied freshmen. Couldn't get his degree without it. So he had to go buy his army shoes. Well, he got the shoe store to send the bill to his old man. His old man is one of these they call 'em pacifists. When his old man gets the bill for his kid's army shoes, maybe you think he don't get the President of this University on long distance and tell him where to head in it. And this kid didn't have to take Military, neither. His old man's a big shot lawyer in the City."

"Yeah, but you got to have pull to get away with that, Charlie."

"That's what I mean, Red. You can get away with plenty in this University if you got the pull."

III

Charlie Wingate loped up the steps of the Administration Building, hurried through the revolving doors, and walked past hissing steam radiators down the long hall to the Dean of Men's office. He was ten minutes late. Before he opened the frosted-glass door he took out a pair of amber-colored spectacles and put them on. Then he went in and handed his summons to the secretary.

"The Dean will see you in a moment," she said. "Please take a chair."

Charlie sat down and gave an amber-hued glance about the outer office. Three dejected freshmen, holding their green caps, were waiting with him. He recognized none of them, so he picked up a week-old copy of the *Christian Science Monitor* and started to read it. But the room was warm and he immediately went to sleep. He had his head propped back against the wall. The newspaper slipped down into his lap. His amber-colored glasses hid his eyes and no one could see that they were closed. He was awakened by the secretary shaking him. She was smiling and the freshmen were all snickering.

"Wake up and pay for your bed, fella!" one of the freshmen called, and everyone laughed heartily.

"I sort of drowsed off. It's so nice and warm in here," Charlie said, apologizing to the pretty secretary.

The Dean of Men got up as he entered and, with his eyes on the slip bearing Charlie's name, said, "Ah, this is Charles Wingate, isn't it?" He grasped Charlie's hand as if it were an honor and pressed a button under the edge of his desk with his other hand. The secretary appeared at the door. "Miss Dunn, will you bring in Wingate's folder—Charles W-i-n-g-a-t-e. How do you like college by now, Wingate? Eyes troubling you?"

"Pretty well, sir. Yes, sir, a little. I wear these glasses."

The secretary came back with the folder and the Dean looked through it briefly. "Well, Wingate, I suppose you're anxious to know why I sent for you. The unpleasant truth is, Wingate, you don't seem to be doing so well in your college work. Your freshman adviser conferred with you twice about this, and this week he turned your case over to me. My purpose, of course, is to help you. Now, to be quite frank, Wingate, you're on the verge of flunking out. Less than a third of the semester remains, and you have a failing grade in English 101, conditional grades in Psychology 51 and Military Training; three hours of F and four hours of D, almost half your total number of hours. On the other hand, you have an A average in Spanish 1 and a B in Economics 150. Wingate, how do you account for your failing English when you are an A student in Spanish?"

"To tell you the truth, sir, I got behind on my written work in English, and I've never been able to catch up. And I don't really have to study Spanish. My father is a railway section foreman in my home town, and he's always had a gang of Mexicans working for him. I've been speaking Mexican ever since I was a kid. It's not the pure, what they call Castilian, Spanish, but I probably know almost as much Spanish as my professor."

"How about this B in Economics? That's a fairly high grade."

"Yes, sir. Doctor Kenshaw—he's my Ec professor—doesn't give exams. Instead he gives everyone a B until he calls for our term papers. We don't recite in his class. We just listen to him lecture. And the grade you get on your term paper is your semester grade."

"Ah! What you students term a pipe course, eh, Wingate?"

"Not exactly, sir. We have to do a lot of outside

reading for the term paper. But I'm counting on keeping that B in Ec."

"That's fine, Wingate. But it appears to me that it's high time you were getting busy on some of these other grades, too. Why can't you dig in and pull these D's up to B's, and this F up to at least a C? You've got it in you. You made an unusually high grade on your entrance exams, your record shows. Graduated from high school with honors. What's the trouble, Wingate? Tell me!"

"I don't know, sir, except I work at night and—"

"Oh, I see it here on your enrollment card now. Where do you work?"

"I work nights for Nick Pappas, down at The Wigwam."

"How many hours a night do you work?"

"Ten hours, sir. From nine till seven. The Wigwam stays open all night. I eat and go to eight o'clock class when I get off."

"Very interesting, Wingate. But don't you suppose that it would be advisable to cut down a bit on this outside work and attend a little more closely to your college work? After all, that's what you're here for, primarily—to go to college, not work in a café."

"I couldn't work fewer hours and stay in school, sir. I just barely get by as it is. I get my board at The Wigwam, and I pay my room rent, and I've been paying out on a suit of clothes. That leaves only about a dollar a week for all the other things I have to have."

"Wingate, shouldn't you earn more than that, working ten hours?"

"I get the regular, first-year-man rate, sir. Twenty cents an hour. It's set by the University. Nick takes out a dollar a day for board. Pays me five dollars a week in cash."

"Can't you arrange for a little financial support from home?"

"No, sir, I'm afraid I couldn't. I have two brothers and two sisters at home younger than I am. It wouldn't be right for me to ask my father to send money out of what he makes."

"But surely you could get out and land something a little more lucrative than this all-night restaurant job, Wingate."

"No, sir. Twenty cents an hour is standard rate for working students, and I haven't found anything better. Nick says he has at least thirty men on the waiting list for this job I have."

"Well, there's this about it, Wingate. The University is here, supported by the taxpayers of this State, for the purpose of giving the young men and women of this State educational opportunities. The University is not here for the purpose of training young men to be waiters in all-night restaurants. And, so far as I can see, that's about all you are deriving from your University career. So it occurs to me that you should make a choice: either find some way to devote more attention to your college work or drop out of school altogether. We are very loathe to encourage students who are *entirely* self-supporting. And yet, I will admit that I know any number of first-rate students who are entirely self-supporting. There's Aubrey Carson, for example. Quarterback on the football team, delegate to the Olympics, president of the Student Senate, and he's a straight A student. Aubrey Carson was telling me only last week that he hasn't had any financial assistance from home since he enrolled as a freshman. Aubrey is a fine example of the working student."

"Yes, sir; but look at the job Carson has. He works for a big tobacco company, and all he has to do is hand out Treasure Trove cigarettes to other students. The tobacco company pays him a good salary for passing out samples of their cigarettes."

"Why, Wingate, you surely must be mistaken about that. I don't believe Aubrey Carson smokes. In fact, I know he doesn't smoke. He's one of the finest all-'round athletes in this country."

"No, sir; I don't say he smokes either. But that's the straight stuff about his job with the cigarette company. They figure it's a good advertisement to have a popular guy like Aubrey Carson passing out Treasure Troves. Sort of an endorsement."

"All the same, Wingate, it doesn't reflect a very good attitude on your part, criticizing the way one of your fellow students earns his college expenses."

"Oh, I didn't mean to criticize him, sir. I was only saying—"

"Yes, yes, I know; but all this is beside the point. We're here to discuss the state of your grades, Wingate. The fact is, you are on probation right now. As you must know, any student who is passing in less than half his work is automatically suspended from the University and must return to his home. Now one F more and out you'll go, Wingate. That's just being frank with you."

"I'd hate to have to go back home like that, sir."

"Well, you'd have to. If you flunk out, the University authorities are obliged to see that you return to your home immediately."

"I'd hate that, sir. I'd hate to go back home and have to live off my family, and that's probably what I'd have to do. I had a letter from mother yesterday, and she says that nearly all the boys who graduated from high school with me are still there, loafing on the streets and living off their old folks. I don't like that idea. Mother's proud of me because I'm working my way through college. You know there are not many jobs to be had nowadays, sir, and I'd hate to have to go back home and loaf."

"It *is* a problem, I'll confess, Wingate. But what's the point in your coming to the University and working all night in a café and then flunking your class work? Moreover, your freshman adviser reports that you make a practice of sleeping in class. Is that true?"

"Well, yes, sir. I suppose I do drop off sometimes."

"Pretty impossible situation, isn't it, Wingate? Well, I've given you the best advice I can. Unless you can alter your circumstances I suggest that you withdraw from the University at once. We have six thousand other students here who need our attention, and the University has to be impartial and impersonal in dealing with these problems. Unless you can find some means to avoid flunking out I suggest withdrawing beforehand."

"Withdrawal would be a disgrace to me, sir. If I withdrew and went back home now, everyone at home would say that I had been expelled. You know how small towns are."

"Ah, now, Wingate, when you begin dealing with small-town gossip, I fear you're really getting outside my province. But I should think you'd prefer honorable withdrawal to flunking out."

"I believe I'll try to stick it through, sir. I'll try to remove the conditional grades, and maybe I can luck through on my finals."

"I hope you can, Wingate. As long as you feel that way about it, good luck to you." The Dean of Men stood up. Charlie stood up too. The Dean put out his hand and showed his teeth in a jovial smile and bore down hard on Charlie's knuckles. "I'm counting on you strong, old man," he said, encircling Charlie's shoulders with his left arm. "I know you have the stuff and that you'll come through with flying colors one of these days."

"Thank you, sir," Charlie said, grinning tearfully while the Dean gave his shoulder little pats. He edged toward the door as soon as the Dean released him, but when he reached it he hesitated and pulled the postal card out of his pocket. "Oh, pardon me, sir, but there's something I forgot to ask you. I got this in the mail today. I've been a little bothered about what to do about it."

The Dean of Men took the mimeographed card and read it quickly. "Why, I should say that you ought to go see what they want, Wingate. You shouldn't ignore things of this sort, you know. It's all a part of the normal activities of college life. No reason for antagonizing your fellow-students by ignoring a request of this kind."

"All right, sir; I'll go see them."

"Why, to be sure, go see them! Always keep in mind that the University is a social as well as an educational institution, Wingate."

IV

Room 204, Student Union Building, was a newly finished, rather barren office that smelled dankly of lime in the fresh plaster. It was fitted with a metal desk painted to imitate painted walnut, a large brass spittoon, a square metal waste-paper basket, a green metal filing cabinet, a large bank calendar, a huge pasteboard shipping case, and Aubrey H. Carson, who had the freshman cap concession.

Charlie Wingate hesitantly opened the door and saw Aubrey H. Carson tilted back in a chair, his feet on the metal walnut desk, reading a copy of *Ballyhoo.*

"Co-ome in! Co-ome in!" Aubrey Carson called loudly without putting down his magazine. "All right, old timer. What's on your mind?"

Charlie held out the mimeographed card. Carson held his magazine a moment longer before accepting the card. He shoved his hat down over one eye, turning the card, looking first at the back, then at the name on the front. "Um-m-m," he grunted. He reached over to a drawer in the filing cabinet without taking his feet down and flipped through the cards. He looked at the name on the postal card again, pulled a card out of the file, and drew his thick lips up into a rosette. He looked at the file card in silence.

"Wingate," he said at last in a severe tone, "you have been dilatory. Indeed, Wingate, I might even go so far as to say you have been remiss. At the beginning of this semester you applied for and received a refund on your student ticket fee. That signifies that you have not attended a single football game this season, and that you have no intention of honoring any of the University's athletic spectacles with your presence this season. Also, the record discloses that you did not register at the Y.M.C.A. freshman mixer. Neither did you respond to polite solicitation for a trifling monetary pledge to the Memorial Stadium Fund. And, most heinous offense of all, Wingate, we find that you have yet to pay in one dollar for your freshman cap, prescribed by your seniors and purveyed to you on a non-profit basis by the Student Committee on Freshman Activities. And yet, Wingate, I find you duly enrolled and attending classes in this here now University. Wingate, what possible excuse do you have for such gross neglect of University tradition? Speak up!"

Charlie said meekly, "Well, I work nights and it's hard for me to get here in the daytime, and I can't afford to buy a cap."

"What's this!" Carson exclaimed, jerking his legs down from the desk top and banging the desk with two flat hands. "Why, boy, this is treason! You mean you can't afford *not* to buy a freshman cap."

"No, I just came to tell you that a dollar has to go

a long way with me and that I need every cent I earn to stay in school. So I wish you'd please excuse me from buying a freshman cap."

Carson's lean, florid face suddenly became rigid and he stuck his jaw out with his lower teeth showing and, in spite of his marcelled taffy pompadour and his creased tailored suit, he again looked very much as he did in all the sporting section photographs. "See here, Wingate," he said, hard-lipped, "You're still a freshman at this University. You'll have to wait another year before you can start saying what you will do and won't do, see? Now we've been patient with you. You've been in school here three months without putting on a freshman cap. Do you realize that over eighty-five per cent of the freshman class came in here and bought their caps before the first week of school ended? Now who do you think *you* are, Wingate—Mr. God? You're going to get you a cap, and you're going to wear it. See? No ifs, ands, or buts about it. And if you don't leave this office with a green cap on your head then I don't mind telling you that we've got ways of getting one on you before another day passes."

"Well, if I buy one it's going to put me in a bad hole. All the money I've got is what I saved out to pay my room rent this week."

"Listen, fella, if we let horsefeathers like that go here, half the freshman class wouldn't be wearing freshman caps right now. Now I've said all I'm going to to you. Do you want your green cap now or will you wait till later? That's all I want to know. I don't aim to give you any high-pressure sales talk on something that's already been decided for you. Take it or leave it."

Carson reached over into the large pasteboard box, groped far down in it, and brought forth a small green monkey cap. He tossed it on the desk. Charlie Wingate stuck his forefinger in his watch pocket and pulled out a small pad of three carefully folded dollar bills. He unfolded them and laid one on the desk and picked up the cap. Carson put the dollar in his pocket and stood up.

Charlie stood holding his cap. He scuffed the cement floor with his shoe toe and began doggedly, "The only thing is—"

"Aw, that's O.K., Wingate, old man," Carson said suavely, "No hard feelings whatsoever." He heid out a freshly opened pack of cigarettes. "Here, have a Treasure Trove on me before you go."

V

That night all the stools along the counter at The Wigwam were filled when Charlie Wingate came in, still dusty from the drill field. He got himself a set-up back of the counter and went into the kitchen. He moved about the steam-table, dishing up his dinner. He dragged a stool over to a zinc-covered kitchen table and sat down to eat. The kitchen was warm and steamy and the air was thick with the odors of sour chili grease and yellow soap melting in hot dishwater. Charlie's fork slipped through his fingers, and he began nodding over his plate.

Fat Kruger, the night dishwasher and short-order

cook, yelled, "Hey, there, wake up and pay for your bed!" Charlie jerked his head up and looked at the ponderous, good-humored cook with half-lidded eyes. "Why'n't you try sleeping in bed once in a w'ile, Charlie?" Fat said in a friendly tone. "You're going to kill yourself if you don't watch out, trying to go without sleep."

"Don't worry, Fat. I can take it," Charlie said.

Almost two hours had to pass before it would be the hour for him to come on, but not time enough for him to walk back to his room and catch a nap, so he took the book on which he had to make an outside reading report in Economics 150 and went up to the last booth to study until nine o'clock. He fell asleep and he did not wake up until Red Hibbert, going off, shook him and told him that it was almost time for him to come on. He closed his book and went back to the washroom. The acrid stench of the mothballs that Nick used to deodorize the latrine cleared his head. He took down his apron and tied it on over his army breeches. Then he slipped into a white coat.

The usual black-coffee addicts came dribbling in. When the telephone rang, Charlie answered it, jotting down short orders to go. The delivery boy came in and went out and banged off on his motorcycle with paper bags full of "red hots" and nickel hamburgers and coffee in paper cylinders. The Wigwam's white tile shone under the inverted alabaster urns. There was a pale pink reflection in the plate-glass window as the Neon sign outside spelled and re-spelled "Wigwam Eats. Open All Night." A party of drunken Betas came in at ten-thirty and seated themselves noisily in the last booth. They tossed Charlie's economics book out into the aisle with a whoop, and he came and picked it up and took their orders in silence while they kidded him about his flap ears and the grease on his white coat. At eleven o'clock the last whistle at the University power house blew for the closing hour, and a couple of lingering "dates" scurried out. Finally the drunks left, after one had been sick in a corner of the booth. The delivery boy came coasting up at midnight and checked in and roared away again on his motorcycle. The long small hours began inching past.

At one o'clock Charlie finished cleaning up the drunk's mess and he had cleared off the last of the tables. The Wigwam was empty, so he opened the book he must read for Ec 150. He had read a few lines when a bunch of girls from the Theta house down the street came charging in, giggling and talking in gasps and screams, their fur coats clutched over their sleeping pajamas. It was long after the closing hour, and they told Charlie to keep an eye out for the University night watchman. They took up the two back booths and they consulted The Wigwam's printed menu card without failing to read aloud the lines "Nick (Pericles) Pappas," "We Employ Student Help Exclusively," and "Please Do Not Tip. A Smile Is Our Reward" with the customary shrieks. Nearly all ordered filet mignon and French fries, which were not on the menu, but two or three ordered pecan waffles and coffee, which were. When he had served their orders Charlie went back to his book again, but the low buzz of their talk and their sudden spurts of laughter disturbed him and he could not read. At a quarter of two they began peering round corners of their booths. They asked Charlie in stage-whispers if the coast were clear.

Charlie went to the door and looked out on the street and beckoned widely with his arm. They trooped out with their fur coats pulled tight, their fur-trimmed silken mules slapping their bare heels. Charlie went on back to clear away their dishes. They had left about thirty cents as a tip, all in cents and nickels. The coins were carefully imbedded in the cold steak grease and gluey syrup and putty-colored cigarette leavings on their plates. Charlie began stacking the plates without touching the money. He carried the dirty dishes back and set them through the opening in the kitchen wall. Fat Kruger came to the opening and Charlie went back to his book.

Fat called, "Hey, Charlie, you leavin' this tip again?"

"You're damn' right, I'm leaving it!" Charlie said. "I can get along without their tips. They leave it that way every time. I guess they think I'll grabble on their filthy plates to get a lousy thirty cents. It takes a woman to think up something like that."

"Charlie, you're too proud. I don't see where you can afford to be so proud. The way I figure it, thirty cents is thirty cents."

"Hell, I'm not proud, Fat. I just try to keep my self-respect. When those sorority sows come in and plant their tips in the dirt and grease of their plates, damn' if I'll lower myself to grub it out."

He sat down on a counter stool with the economics

book before him, trying to fix his mind on it. He read a page. The print became thin blurred parallels of black on the page. His eyelids kept drooping shut and he propped the muscles with his palms at his temples, trying to keep his eyes open. His head jerked forward and he caught it and began reading again. Soon his face lowered slowly through his hands and came to rest on the open book.

Fat Kruger came through the kitchen swinging door and tiptoed up front. Fat stood grinning, watching Charlie sleep. Cramped over with his head on the counter, Charlie snored softly. Fat gave his head a gentle shove, and Charlie started up to catch his balance.

"For God sakes, guy, you're *dead!*" Fat howled. "Don't you never get no sleep except like that?"

"What time is it?" Charlie said, yawning and arching his back.

"Half-past two."

"Jees, is that all?"

"Charlie, go back there and lay down on the kitchen table. I'll watch the front for you. Nobody'll be coming in for a while."

As he was talking old Uncle Jim Hudson ambled in, a bundle of sweaters, overcoats, and grizzled dewlaps, his black timeclock slung over one shoulder by a leather lanyard. Uncle Jim laid his long, nickled flashlight carefully on the counter and eased himself onto a stool. He ordered a cup of black coffee and in a lecherous wheeze began telling dirty stories selected from his twenty years' experience as a campus night-watchman. Fat Kruger nickered loudly after each telling, and Charlie jerked his eyes open and smiled sleepily. It was three-thirty when Uncle Jim left. Charlie opened his book again.

"Charlie, I wouldn't put my eyes out over that damn' book if I was you, when you're dyin' for sleep," Fat said.

"I've got to get it read, Fat. It's my outside reading in Economics and the whole semester grade depends on it. It's the hardest book to keep your mind on you ever saw. I've been reading on it for over a month and I'm only half through, and he's going to call for these reports any day now. If I flunk Ec I flunk out of school."

"Why mess with reading it? I know a guy over at the Masonic Dorm who'll read it and write your report for two bucks. He writes all my English themes for me, and I'm making a straight A in English. He only charges fifty cents for short themes and two bucks for term papers. You ought to try him."

"Hell, Fat, you get five dollars a week from home. Where am I going to get two dollars for hiring a guy to read this book?"

"Charlie, I just can't figure you out. You never do get any real sleep. You sure must want a college education bad. It don't look to me like you would figure it's worth it."

"Oh, it's worth it! It's a big satisfaction to my folks to have me in college. And where can a man without a college degree get nowadays? But I'll tell you the truth, I didn't know it was going to be like this when I came down here last Fall. I used to read *College Humor* in high school, and when fellows came home from University for the holidays, all dressed up in snappy clothes, talking about dates and football and dances, and using college slang—well, I had a notion I'd be like that when I got down here. The University publicity department sent me a little booklet showing how it was easy to work your way through college. So here I am. I haven't had a date or been to a dance or seen a football game since I enrolled. And there are plenty of others just like me. I guess I'm getting a college education, all right—but the only collegiate thing I've been able to do is go to sleep in class."

"How you get by with sleeping in class, Charlie?"

"I wear those colored spectacles and prop myself, and the profs can't see I've got my eyes closed."

Fat waggled his heavy face mournfully. "Boy, it sure is tough when a man don't get his sleep."

"Yeah, it is," Charlie said, looking down at his book again. "I'll get a break pretty soon, though. I'd rather chop off a hand than to flunk out of University before I'd even finished one semester."

VI

The tardiest of the hundred students enrolled in Dr. Sylvester C. O. Kenshaw's Economics 150 straggled into the lecture room and made their ways to alphabetically-assigned chairs with much scuffling and trampling of toes and mumbled apologies. Ec 150, renowned as a pipe course, was always crowded. Doctor Kenshaw was the celebrated author of seven textbooks on economics, five of which his students were required to buy each semester. Doctor Kenshaw's national reputation as an economist permitted him to be erratic about meeting his classes, but fame had never dimmed his fondness for student flattery. The only students who ever flunked Ec 150 were those who gave affront to Doctor Kenshaw by neglecting to buy his textbooks or by not laughing at his wit or by being outrageously inattentive to his lectures.

Doctor Kenshaw was late that morning. Charlie Wingate sat in his chair on the back row in an agony of waiting. He had on his amber glasses and he could fall asleep as soon as Doctor Kenshaw opened his lecture. But he had to stay awake until then. There was a slow ache in the small of his back. The rest of his body was numb. He had not taken off his army shoes for twenty hours, and his feet were moist and swollen. Every time he shifted position his arms and legs were bathed in prickling fire. He kept his eyes open behind the amber lenses, watching the clock. Small noises of the classroom came to him as a low, far-off humming.

When the clock on the front wall showed nine after eleven the seated class began stirring as if it were mounted on some eccentric amusement-park device. Excited whispers eddied out on the warm air of the steam-heated lecture room. "He's giving us another cut!" "He's not meeting this class today!" "He's got one more minute to make it!" "Naw; six more! You have to wait fifteen minutes on department heads."

There was a seething argument on this point, but when the clock showed fourteen minutes after eleven a bold leader sprang up and said, "Come on, everybody!" All but five or six especially conscientious students rose and milled after him toward the door. Charlie Wingate followed, thoroughly awakened by the chance of getting to bed so soon. The leader yanked the door open and Doctor Kenshaw stumbled in, all out of breath, his eyeglasses steamed, his pointed gray beard quivering, a vain little man in a greenish-black overcoat.

"Go back to your seats!" Doctor Kenshaw commanded sternly as soon as he could get his breath. He marched over to his lecture table and planked down his leather brief case. He took off his overcoat and began wiping the steam from his eyeglasses while the students hurried back to their chairs. "It does seem to me," he said, his voice quavering with anger, "that it would be no more than courteous for this class to await my arrival on those rare occasions when I am delayed. Day after day you come lagging into my classes, and I have always been extremely lenient in giving credit for attendance, no matter how tardy your arrival. Certainly it is no more than my privilege to ask that you wait for me occasionally."

A few students exchanged meaning glances. They meant, "Now we're in for it. The old boy has on one of his famous mads."

"Today, I believe I shall forego delivering my prepared lecture," Doctor Kenshaw went on in a more even voice, but with elaborate sarcasm, "and let *you* do the talking. Perhaps it would be meet to hear a few outside reading reports this morning. All of you doubtless are aware that these reports were due last week, although I had not expected to call for them at once. I trust that I have impressed you sufficiently with the importance of these reports. They represent to me the final result of your semester's work in this course. The grades you receive on these reports will be your grades for the semester. Let us begin forthwith. When your name is called, you will rise and read your report to the class." He opened his roll book.

"Mr. Abbott!" he called. Mr. Abbott stammered an excuse. Doctor Kenshaw passed coldly on to Miss Adams, making no comment. All through the A's it was the same. But with the B's an ashen, spectacled Miss Ballentyne stood up and began reading in a droning voice her report on *The Economic Consequences of the Peace*. Obviously Doctor Kenshaw was not listening to her. His hard little eyes under craggy brows were moving up one row and down the other, eager for a victim. On the back row, Charlie Wingate's propped legs had given way and he had slipped far down into his seat, fast asleep. When Doctor Kenshaw's preying eyes reached Charlie they stopped moving. Someone tittered nervously and then was silent as Doctor Kenshaw jerked his head round in the direction of the noise. Miss Ballentyne droned on.

When she had finished, Doctor Kenshaw said dryly, "Very good, Miss Ballentyne, very good, indeed. Er—ah—would someone be kind enough to arouse the recumbent young gentleman in the last row?"

There was a murmur of laughter while everyone turned to look at Milton Weismann nudging Charlie Wingate. Doctor Kenshaw was running down the list of names in his small record book. Milton Weismann gave Charlie another stiff poke in the ribs, and Charlie sprang up quickly. Everyone laughed loudly at that.

"Mr.—ah—*Wingate,* isn't it? Mr. Wingate, your report."

"Pardon me, sir?"

"Mr. Wingate, what was the title of the book assigned to you for report in this class?"

"*Theory of the Leisure Class* by Veblen, sir."

"Ah, then, that's the explanation. So you were assiduously engaged in evolving your own theory of the leisure class. Is that right, Mr. Wingate? You have evidently concluded that Economics 150 is the leisure class."

The class rocked with laughter. Doctor Kenshaw, pleased with his pun and flattered by the response to it, found it hard to keep his face straight. Suddenly he was back in good humor. "Mr. Wingate's theory is quite apparently one to which the majority of this class subscribes. Now I try to be lenient with students in this class. Surely no one could describe me as a hard taskmaster. But I resent your implication that I have been too easy-going. Now these reading reports were assigned to you last September, and you have had ample time to prepare them. I'll not call for any more of them today, but at the next session of this class I expect every one of these papers in. As for you, Mr. Wingate, if you'll see me directly after class, I'll be glad to hear any explanation or apology that you may wish to make. I want most of all to be fair. I have always given every student the benefit of the doubt until a student deliberately flouts me with his indifference. But I am capable of being quite ruthless, I assure you."

"Thank you, sir," Charlie mumbled. He suffered a

slow torture, trying to keep awake until the class bell rang. He rolled his hot, red-veined eyes up with drunken precision to see the clock. Fifteen minutes had to pass before the bell would ring.

When the bell rang the class arose quickly and began clumping out. Several co-eds and men, politickers and apple-polishers wangling for A's, crowded about the lecture table. Doctor Kenshaw always remained behind after each class to accept their homage. But today he looked up over the heads of the eager group. He silenced their inane questions and flagrant compliments by placing his right forefinger against his thin, unsmiling lips. "Sh-h-h!" he said. The apple-polishers turned their heads in the direction of his gaze and then, giggling softly, tiptoed away. When the last had gone out, Doctor Kenshaw unscrewed his fountain pen and opened his roll book. He ran his finger down the list until he came to "Wingate, C." and in the space opposite under "Smstr Grd" he marked a precise little F.

A whiffling snore escaped Charlie Wingate in the back of the room. Doctor Kenshaw looked back across the varnished chair rows with a frown of annoyance. He took his overcoat from its hanger, slipped into it, and strapped up his brief case. He jammed on his hat and strode out of the lecture room, slamming the door. The noise made a hollow echo in the empty room, but it did not disturb Charlie Wingate. He slept on behind his amber glasses.

6

REVENGE

WE WERE all very proud when school opened again that Fall, because we were going into the sixth grade. The grades before the sixth were on the ground floor of the school building, but the sixth was upstairs with the higher grades. We had been wondering for a long time how it would feel, marching in from recess, to go on up the stairs instead of turning in at a room on the first floor. The year we were in the fifth we envied the sixth-graders almost as much as the eighth-graders envied the high-school freshmen.

There were other things that had made the sixth grade one that we were eager to be in. One thing was that we could have ink in the inkwells. Some of the desks in the fifth grade had nothing but round holes where the inkwells should have been, and we had kept the few inkwells there were stuffed with chewed-up paper. We had used only pencils. But in the sixth, we knew, we would use ink. That would be something new.

We had a new teacher from the State Normal School that year, too. We were curious about her, and the ones who had been lucky enough to get first sight of her were questioned anxiously. Already the rumor had gone around the school-yard that first day, telling that the new teacher was a funny looker, and that she wasn't in favor of whipping. That was good news for several of us. Miss Spandrel, the fifth-grade teacher, had been strong on whipping. Boys who knew said that she whipped harder than Professor Butler, the superintendent, who kept a length of rubber tubing in his desk drawer and used it to wear out anyone who was sent up to him.

The new sixth-grade teacher wasn't out to watch the lines pass that first morning. She was sitting at her desk when we marched in. We all took seats, some of which we had spotted the year before. We sat up very straight with our hands folded in front of us, fresh and clean for the first day of school, and very happy to be starting the sixth grade. The new teacher sat plucking her lower lip and looking us over distantly. We gazed back at her. She was a neat, starched woman, with a square-tipped pink nose and an upper lip too short to cover her teeth.

After she had looked at us a while, she said, "You two boys sitting in the back seats bring your books up here to the front seats. I know about boys who always take the back seats the first day of school. I like to have them up here by me."

We all laughed heartily at that, and Loppy Crashaw and Gus Belcher took their second-hand books and brand-new pencil tablets out of the back desks and came slowly up to the front of the room with them.

The new teacher went to the front blackboard and wrote, "*My* name is *Miss* Manchester," on it in round letters.

While she had her back turned, Loppy Crashaw, who was the meanest kid in our grade, tripped Gus Belcher.

That made a big clatter, because Gus, the big cow, dropped all his books, and everyone began laughing again.

Miss Manchester turned around quickly and rapped on her desk with a ruler. We stopped laughing. She stood glaring at us so hard that her eyes, as round and hard blue as china taws, seemed ready to pop out of her head. Later we learned that glaring was one of Miss Manchester's punishment methods. We never did feel hurt by it. It only made her look funnier, her eyes starting out of their sockets like that. But as soon as we found that she meant it for punishment, to keep her from doing anything worse, we always tried to look shamed and uncomfortable when she glared at us.

She shifted her glare to Gus Belcher and she kept it on him until he had finished picking up his books and had taken a front seat. When everything was in order again, Miss Manchester said, "I may as well tell you at the beginning that I do not believe in whipping pupils. But that does not mean that I do not believe in punishment.

"I have my own system of punishments. Of course you all know that there are certain things we can't have. Among them are: whispering, chewing gum in the classroom, note writing, bringing candy, or marbles, or tops, or any kind of plaything into the classroom, throwing paper wads, speaking out without permission, using ugly words or names, such as liar and fool, and several other things which I shall mention later. I shall give demerits for each of these, one demerit for some offenses, as many as five demerits for others.

"When any pupil gets five demerits within one month, he will have shown that he can't behave as a big boy or girl should, and I shall punish him just as Mrs. Wellborn punishes her little primary pupils downstairs. When any pupil gets five demerits he will be made to sit on the floor under my desk for two hours.

"When any pupil gets ten demerits in one month he will have to stay in after school and commit to memory twenty-five lines of poetry. They won't be these little short lines of poetry, either. Let me tell you that!

"When any pupil gets fifteen demerits he will have to stand at the front blackboard for one hour with the tip of his forefinger in a small chalk circle which I shall place up as high as he can reach, standing tiptoe." Miss Manchester went over and took a piece of chalk and high up on the blackboard she drew a circle about the size of a quarter. "And if any pupil lets his finger slip and smudges the circle," she went on, "that will add fifteen minutes more to the time he must stand there.

"Perhaps I should add here that I have some special punishments for special offenses. For example, when one of you is guilty of continual whispering, I shall seal your lips with a piece of adhesive plaster. I believe that that punishment is more effective than demerits for boys and girls who whisper."

Miss Manchester paused for a moment, and then, glaring hard at us all, she said in a slow, tense voice, "*And* when any pupil gets *twenty* demerits before the end of the month, I shall send him in to have a little talk with Professor Butler, the superintendent."

What difference did it make if Miss Manchester

didn't believe in whipping? We all knew what would happen to anyone who got sent in to have a little talk with Professor Butler.

II

The school year hadn't got very far along before most of us were sick and tired of Miss Manchester and her new system of punishments. Sometimes, when our backs and legs were aching from the strain of standing tiptoe with our fingers in the chalk circle, or when the lines of *Hiawatha* wouldn't stick in our memories, we thought that whipping would have been much easier.

She was near-sighted, and she was always getting the wrong person. She wouldn't listen to any explanation.

"Why, I wasn't doing anything!" one of us would complain.

"Oh, so you weren't doing anything?" she would say. "Well, why weren't you, then? You're not coming to school to sit idle, are you?" And she would double the punishment.

The only boy in the room who escaped her, those first months, was Loppy Crashaw, and he was the meanest kid in our grade. He had had some kind of sickness when he was a baby, and one of his legs had never grown to full size. We called him Loppy because he was lopsided. But sometimes we wouldn't have minded being like him. He could do almost anything without fear of punishment. Teachers never had done anything to him, because he was crippled.

Back in the fifth grade Miss Spandrel thrashed all the other boys, but she never did lay a switch on Loppy.

One day, in the fifth, Loppy kept shooting Gus Belcher with tinfoil wads. He shot them with a rubber band and they stung hard. Gus stood it as long as he could. Then he jumped up and knocked Loppy clear out of his seat. Miss Spandrel came over and grabbed Gus by the collar. She didn't ask any questions. She got out the bamboo stick and she whipped Gus until his stocking legs showed blood. "You great big brute!" she said. "I'll teach you not to strike a poor little crippled child!"

It didn't do any good for us to catch Loppy out and beat him up after school hours, because he always tattled, and that meant our getting whipped harder than ever when we came back to school the next day.

He was good in his books, and that gave him time to think up tricks to play while school was going on. Many of us suffered long hours with our fingers stretched up to the chalk circle for things that Loppy pulled. If he put a pin in the toe of his shoe and stuck somebody with it, the one who cried out in pain was the one who was punished. If he made a funny face that caused some girl to giggle, the girl was the one who stayed in after school. If he threw an apple core across the room, the one who got hit and yelled had to take the blame. Miss Manchester had put Loppy up in a front seat the first day of school, but he was too slick to let her see him do anything.

That was why the rest of us were tickled, even though it was too late then for us to get any great satisfaction out of it, when we heard how Loppy and Miss Manchester had been made victims of a strange revenge—strange, because neither the ones whom it caught, nor the one who caused it, knew that the score had been evened.

We never did forget the dirty trick Loppy Crashaw played on Rolland Gentry.

Rolland was a big country boy. He was five or six years older than any of the rest of us. His people had kept him out of school to pick cotton so much when he was little that he had got a late start. But he had his mind made up that he was going to get an education, and he came to town to school after he was almost ten years behind his grade. He was getting along fine, though, making two grades each year. He was passed on from the fifth to the sixth at Christmas, and Miss Manchester had told him that if he worked hard enough in the sixth he might be able to skip the seventh grade altogether. Then he could go into high-school from the eighth at Christmas the next year and he would be almost up with pupils of his own age.

Rolland soon took his place as the brightest boy in our grade. He always had all the problems in arithmetic, he made 100 in spelling every month, and he answered questions in geography and physiology that stumped the rest of the class.

But Rolland looked funny sitting up there in the back seat, way too small for him, and the desk too low. Even if he was taller than we were, we thought that he was a big sissy. He had kidney trouble, and we thought that that was a sissy thing to have. He was pale and blue-veined, with blond, curly hair and long, nervous fingers. He had won a gold medal for penmanship in the county contest the Spring before, and he wore the medal on his coat lapel. He was so nervous he couldn't sit still when the teacher asked a question. He would wave his hand wildly. The teacher wouldn't call on him often, because she knew that he always had the right answer. He never swore, or fought, or played marbles for keeps on the playground. Rolland was too nice.

Loppy Crashaw had been the brightest boy in the sixth grade until Rolland came up from the fifth that Christmas. Loppy had even made the highest grades in penmanship. His sentences were almost exactly like those in the copybook. Then when Rolland Gentry came up from the fifth it wasn't long before Loppy had to take second place in everything. That made him dislike Rolland. He was always picking on the big country boy. He knew that Rolland was too goodie-goodie to do anything back, even if he was big enough to clean up on any two of us.

One of Miss Manchester's new methods was the way she had for letting us go out. She had a little wooden paddle hung up by the door. On one side it had "In" printed, and on the other side "Out." When one of us wanted to be excused we had to turn up the side that had "Out" on it, and then no one else could go out until that one had come back and turned up the "In" side again.

Miss Manchester said, when she was explaining this new system to us, "Now in the lower grades, I know, you have been accustomed to holding up two fingers when you wished to be excused. But in the sixth, of course, we are getting a little more grown up, and we can adopt a new method. More than one person's being out of the room at a time leads to disorder and confusion. So when the 'Out' side is showing, you all will know that some person is out of the room, and you must wait until he or she returns. So please do not hold up your hands to be excused any more, because only one person will be permitted to leave the room at a time."

One day, just as the study hour before noon was beginning, the "In" side of the paddle was showing, and Rolland Gentry left his seat and started toward the door. But Loppy Crashaw looked back and saw him coming down the aisle. He jumped up from his front seat and turned the paddle and went limping out.

Rolland went quietly back to his seat. Miss Manchester was sitting at her desk, reading, and she did not see what had happened.

Loppy stayed and stayed. Rolland began twisting around in his seat and sliding back and forth. Finally he raised his hand with two fingers up. Miss Manchester glanced up from her book and frowned and shook her head. Rolland put his hand down.

After a few minutes he put it up again, and began snapping his fingers. Miss Manchester looked up from her book again, glared hard, and said, "No!" loudly. Then she looked down at her book again and went on reading.

Rolland shuddered violently. All at once he put his head down on his arms and began sobbing. Miss Manchester snapped her book to. Then she went back and stood by Rolland's desk. She could see that she was too late. There was a big puddle on the floor. But she said softly, "You may leave the room now, if you wish to, Rolland."

But Rolland wouldn't raise his head. He kept his face buried in his arms, sobbing, a big boy like that.

Loppy Crashaw came back just before the bell rang for noon. Miss Manchester turned her glare on him. "How long have you been out, young man?" she said.

"Just a few minutes," Loppy said.

"Well, you stayed out too long, and I'm going to give you two demerits."

When the bell rang for noon, Miss Manchester said, "Attention!" but Rolland did not raise his head.

"Turn!" said Miss Manchester. We pivoted our legs out into the aisles, but Rolland didn't move.

"Stand! March!" said Miss Manchester, clapping her hands for the march-step.

When we glanced back, leaving the room, we saw Rolland still hunched up with his face hidden on his desk. That was the last time we ever saw him at school.

III

Some of the older girls used to get up in the sixth-grade room and practice dancing in the latter part of the noon hour, before the teacher came in. They played the phonograph and kept a sharp look-out for Miss Manchester, who was a strict Baptist.

There were some good-sized girls in the sixth grade, and girls get interested in dancing before boys do. They would waltz around with an imaginary partner, sashaying up and down the aisles and around the front of the room, humming the tunes. We would make fun of them, but they would only make slapping motions at us, and go on. They didn't know how silly they looked.

One day in April, a few minutes before time for the last bell at noon, Loppy Crashaw went up to a big girl named Anna Lance, who was feisting around, trying to dance. He grabbed her around the waist, pretending that he was going to dance with her. Anna gave Loppy a big shove, but as he went stumbling backward, he yelled, "Oh, Anna's got on a corset! I felt it on her just then! Anna's got on a corset! Anna's got on a corset!"

About that time Miss Manchester came into the room. She grabbed Loppy by the shoulders and began shaking him. Loppy was so surprised he didn't know what to do. That was the first time any teacher had ever punished him. It was the first time he had ever been caught outright. He whimpered.

"You dirty-minded little *thing*, you!" said Miss Manchester. "I'll teach you that you can't talk that way to girls. Now you get under my desk there, and don't you come out until I give you permission."

She kept Loppy under her desk until recess time.

That same afternoon Miss Manchester was keeping some of us in after school for punishment. She had caught me chewing gum, and I had to write "I must not chew gum in the classroom" two hundred times.

Reverend Reynolds, the young man who had the Baptist pulpit for a while, used to come around to keep Miss Manchester company while she was keeping us in after school. He was there that afternoon, and they had been talking together in low voices. She was tidying up around her desk, straightening up the theme papers, emptying the pencil sharpener, and cleaning out the desk drawer, while she talked to the preacher.

I finished my two hundred sentences and came up to hand them in. When Miss Manchester took them, I said, "Gee, my arm is about give out from all that writing."

Reverend Reynolds frowned at me and said, "Any boy who takes the Name of the Lord in vain like that ought to be made to write the Third Commandment two hundred times."

I hadn't known that there was anything wrong with "Gee," (I didn't discover until later that it was short for "Jesus") and I was standing there trying to figure it out when Miss Manchester picked up her desk drawer, the wide, flat one that went under the top, and turned it upside down to shake the dust out of it.

We all three saw it at the same time: a sentence about Miss Manchester chalked across the bottom of the drawer. It had one word in it that caused the preacher and the teacher both to turn red. It was written in good handwriting, almost as good as that in the copybook. Loppy Crashaw had been under the desk that afternoon, and, since Rolland Gentry had left school, Loppy was the only boy in the room who could make such a graceful capital F.

Miss Manchester put the drawer back in her desk quickly, and, with her face as red as beet, said to me, "You may go."

The next morning when school took up, Miss Manchester glared at Loppy for several minutes. Then she said, "Young man, your dirty-mindedness is going to get you into very serious trouble one of these days."

"What about?" Loppy asked boldly.

"You know what about," the teacher said, blushing.

The last week of school, a month later, we had an oral spelling examination. We were divided up into sides, standing along opposite walls of the room. Anna Lance was the last one left standing on her side, and she was standing near Loppy Crashaw's desk.

Anna Lance had spelled down all but two or three on the other side, but she was faltering because she felt her underpants slipping down. Finally they fell down around her ankles. Miss Manchester had her back turned, giving out a word to the other side. Anna quickly kicked the panties under Loppy Crashaw's desk. Loppy had already missed a word, and he was in his seat.

Nearly all of us saw what Anna had done, and we began to giggle. Miss Manchester stopped giving out words and came over to that side of the room. She looked down and saw the white drawers under Loppy's desk.

"What is this?" she said, dragging them out into the aisle with her toe.

"They're hers," Loppy said calmly, pointing to Anna.

"They are not!" Anna said loudly. She started crying. "He's been tormenting me with them. He just brought them to school to torment me. He's been tormenting me like that all year." Anna sobbed wildly.

"Why she's a big liar!" Loppy said.

"What was that word you used?" said Miss Manchester.

"I said, she's a liar," Loppy said firmly.

"Young man, do you remember what I told you about your dirty-mindedness getting you into very serious trouble some day? I've had some experience with your nasty tricks, myself. I haven't forgotten that vulgar sentence you wrote on the bottom of my desk drawer that day I put you under there."

"What sentence?"

"You know very well what sentence."

"I never wrote nothing on the bottom of your desk drawer."

Miss Manchester was aghast. "Oh, I suppose you're going to try to tell me that I'm storying, too," she said, sarcastically.

Loppy looked down at the floor. "You're lying if you say I wrote anything on the bottom of your desk drawer," he mumbled, but loud enough for everyone to hear.

That made Miss Manchester so mad she couldn't keep her feet still. "I heard what you said!" she cried. "I heard what you said, young man! There's a limit to what a teacher can put up with. Now you hustle right out and cut me some switches. There's only one punishment for a boy of your type."

That Spring the Ladies' Civic Club had planted shade tree slips all along the sides of the cement walk leading up to the school building. They were Lombardy poplars. Shade trees were scarce around there, and the *Weekly Recorder* had given the tree-planting a big write-up. When Loppy came back he had an armload of Lombardy poplar switches. They still had the nursery tags on them.

Miss Manchester shrieked, "Oh, what have you done! You nasty little brat, you! Don't you know that those shade tree slips cost three dollars apiece?"

Loppy let the bundle of switches fall clattering to the floor. "I cain't he'p what they cost," he said sullenly. "You told me to get switches, and them's switches, ain't they?"

Miss Manchester grabbed up one of the sticks and took hold of Loppy. She began striking him across the back. She had given him about three licks when he twisted out of her grasp. They stood there glaring at each other, both breathing hard and trembling.

"I never done nothing, and I ain't going to take any whupping off of you, you danged old fool!" Loppy yelled. "You and your new-fangled ideas. Pooh! I thought you wasn't in favor of whupping!"

"I'm not, but a good, sound thrashing is the only way to appeal to a boy like you," Miss Manchester said in a strained, high voice. "Come here to me!" She made a grab for Loppy, but he jumped nimbly out of reach. "Come here to me!" she shrilled.

"Yah, what do I want to come there to you for, you blamed old near-sighted fool, you! You won't lay hand on me!" Loppy turned and went limping toward the door.

"If you leave this room, I'll fail you!" Miss Manchester called after him. "If you go out of that door, you needn't come back!"

Loppy went on out and slammed the door behind him.

While this had been going on the rest of us had been sitting with our mouths open. Miss Manchester sat down at her desk. She was trembling so hard she couldn't hold a book. She turned her glare on us.

"I don't think any of you have any time to be idling," she said, "because we're having the final examination in arithmetic the first thing after recess."

None of us was prepared for the final examination in arithmetic, because it had been promised for the next day, the last day of school. We were frightened.

When we came in from afternoon recess Miss Manchester was writing the problems on the board. We were all feeling sick and weak, waiting to see how hard the examination was going to be. The first example looked pretty hard.

She had finished putting on two problems when the door flew open and in marched Mrs. Crashaw, a big, black-haired woman. Loppy followed along behind her.

"Did you strike this pore little cripple' child of mine?" said Mrs. Crashaw in a loud, trembling voice.

Miss Manchester was startled. "Why, I—" she said.

"Do you know what ought to be done with any grown woman that would whip a cripple' child?" Mrs. Crashaw stooped over and picked up one of the sticks from the bundle in the corner. She began switching Miss Manchester about the legs. Miss Manchester started screaming and grabbed Mrs. Crashaw by the hair.

Professor Butler, the superintendent, heard the screams and he came dashing into the room, his dyed, purplish-black pompadour waving and his glasses askew.

"Here, here! Ladies! Ladies! What's the meaning of this?" He thrust himself between Miss Manchester and Loppy's mother.

Mrs. Crashaw, with her hair all down, looked like a wild woman. She still held her switch. "I'll show *you* the meaning," she yelled and she turned around and started hitting Professor Butler. As soon as she got loose, Miss Manchester went running out of the room. Professor Butler turned and ran out too. Mrs. Crashaw ran after him, cutting at him with the switch.

We heard the door of Professor Butler's office bang to down at the end of the hall. Then we heard Mrs. Crashaw pounding on it, calling to them to let her in. No one laughed. Everyone sat very still for a while. Loppy was sitting at his desk, looking very solemn. Pretty soon Mrs. Crashaw came back down the hall and put her head in at the door. She said, "Come on, son." Loppy got up and picked up his books and went out.

We had started throwing chalk and whispering loudly by the time Professor Butler came back into the room.

"Miss Manchester is not feeling well," he said, "and she will not be able to give the final examination in arithmetic. But she asks me to tell you that you are all passed to the seventh grade next year." He smiled thinly. "So it will not be necessary for you to come back to school any more this term. Your report cards will be mailed out to your parents. Pass out quietly so as not to disturb the other rooms. Dismissed!"

IV

Outside it was late May and the afternoon was warm. It was about three o'clock. When we came out of the school building into the bright air, we felt dizzy. We didn't even whoop because it was the end of school. Too much had happened that day. We were dazed by all that.

Gus Belcher said, "Let's go out to Edwards' tanks and go swimming."

None of us had been swimming that year, and two or three thought that the water was still too cold. But the rest of us scoffed at that. Everything was perfect that day. Everything had come out right. So we went on, five or six of us, walking out to Edwards' cattle pond.

We were still wearing our shoes and stockings. When we were about a mile out of town we sat down and pulled them off. We wriggled our tender toes in the warm dust as we walked.

We were cutting across a pasture when we saw a tall boy over in the next field, chopping cotton. He looked toward us and leaned on his hoe and called out, "Hi, there, you fellers!"

We walked over to the barb-wire fence, and when we got up close we saw that it was Rolland Gentry. It had been two months since we had last seen him, and he didn't look so sissified any more. When he pulled off his straw hat we saw that he had had his curly hair cropped close to his scalp. He was chewing a big quid of tobacco. But he was wearing his gold penmanship medal on his overall bib.

He came over to the fence where we were standing. "Hello, Rolland," we said. "Where have you been keeping yourself?"

"Oh, me, I been doing a little share-cropping. This here is my stand of cotton. And making some corn whiskey on the side. There's where the real jack is." He talked louder than he ever had before. He spurted tobacco juice a long way. He had got pretty tough and we were awed.

"Are you coming back to school next year, Rolland?" Gus Belcher asked him.

"Me! Naw, I'm not never coming back to school," he said. "I don't like them educated fools they got teaching over there. What does a man like me want with schooling?" He began cursing, calling Miss Manchester all kinds of names. We never had heard Rolland talk like that before.

We wanted to tell him about what had happened at school that afternoon, but he swore so hard it made us timid. We sought an opening. I asked him, meekly, "Say, Rolland, what did the teacher say to you that day you—aw, uh—that noon after all the rest of us had marched out?"

Rolland scowled. "She didn't say nothing to me, the damned old rip. She knew better than to, because I was all set to get her told. She hung around awhile, like she wanted to make it up to me, but finally she went on off to dinner and left me there."

He chewed tobacco for a while and looked at us with

squinted eyes. None of us dared say anything more about his shame.

"Well," he said musingly, "all I hope is one thing. All I hope is that the blamed old heifer found that about her what I chalked on the bottom of her desk drawer. I told her what she could go do, all right. If she ever sees that, that'll fix her."

7

SUGAR BE SWEET!

SPRING was a soft green cloud hovering over the willow tree in the corner of Whalen's front yard the day that Marion died.

Mrs. Whalen wheeled her out on the front porch in her invalid's chair after the noon meal so that she could take in the sunlight. She had been in high spirits all morning, excited about Spring's coming back. She talked cheerfully and she even suggested to her mother that she might be getting up soon. She wanted to go into the woods to pick violets.

It was the first fine day of the season. And yet, beneath the warmth of the breeze, there was a reminiscent chill. Mrs. Whalen was careful to tuck the blankets snugly about her daughter. There were still to be rain and bitter days, it is true, but the motes of renascence were in the air. All about there was a quickening stir, and it was inconsistent that a body should die at such a time. It refurbished all the platitudes about death.

Walter Whalen was the one who heard the last words his daughter ever spoke. He reënacted the scene many times, in his own mind and for other people, with as many tears and hiccups as a sober strong man is permitted, all up until the funeral. But after the funeral he never thought of his distinction again, or if he did, he never said anything to anyone about it.

The way it was, he recollected, he had finished his noon meal, a hearty dinner, and had got up and gone out into the hall to get his hat. He was about to leave the house when he felt in his vest pocket and found that he didn't have any toothpicks. So he went back into the dining room to get a few. The ruby glass toothpick-holder stood on the sideboard empty.

Now where emptiness was there Walter Whalen found a pinch of chaos. Later he was glad that he had not made a scene on finding the toothpicks all out that noon. He pondered his restraint vaguely as something portentous in itself. He would never have got through blaming himself, he thought, if he had raised a commotion in that last hour of his daughter's life. So he was pleased to recall that there had been more of reproach than of irritation in his voice when he spoke to his wife that noon.

"Clara," he said loudly, "what have you done with all the toothpicks?"

Mrs. Whalen was at that moment tucking the blankets about Marion against the faint chill of the April wind. She gave the covering a hurried final pat and hastened back into the house.

"Just a minute, papa, and I'll get some toothpicks for you," she said in her mild, faded voice. And she apologized as she disappeared into the kitchen, "I should have filled the glass this morning but I didn't notice that it was getting low."

She took the box of toothpicks down from the kitchen

cabinet and put a handful of them into the little ruby glass tumbler. It was a souvenir and it had "Greetings from the St. Louis World's Fair, 1904, Walter R. Whalen," etched in ornate script around the red barrel. She hurried back into the dining room and placed the refilled holder on the sideboard.

"There's the toothpicks, papa," she said, turning back to the kitchen.

Walter Whalen came into the dining room. "Where are they at?" he said, still surly.

"Right there on the sideboard, Walter," Mrs. Whalen said patiently.

The sight of the fresh, complete little bundle placated him. He took out a dozen, rolling the smooth white slivers between his thumb and forefinger, enjoying the feel. He put one in the corner of his mouth and stuck the others in a vest pocket.

"You want to watch that toothpick holder, Clara," he said, not unkindly, going out.

He appeared through his front door, making little chirps between his teeth while he prodded them, smoothing down his vest with one hand. He and Marion were alone there on the porch. Mrs. Whalen, chastened, stayed in the kitchen. That was how it came about that the father was the only one to hear the girl's last words.

The Buick sedan stood in the driveway, its nickeled radiator throwing off little lances of sunlight.

Walter Whalen glanced at his only child. She lay back in the wheel chair, so fair, so bloodless, and beautiful. There were shadowy blue veins in her neck and a faint lacework of them at her temples where the breeze lifted a wisp of her golden hair. Against her face's cool, transparent whiteness lay the soft crimson braces of her lips. Her eyes were closed, as she lay there in the sunlight, and Walter thought she was asleep.

He stood on the porch steps and tossed his frayed toothpick into the sear honeysuckle vines along the balustrade. He took out a cigar and cut the end with his small knife. A belch rose from his well-stuffed stomach and he suppressed it, causing the elk-tooth fob on his paunch to bobble. Then he lighted his cigar and started down the walk.

"Aren't you going to take the Buick, papa?" Marion called, fluttering her eyelids. She had a dainty voice.

Walter Whalen halted and half turned. "Oh, I thought you was asleep," he said in embarrassment.

Marion said, "No, I've been awake all the time. But are you walking to town? Aren't you going to take the car?"

"No, I guess I won't take the car this afternoon," Walter Whalen said. "I kind of thought I would walk to town this afternoon. It's too pretty a day not to walk. A day like this makes you feel like walking."

"Isn't it a perfectly gorgeous day, though, papa!" Marion said, lilting.

"Yes, it's a fine day, all right. I guess Spring is here, sure enough. I mean I don't think we'll have much more Winter after a day like this. It sure makes a person want to get out in the open."

"Oh, doesn't it, though," Marion said ecstatically. "It just makes one feel closer to God!"

Two hours later Walter Whalen found significance

and solace in these words, which he chose to remember as the last his daughter ever uttered. At the moment, however, he was abashed by her demonstrative sentiment. It made him feel ludicrous to hear people say things like that. He was miserable with an eagerness to get away. He said, in brief agreement, "Yes, it's mighty fine weather today," and turned abruptly to go on down the walk.

Then Marion called tenderly, "Good-by, daddy!" and those were her last words. Those were really the portentous words.

"Good-by," Walter called brightly, waving his arm.

II

Walter Whalen, the hearty, the well-filled, the munificent, dealer in automobiles, a car for every pocketbook, walked to town in the sunlight. He experimented with deep breathing for a block or two, inhaling jerkily, taking an extra sniff each time to insure capacity and exhaling with a suddenness that left him slightly disconcerted. He tried to time his breathing to his footsteps, but the effort wearied him. Before he had gone far he felt that he had had enough of it for one day. He realized though that it was time he was beginning to think about getting back into condition. Every Spring his thoughts turned to the danger of his growing flabby.

"No use talking," he murmured to himself. "I've got to take off some of this belly. Must begin to get out and take more exercise." But he contented himself with bringing his rubber heels sharply down on the concrete sidewalk, feeling a satisfying resilience.

He was a large man, large in body, large in spirit too, any person in town would tell you. Walter Whalen was no man's debtor. He paid as he went and he was as substantial as he looked. Even his paunch, sweeping down from his lower ribs in a magnificent cataract of flesh, was there to buttress the breadth of his shoulders. His hair was beginning to gray, but it was the iron-filings gray of stalwart middle-age and not the yellowed gray of infirmity. Walter was proud of it, but the prospect of baldness gave him anxiety. He doused and massaged and trained tendrils of side hair against the shining pink encroachments of his forehead.

He was beginning to study about age more often lately. That was why the promise of Spring plagued him a bit. But it reassured him just as much. He felt his inner juices expanding in the mellow warmth of the early Spring sunshine and he was ebullient with a great affection for all the redundant world. The forty-eight years of his life dwindled to short yesterdays. He felt very youthful.

Two thin squirrels were racing in the Presbyterian churchyard. Walter paused to watch them until they scrabbled up a big oak, still leafless, and disappeared down a sprawling crotch. He smiled on them benignly and winked to himself, pleased with the surge of blood that came after his fleeting meditation of lustful joys.

Walter Whalen walked on. The fusty smell of turned earth came to him, cool as a cave, and all along his passage he called cheerful howdies to towel-turbaned housewives digging in flowerbeds, beating rugs, and sweeping off front porches. They replied to his genial bellows with smiles and pleasant comments on the weather and the new season.

He strode on toward town and an afternoon's confinement in his automobile sales and service office with every assurance that the world was a fine place to be living in. He continued to exchange brief comments on the weather with everyone he met: "Scrumptious weather we're having, eh, Ed?" for "Yes, sir-ee, Walter, fine day." Once or twice, to be sure, there were faint disturbances in his stomach, weighted with its heavy noon meal. He drew in his chin with little jerks to suppress the gases that rose in his throat and he threw away his cigar.

When he came out on Broadway, the main business street of the town, he stopped short in his tracks and regarded that thoroughfare with amazement.

Broadway was a fluttering mass of color. Hitched to the cast-iron electric-light standards, segments in the White Way, that symbol of the progressive community, were ropes stretched from side to side bearing a carnival array of colored pennants. Many store windows along the street were decorated with bright paper crescents.

The vision puzzled Walter. Broadway, when he had left his office for dinner a short while before twelve o'clock, had been neat and drab and almost without activity of any kind. There seemed at first no logical way in which this sudden transformation could be explained. He looked at the gay pennants more closely and saw that each of them was lettered.

"Lucky Moon Auction Sales," Walter muttered.

"What in the name of goodness have the boys got up now?"

He walked on a few doors up the street to where Virgil Clay (You-furnish-the-girl-and-let-Clay-furnish-the-home) stood leaning against a door-post in front of Clay's Furniture Store.

"What's all this, Virge?" asked Walter. "How come all the decorations?" He noticed that the furniture store windows also were plastered with the crescent posters.

Virgil Clay's smooth round face wimpled and broke. "Why, ain't you heard, Walt?" he said. "It's a trade stimulator scheme that they've got pret' near ever' leading merchant in town signed up on. I allowed you'd be the first one to get in on it."

Walter frowned. "Well, now that you mention it, it does seem to me like there was a man come in to my place last week talking about it. But these birds have always got something going, and I didn't pay much attention to him. You can just figure that the main thing they're interested in is making some money out of you, instead of having any idea that would help you make money. A thing like this," Walter gestured heavily toward the decorated street, "don't do me any good in my business."

"Wait a minute now, Walt!" Virgil exclaimed. "You don't even know how this Lucky Moon proposition works. We got to have something like this to stir things up ever' once in a while. The farmers like it, and it does draw trade. That's an absolute proved fact. And this here Lucky Moon proposition is a new wrinkle that beats anything of the kind I ever heard of. Better than one of them automobile drawings anyhow." He chuckled and nudged Walter.

"Oh, now, I don't know, Virge," Walter Whalen said with only the flicker of a grin. "Last Fall when the merchants had that big trades-day drawing and give away that Chivy touring from my place, this street was just packed solid. You know that. And I bet that's the biggest Saturday crowd this town ever did have. I let the Chamber of Commerce have that Chivy at cost. From all I ever heard that automobile drawing was satisfactory to ever'body."

"Yes, but you know how it is, Walter. Having one big prize like that, only one person can draw it. The country people all gets suspicious, and then somebody living right here in town generally always gets the prize —you know, somebody that don't need it at all—and then all the farmers claims that it's just a frame-up. You can't argue them out of it, neither. I never seen an automobile drawing like that yet that it didn't cause a lot of hard talk and ill feeling among the country people."

"So you figure that this Lucky Moon Auction Sale proposition is a better one than a trades-day automobile drawing, do you, Virge?"

"Yes, sir, Walter, I do. I was sold on it right off. The way it's worked out, I look to see it cause a right smart pick-up in business around here. And, Lord knows, this town certainly needs it. Just here last week a furniture drummer come in and he says to me, 'Well, how's business, Mr. Clay?' And I looks at him and says, 'Well, sir, the best I can remember, the last business

I had was pretty darn' good.' " He laughed at his own witticism, his face as ruddy as a tomato.

"Yes, but tell me one thing, Virge. How does this proposition work? You speak so high of it, I might of made a mistake not to get in on it."

"You sure did make a mistake, Walt. It's only offered to one line of business in a town, and I see they already got the Ford Garage signed up on it. We're going to have circulars out some time today, giving all the details, but it don't take but a minute to tell how the plan works."

"Well, let's hear then. The fellow that come in to sell me last week tried to high-pressure me, and you know that high-pressure stuff don't work on me, Virge. Not on Walt Whalen. So I didn't pay much attention to his line. Just told him that I couldn't be interested and sent him on his way. Then the first thing I know the whole street blooms out with these colored flags. They didn't have none of them up before I went to dinner."

"No, none of them was up before noon. They put them all up during the noon hour," Virgil Clay explained. "They come in by express on the 10.45. But the way this Lucky Moon Auction Sale works: fourteen of us is signed up on it, Epstein's Clothing Store, and the O.K. Butcher Shop, and Ira Cunliff's grocery, and the Luxor Barber Shop, and, now let's see. Luxor, O.K. Butcher Shop, Epstein's. And Milady's Style Shop-pe and the *Record-Democrat*. And my place. How many is that? Anyway, there's fourteen of us signed up on it. I can't call everyone to mind right now, but the whole list will be on these circulars we're getting out today.

"Now, the idea is ever' time a customer makes a cash purchase, we give him a coupon with the amount he spent on it. Coupons just issued for cash purchases, or for payment on account. Double coupons issued whenever merchant so desires. Then we have a bunch of premiums put up on display somewheres, a big variety of premiums, just like prizes. Each merchant furnishes a premium for each and every auction sale. All kinds of things from radio sets to groceries. Sensible things that people would have to spend real money for. No gimcracks.

"Now then, ever' two weeks we have an auction sale, and these coupons we put out count just like real money at these auctions. The customer, of course, is supposed to take and save up these coupons until he gets enough on hand to do some bidding. He uses his coupons to bid on any of the articles he wants that we have put up for auction, just like the coupons was cash money, see?

"So you see, ever'body has a chance at something. It works a whole lot better than a drawing, because it's all out in the open. Anybody can see that there ain't no monkey business to it. All premiums are on display ahead of time. And all that it costs the merchant is for the coupons, which we have to buy from this concern that got up the idea. And we all have to chip in with some article from our place of business worth at least five dollars in value—some little piece of merchandise that would make a good premium. In that way all premiums is purchased at wholesale, right here from home-town merchants, keeping home money at home. And lots of times a merchant might be able to work off a slow-moving piece of goods for a premium. This company that puts out the proposition loans us all these decorations free of charge. The only cost to us is the coupons. That's the whole proposition in a nutshell."

"Oh, I see, I see!" said Walter, looking very grave. "And of course some of these farmers around here will take to killing off their families just so they can come in and pay you cash for coffins so as to get Lucky Moon Auction Sale coupons!"

Virgil Clay, unsmiling and serious, said, "Well, Walt, I sure hope that nothing like that don't happen. But I tell you the truth, I do believe that this is going to stir up a lot of interest after it gets good and started. And if anybody was to come in here and pay me cash for mortician's work, or a coffin, or anything, I'd issue them coupons, just like I would if they had bought a bedstead, or a rug, or a refrigerator. I sure would!"

Whalen chuckled. "That's the spirit, Virge! All I've got to say is, I hope this proposition will stimulate business as much as you seem to think it's going to."

He pulled out his watch and glanced at it. "My God!" he exclaimed, snapping the case sharply. "Here I stand gassing with you, and it's darn' near two o'clock. I'll be seeing you, Virge!"

"Sure thing, Walt!" The furniture man turned his gaze back to the fluttering, bright-hued Lucky Moon Auction Sale pennants.

III

Clara Whalen finished washing and drying the dishes from the noon meal. She tidied the kitchen methodically and then she went over the parlor with the vacuum sweeper. She hurried about her household routine, a noiseless, mousy woman who had not had an independent thought in twenty years. Her blue eyes had lost color and expression, her golden hair had turned ashen, and yearly she had grown more dun and shy. Sometimes it would occur to people to remark, as if they had suddenly made a startling discovery, "You know, anyone can tell by looking at Walter Whalen's wife that she must have been a right pretty woman in her day."

There was a relationship between Clara Whalen and her daughter, however, that sometimes made Walter Whalen feel as if he were an awkward stranger in his own house. He was undisputed master there, but Marion and her mother kept an understanding that transcended filial affection. They would sit for long hours in the same room, sewing perhaps, or, when the work was all done in the afternoon, gazing vacantly, silent and content to be with each other. A long period would pass without either of them speaking. Then, when one of them said something in a low, soft voice, almost cooing, neither would be surprised to find that the one who had spoken had added a word to what the other had been thinking. They seldom made any outward sign of their affection, no embraces, no tender kisses. They did not use terms of endearment: Marion was "Sister" and Clara Whalen was "Mamma." But from the time Marion was a baby until she was a young woman the bond between them was complete. And, when Marion was near death that last Winter of her life, Mrs. Whalen sat by her bedside wan and immobile until one had the uncanny feeling that as Marion sank life was ebbing away from Clara Whalen too. The doctor said that the mother's constancy had probably brought Marion through the Winter.

So Mrs. Whalen, too, felt a buoyancy that Spring day. Not even her husband's displeasure could dispel it for long. She knew that she had been at fault in letting the toothpick holder get empty, and she had gone back to the kitchen in humiliation. But by the time she had finished straightening up the sitting room she caught herself humming a happy, if tuneless, song. She left off quickly, pursing her lips with chagrin. Then she took off her kitchen apron and came out on the front porch, tucking at her hair.

She noticed that Marion's eyes were open, so she said, "Does that sunlight feel good on you, Sister?"

Marion did not answer. Then Clara Whalen went over to her, and she saw the cold glaze on Marion's beautiful eyes and she saw Marion's sweet lips parted in the gape of death.

So it was all very seemly when the neighbors came in answer to Clara Whalen's cries. The incongruousness of a girl's death on a day when all the earth was stirring with new life was not mentioned by them.

"So sweet," murmured the misty-eyed ones who refrained from sobbing loudly. "So sweet. So peaceful and all. Just like she had went to sleep. She didn't suffer at all, Mrs. Whalen, or else she wouldn't be laying back so sweet and gentle there. Such a beautiful way to die, Mrs. Whalen."

They buried Marion on a Saturday. The church was crowded. She had a fine funeral, and no one was disappointed. Walter Whalen was never a man to stint on anything.

IV

Two Saturdays later Walter Whalen stood in his automobile showroom, gazing out through the plate-glass window at the preparations for the first Lucky Moon Auction Sale going on in the vacant lot opposite.

Already the farmers and their families had started gathering. They stood about, staring hungrily at the proceedings. Many of them held wads of coupons in their hands and they would re-count their hoards from time to time, thumbing the colored paper slips and peering with covetous side glances at the savings held by their neighbors.

At 2.30 a truck drove up, hauling the premiums that had been on display for two weeks in the south show window of Epstein's Model Clothing Store. That was a large array of desirable merchandise. None of your cheap, shoddy premiums, but articles contributed by local merchants sponsoring the plan—usable, substantial articles all, things for which one ordinarily would have to pay real money. Ladies' rayon hose from Milady's Style Shoppe, a red-lacquered end table from Clay's Furniture Store, a boy's roller coaster from the Green Front Hardware Company, a set of inner tubes from the Ford Garage, a hundred-pound sack of sugar from Ira Cunliff's grocery, a cured ham from the O.K. Butcher Shop; and a dozen other items equally indispensable, including some intangible ones represented by show-cards such as five dollars' worth of printing at the *Record-Democrat's* job shop and twenty shaves at the Luxor Barber Shop.

Ready hands began unloading the premiums from the truck. It was about time. Walter Whalen strolled across the street and joined the throng.

A loose plank platform had been erected in the center of the lot. The goods were stacked on it.

Major Cummings, the town auctioneer, had been retained for the occasion. It took the jocose major to make an auction sale a gala event. He was already warming up, prancing up and down the rickety platform, his broad black Stetson pushed back on his head, his black windsor tie flapping when a stray breeze caught it.

"Ah, yes! Ah, yes!" he bellowed as he paced the unsteady, rattling planks. "Draw right on up close, folks. Come right on up near so as you won't miss no bargains. We're going to start this sale off with a bang pretty quick now. Don't be bashful, neighbors. They's plenty of room down in front here."

He caressed his broad belly complacently. Two hundred successful farm auctions had convinced Major Cummings that he was a master of men.

He coaxed the gaping farmers and their timid wives in a loud, generous voice, but when some of the small boys down in front got pressed against the platform and began scuffling and jostling, he put by his sugary tone to say to them in a low, mean aside, "Watch out there! Stand back away from that there sawhorse! You'll have the whole blamed works down on the ground the first thing you know."

Then, looking out over the adult throng again, he resumed his louder, wheedling, mellifluous tone. The corner lot was a squirming block of people. Farmers and their wives had come from miles around. They were still skeptical about whether the Lucky Moon coupons were worth anything, but they clutched their accumulations in fists none the less tight and looked out for some shady dealing.

Major Cummings started the auction by holding up a box of rayon hose, "Hey, look'ye, look'ye! Five pair of gen-u-wine rayon silk hose in five diff'runt shades. Now what am I bid? These here stockings will give any womern's limbs that come-hither look. Gals, when you stick your limbs into a pair of these here hose, you won't have to worry no more about how your face looks."

This risqué quip caused an outburst of raucous, embarrassed laughter, and a hundred elbows moved in nudges. The Major went on, "What do I hear for this ass-sort-ment of gen-u-wine rayon silk hose? Five pair, five, and no two shades alike. Who'll say twenty? Twenty-twenty-twenty! And the young feller with the front teeth in his mouth over there says uh ten! I betcha he's got his eye on the gal he's going to give 'em to already."

Rowdy laughter greeted this remark, but the Major paused for serious explanation: "Remember, friends, them Lucky Moon coupons counts just like U. S. A. cash money at this sale. Only you couldn't use cash money here if you was wanting to. Everything here goes for the Lucky Moon coupons and the Lucky

Moon coupons only. They come to you free; now let's let 'em go free. You didn't have to strike a lick of work to get 'em. Come to you just like they had been willed to you. So let's hear a good bid now! I'm bid ten. Let me hear uh twenty! Twenty-twenty-twenty! And uh twenty from the young lady over there with the black hat on. Who'll bid me thirty? Do I hear uh thirty?"

So the sale progressed. As soon as the rayon hose had been knocked down to a young farm hand for thirty-two-fifty, the Major, giving out exaggerated grunts, hoisted aloft a cured ham.

"Now, ladies and them that run after you, here is something that you can sure enough bid on. The ham what am! Hang it up in the old smoke house and put it by for winter. A few slabs of this would go mighty good to lay up against your ribs on a frosty mornin'. All smoked and preserved and she'll tip the beam at twenty pounds easy. So don't let me hear any of them measly little bids on this here great big fine cured ham! Let me hear uh hundurd. Uh hundurd! Am I bid uh hundurd?"

As the people grew accustomed to the large denominations of their imitation money, which had been issued generously in a hundred side-deals and which had been carefully collected from less provident neighbors, the bidding grew high and reckless. The farm auction was always an event with its social as well as its business aspects, and the Lucky Moon Sale resembled a farm auction closely enough to be an enjoyable occasion.

Farmers and townspeople alike took vast pleasure in dealing with the large, imaginary sums printed on their coupons.

V

That evening at the supper table Mrs. Whalen said, "Walter, the boy from the garage brought out a hundred-pound sack of sugar on the truck a little while before you came. I'm glad you thought to get it, because we were almost out of sugar. Tomorrow is Sunday, and I would have had to run over to Mrs. Fitz to borrow a cupful, or we wouldn't have had a grain of sugar in the house."

"Well, that hundurd-pound sack ought to last us a while," Walter said, helping himself to the gravy.

"Yes, it'll soon be canning season, and it won't be a bit too much."

"I sort of figured we could use it," Walter said.

"Did you get it at a bargain?"

"Did I get it at a bargain? I'll say I got it at a bargain," he said proudly. "And I would of got it at a whole lot better bargain if a bull-headed German farmer from out here east of town hadn't been bidding against me."

"Bidding against you?"

"Yeah; I got it at that Lucky Moon Auction Sale they're putting on."

"Oh, Mrs. Fitz was over here yesterday asking me whether I was saving those Lucky Moon coupons. But I didn't get it straight in my head how the auction part worked."

"Well, it's just like a drawing, only they issue you

these coupons, and you use them to bid just like money. They're supposed to issue them, a dollar coupon for a dollar spent, but some of the merchants in on the deal have been issuing double coupons. Before long they'll be issuing triple coupons; I wouldn't be surprised. I would of got that sack of sugar for half of what I did, because I had ever' one else bluffed right on the start. But this farmer (it was old August Schaeffer from out here east, that's who it was), he kept running the bid up on me. Somebody told me that he had bought him a tractor from the Green Front Hardware last week, and they issued him double coupons on the deal. He had a bunch of coupons there big enough to choke a yearling heifer. I had to bid eight hundred dollars, all the coupons I had, before I could get him stopped."

"Eight hundred dollars' worth? My goodness! Where did we get eight hundred dollars' worth of coupons?"

"Where do you suppose?" Walter said, sharply, his head turned down toward his plate. He reached out for the sugar bowl to sweeten his coffee. His spoon grated against the bowl's crusted inside.

"Walter, you don't mean from—"

He flung down his spoon and interrupted her loudly, "Clara, you've let the sugar bowl get empty again!"

She sat very still, staring at him.

He addressed her with pursed lips, in mincing, mock-politeness, "Madam, would you be so kind as to get up and fill that sugar bowl like you ought to of done before supper?"

She did not get up and she did not move.

Walter Whalen pushed back his chair angrily. "All right!" he shouted, his face gorged with blood. "All right, then!" he shouted, making for the kitchen with the empty sugar bowl in his hand. "If you're going to be a goddamn' fool about this, I'll go fill the sugar bowl myself."

Clara Whalen sat very still, her eyes hard with loathing.

8

A PRETTY CUTE LITTLE STUNT

WELL, R.A., I wish you could of been out to Rotary today. You certainly missed a treat. They pulled off a pretty cute little stunt, and I'm right here to tell you it would of give you something to think about, you old potwalloper, you!

Well, sir, it was a pretty cute little stunt the way they pulled it off. Just as slick as you please. The way it happened, the Chief called me up on the 'phone about 11.30 and says, "Harry, we've got a bum in jail down here, and he claims that he's an old ex-member of Rotary. He's been aggravating the life out of us, telling us that he's got a message that he's got to get to you boys some way."

The first thing that occurred to me was that it was some kind of a joke. You know how the Chief is, yourself, R.A., always up to some kind of monkey-business. Sure you do, though, because I remember how the Chief helped pull that fake pinch on you at the station last year, the day you and Alice was starting on your honeymoon. Handcuffed you right there as the train was starting up, and Alice sticking her head out the window, yelling and crying when the train pulled out. I thought I'd 'a' died laughing at the look on your face that day, the way you sputtered when the Chief snapped on those bracelets. And that flabbergasted look of yours all the way on the road when we was making sixty per hour trying to get you to the next station in time to catch up with your missus!

It took you quite a while to catch on to the joke. And, come to think of it, R.A., I don't think Alice ever has acted the same toward we boys since that day she lost her temper. Well, I thought they was carrying the joke a little too far, myself, but I never saw a woman yet that could take a joke in the proper spirit. The way she turned loose on the Chief when we finally caught the train! I mean Alice ought to of seen that the Chief was just helping we boys kid you a little. I mean the Chief was only doing like we asked him to.

But to get back to what I was telling you, I thought to myself, "This is just some horseplay the Chief's pulling off." So I says to him, "Oh, yeah?" You know. Like that. "Oh, yeah?"

The Chief didn't let on a bit, though. He was just as serious as he could be. He says, "Yes, he's got the Rotary button and the credentials, but of course he could of stole those some place. But he tells a pretty straight story, and if you've got time, I wish you'd come down to the station and take a look at him."

Well, just as soon as I saw that the Chief was serious, I quit kidding right away. I says, "Sure thing, Chief, I'll be right down." So I hung up and got in my Chivy and drove right on down to the station.

I wish you could of seen this bird the Chief come leading out, R.A. Dirty as rot and looked like he didn't have a shave in a week. He had on an old, worn-out-looking blue-serge suit, all out at the sleeves, and it looked like he didn't have on any shirt, because he had his coat-collar turned up and pinned at the neck with a safety pin.

I was still kind of leery when I walked into the station, but I didn't have no more doubts after I saw this bum the Chief come leading out. He was a little short fellow that looked like he might of seen better days in his time. But it certainly looked like it had been many a day since he had. I mean he had a pretty good-sized stomach on him and he was wearing horn-rim glasses, but I wish you could of seen the way he looked. He just had down-and-outer written all over him.

The Chief introduced us, and I shook hands with him. Then he started in to explaining how he had been setting there in his cell thinking about things, and how good-for-nothing he had got to be. Then he said he just happened to remember that, a little while before the police picked him up, he had seen one of our Rotary-wheel signboards with "Rotary meets on Mondays—Visitors welcome" on it. Well, the long and the short of it was that he said that he had used to be a Rotarian before he went to the dogs, and he just got to thinking that he would like to meet with the boys again and give them a talk.

He showed me his credentials, they were so dirty and worn I couldn't hardly make out the writing, and his button. He wasn't wearing his button. He was just carrying it in his pocket.

I could see that his feelings were working on him

pretty strong. I looked to see him break down and start crying any minute. He was so pitiful I just didn't know what to do about him. But at the same time, I begun to wonder what the boys would think if I was to come walking in with a filthy bum like that to eat with us. You'd have to of seen him to appreciate it. He looked like something somebody had drug up the streets with. Well, I knew that I'd have to decide something quick. It was getting close to noon then. So I says to him, "You wait here just a minute." I steps over to the 'phone and calls up Gay Harrison, the secretary.

"Gay," I says, "what have we got on the program today?"

"Not a thing that I know of, Harry," Gay says, "why?"

"Well," I says, "the Chief's got a bum in jail down here that claims he's an old former ex-Rotarian, and this bum wants to come up and eat with us today, and then give us a talk after we eat. What's your reaction?" I says.

Gay fell right in with the notion. He says, "Harry, that strikes me as being a pretty cute little stunt. Bring him right along!"

And I want to say it *was* a pretty cute little stunt, too.

I went back in to where the bum was standing by the desk, waiting. I hadn't quite caught his name, so I says to him, "I didn't quite catch what your name was, brother."

"Just call me Oscar," he says. "That's the old Rotary spirit."

I kind of grinned when he said that, but when I looked at him, just as solemn as a judge when he said it, I didn't lose any time wiping that grin right off my face. I felt kind of ashamed, R.A. I mean the way he looked at me made it seem kind of heathenish to grin at Rotary spirit like that, R.A.

I turned around to the Chief and said, "Chief, I guess you haven't got any objection, have you, if I took Oscar to Rotary with me today."

The Chief didn't crack a smile. He said, "Well, Harry, it's a little irregular, but if I go along to keep him in custody, I guess it'll be all right. I mean we've got him booked on a vag charge here, you see, and we'd be held liable for him."

Before we started out, though, I looked the bum right straight in the eye and says, "Before we start, though, Oscar, I want it distinctly understood that there's to be no begging for alms done. The boys wouldn't stand for that. We're glad to have you come eat with us, and to hear your message—but no begging speech, remember that."

The bum kind of drew himself up and says, "Why, of course I have no intention of begging for alms. Of course not. That wouldn't be Rotary," he says. And somehow or another he made me feel pretty cheap again, the way he said that, "It wouldn't be Rotary."

II

Well, the upshot of it was, we all piled into my Chivy sedan, the Chief and the bum and me, and drove right up to the Hotel Beckman just like we was a delegation of millionaires. I wished you could of seen that big nigger doorman they got there at the Beckman, R.A., when we come piling out of my Chivy. That nigger's eyes just bulged out like stoppers on an organ. I'd give a pretty to know what he was thinking.

When we walked through the lobby I could see ever'-one craning to get a look at us, and when we come into the dining-room they had already started eating. But ever'one put down their knife and fork when we walked up and took our seats at the speakers' end of the table. They didn't know what to make of it.

And I wished you could of seen that fellow lay away the grub. He ate like he was half-starved. He just ate up everything in sight and was ready for more before anybody else had got good and started. Ever'body was staring down in our direction, and I was turning about seven different colors. I couldn't hardly eat, myself, and I was kicking myself for a sucker all through the meal.

After the meal Gay Harrison got up and said, "I don't believe there are any visitors today, so we'll proceed with the business." Some of the boys began clearing their throat and laughing a little, and I want to tell you I was about ready to sink right through that floor. Then Gay says, "Oh, I beg pardon. Harry has a guest. Harry, will you introduce your guest."

I could of kicked Gay around the block for the way he said that, but I saw then that I was going to have to go on through with it, so I gets up and kind of grins, and says, "Well, boys, this was all about as big a surprise to me as it was to you. And Gay there is letting on like he didn't know nothing about it, but he knows just as much as I do. About 11.30 I got a telephone call from the Chief saying that he had an old ex-Rotarian in jail, and that this fellow thought he had a message for us. I called up Gay and he said it would be all right. So I want to introduce Oscar," I says, "and if he'll get up now he can do his own explaining."

I set down, and this bum, just as ragged and dirty as a Turk, stood up. The boys clapped for him, but they was all about to bust laughing. This bum just kind of looked around over the table, and it got still enough so as you could of heard yourself think. You talk about magnetism, R.A., well that man had it. He used psychology on them. Nobody there knew any more about him than I did, but he stopped that laughing, don't you forget it.

I wish you could of heard that man talk. He started right in.

"Boys," he says, "you don't know me, and I guess none of you care very much who I am, or what I was once upon a time. And I'm not going to dwell on that," he says. "I came into your fair city unannounced and I'll be lucky if I can go out the same way," he says. "The way you see me now," he says, "I'm on the dog, just a poor down-and-outer. But," he says, "I'm not here to play on your sympathies. I just want to talk to you a little about Rotary fellowship, and then I'm through," he says.

"This morning I was setting in my jail cell meditating," he says. "You know that's one thing about being in jail, you get a chance to do a lot of meditating," he says. And then he went on to describe about how the early disciples of the Church had all spent a lot of time in jail, and about how that had give them time to do a lot of meditating, and that had a lot to do with the purity and inspiration of their message, and so on and so forth. Well, R.A., it seems like he was setting there meditating and all of a sudden he got this inspiration that if he could just give a talk to Rotary once more, he had a message for them that was worth hearing.

"I used to be a member of Rotary in good standing," he says. "I'm not going to say where it was, because that don't make any difference," he says. And then he talked a little more and went on and recited that poem, you know that poem that goes:

I want to live in the house beside of the road,
And see the men go by,
The men who . . .

Well, I don't remember now just how it goes, something like that, but anyhow it ends up:

I want to live in the house beside the road,
And be a friend of man.

This bum recited the whole poem from start to finish, and when he got through, he says, "Now, that poet had it all wrong," he says, "because that's not Rotary. To be in keeping with Rotary you have to get out in the middle of the road, and live out in the middle of the road. You've got to be out in the middle of the road *meeting* with men and *mixing* with men, if you're going to be a friend of man," he says. "This old setting down beside of the road watching men go past won't do at all," he says.

Well, R.A., his talk was just full of sharp little points like that, and they hit home, too. A pretty cute little stunt, I want to say.

Another place there he went on and told about how in a town where he had been a Rotarian one time Rotary had taken all the kiddies in town, all the poor kiddies, out on an outing out in the woods. Well, he was a respectable business man back in those days, and he was getting around among the kiddies, seeing that they all had a good time, and he come across a little cripple boy standing over by a tree just crying like his heart would break.

He went up to this little cripple boy and says, "What's the matter, sonny?"

And the little cripple boy sobbed out, "Oh, I can't have any fun. All the other kids can go around and get red lemonade and ice cream cones and hot dogs and ever'thing, but I can't. I'm crippled."

About that time he looks up and he sees a big strapping boy coming up, and he sneaks around on the other side of the refreshment tent to see what this big boy is going to say to this little cripple.

Well, the big boy come up and says, "What's eatin' yuh, kid?" And the little cripple starts to crying again, and the big boy says, "Aw, shucks! Come on here and get up on my back." And he stooped over and got the little cripple up on his back and pretty soon he was loping him all over the picnic ground, handing him up soda pop and hot dogs and ever'thing and the little cripple was having just as good a time as anybody.

R.A., I'm right here to tell you that when that ragged bum finished that story ever'one around that table was a sniffing and a snubbing and making dabs at their eyes and trying to grin and make out like they wasn't crying at all. If any speaker ever had magnetism, that man certainly had it. The way he used that psychology on them wasn't even funny.

Well, he finished up by saying that all his message was that if he could just get us to live a little more like the Master Rotarian, and follow in His footsteps, his mission would be fulfilled, and, even if he was a ragged bum, he would 'a' done something worthwhile.

He says, "Now, boys, you're going to forget me. I'm just a ragged old bum, and I'm going to pass out of your lives. But the idea of fellowship is what I wanted to get across today. The bums and the jailbirds need the grip of a manly hand sometimes. Fellowship, that's all!"

He says, "Now I know what a lot of you boys been thinking I've been leading up to, but you're wrong. I'm not going to make any plea for money, or for aid of any kind. If you was to offer it to me, I wouldn't take your money. Because that wouldn't be Rotary. But just remember what I told you about fellowship, and try and be a little more like that Master Rotarian of long ago."

Then he turned around quick and says to the Chief in a kind of tired-out voice, "Come on, Chief, let's be going."

The Chief got up and took him by the arm, and they had almost got to the door when old Cliff Oliphant—you know old Cliff, R.A., just as kind-hearted as they make them—jumped up with his eyes streaming tears and began trying to say something.

Well, the whole place was in a hub-bub, and I guess they would of passed the hat, if Gay Harrison hadn't stood up about that time and started to tapping on a glass with his knife. "Hold on just a minute, boys," Gay says. "Hold on there just a minute."

And then he beckoned to the Chief, and the Chief come leading the bum back to the head of the table.

"Boys," Gay says, "I want to introduce you to the Reverend Oscar D. Sneathen, pastor of the First Christian Church over at Garden City."

The bum reached up and undid the safety pin at his coat collar and threw back his ragged old coat and showed that he had on a collar and tie and a suit just as good as any of us!

III

Well, R.A., we all just set around and goggled and nobody could say a word. It was a regular shock to us to find out that this ragged bum had been a respectable minister of the gospel all along.

And the funny part about it was, none of us suspicioned anything right up to the last. Nobody but Gay and the Chief had been in on the know. It fooled ever'-one of us.

I mean, there we was, all ready to show our fellowship to this ragged bum, and shell out some coin if we had to make him take it, and it kind of hit us when we found out he couldn't use our money. But he certainly got his message across. It was a clever little stunt, just as cute as it could be.

Gay made a little talk, telling how Reverend Sneathen had been going around over the State pulling this stunt at Rotary luncheons, and asked us not to give it away to no one, as that might spoil the effect somewheres else.

It done a lot of good, too, even if it was just a trick. I was talking to Otis Bailey, riding back to the office after it was all over, and he says to me, "You know, Harry, that bum had it just about right, after all. We've got to get back to fundamentals in this country. After all, a bum is just a human being like us."

Otis said he wasn't in favor of any new experimenting in this country, like this Dole's System and so on. But he said his point was that we couldn't just let these bums starve.

I told him, "Sure, Otis, sure. And the way I look at it, that's right where some of this fellowship the speaker was talking about is going to go a long ways toward solving the situation."

So that just goes to show you, R.A., how a clever little stunt like that can be a big inspiration by getting people to discussing a question.

To get back to what I come to see you about, though, R.A.: Reverend Sneathen is going around over the State putting on this little stunt at Rotary luncheons, and he's out to quite a little expense for traveling expenses and so on. Gay told me to draw $25 out of the entertainment fund for him, but there was only $3.65 left in the treasury after we sent that marble-contest kid to New Jersey to the finals last month. So we're asking the boys all to chip in a dollar or so apiece for the reverend.

It's a pretty cute little stunt he pulls off, all right. I wish you could of been there. I mean it would of give you something to think about, R.A. Well, R.A., give me a ring when it's anything in the insurance line.

9

BOY AND SNAKE

DENNIS thought that he was getting old enough to make some real money that summer vacation, so early one morning he started walking out to Kuykendall's farm where they were threshing. He had heard that there was a chance to get a job carrying water to the threshers and that there was a dollar and a half a day in it.

It was a morning in June and the first level rays of the sun were changing the dew-drenched fields into squares of shattered color. Dennis walked along in the wet gray dust, curling his bare toes and shivering a little, because the morning was cool and the warmth of bed was still with him.

He walked along very rapidly, doing arithmetic sums in his head with one dollar and fifty cents and faltering only when a meadow lark whirred at the roadside. After a while he came up over the rise past Humphrey's place and he saw the black smoke from the threshing machine piling up against the washed-blue sky. The men looked very small in the fields below and they moved like mechanical toys, pitching the bundles.

Dennis could hear their faint shouts to the plush horses and his heart got a weak feeling. They had already started the day's work. He was too late to get a job. And it was still so early! He plodded on, a little bitterly, grimly nursing his faint hope that they would still need a water-carrier.

When he came up to the threshing machine he stood there for a while trying to summon enough courage to speak to Mr. Kuykendall, who was shouting orders to the threshing hands. Mr. Kuykendall was unused to a position of authority, and he was very officious and blustering about giving the men directions.

Then Dennis watched the pistons on the threshing machine flash in and out, in and out, for a little while, until Archie Gibbons, the fireman, shouted something to him and bared gleaming teeth at him in a sooty smile. That buoyed Dennis up somewhat. He walked on over to where Mr. Kuykendall was standing with his feet apart and waited for him to get through shouting.

He said, "Say, Mr. Kuykendall, I heard that you needed a good water boy to carry water to the threshers."

His voice was so timid that the big man did not hear him the first time. Dennis cleared his throat and said loudly, "Say, Mr. Kuykendall, you wasn't needing an extra hand today was you?"

Mr. Kuykendall looked down at him a little impatiently, but when he saw that it was Dennis, he said, "Why, no, Denny, we've got all the men we need right now. But you go on up to the house and play with the kids, and tell Mamma I said we'd have an extra man eating dinner with us."

Dennis smiled a quivering smile, but very broad, and said, "All right!" tremulously. He walked off toward the house very much relieved that he had got it over with and rather glad that he would get to play that day after all.

II

He played "Banner" with the Kuykendall kids all morning. Usually Dennis felt inferior around country boys when he was out in the country, but the Kuykendall kids were a dumb outfit. He could banner them so easily that it wasn't very much fun. They wouldn't even follow him when he jumped off the wagonshed onto the manure pile.

When noon came Mrs. Kuykendall walked out across the yard and rang a bell and all the farm hands began coming in. There was a long plank table out in the back yard in the shade of the house and they brought the food out of the kitchen to put in the center of the table. Mrs. Kuykendall's two oldest girls did the serving, and Mrs. Kuykendall stood up at the head of the table waving off the flies with a locust branch.

As they sat down at the table each thresher took up the little cake with the pink icing on it by his plate and covered the icing with spittle to keep any of the other hands from swiping it.

Dennis sat at the table with the others. There were, among other things, cabbage and hominy and baker's bread. Dennis liked hominy and baker's bread, but until that day he had never liked stewed cabbage. That day he learned how to douse it with pepper sauce. That made it good, and he ate cabbage until Mrs. Kuykendall called out, "My gracious, papa, look at that Denny eat cabbage! The way he lays it away a body'd think that he'd been making a hand in the field with you-all today."

Dennis called for another helping of cabbage. After Mrs. Kuykendall said what she did he felt that he had a record to set. He ate so much cabbage that his insides made a funny slushing noise when he moved. He was too full to play very much with the Kuykendall kids that afternoon. They were so dumb anyway. But after a while he strolled back out to the fields where the threshing machine was. He watched the threshing machine some more, following with his eyes the lacing as the leather drive belt slapped around the fly wheel. When Arch Gibbons sat down on the steps of the engine and said to him, "Well, Dennis, you been sparkin' any good-lookin' girls here lately?" he kicked at a wheel and said, "Naw!"

III

Along about three o'clock in the afternoon one of the bundle-pitchers picked up a shock of wheat and uncovered a large rattlesnake.

He jumped back and in his fright he slammed his pitchfork at it and the pitchfork tines went plumb through it, pinning it to the ground. Then he began yelling loudly, "Snake! Snake! Killed a rattlesnake!"

All the others came running, and Dennis was one of the first to get there. Dennis was very proud of the way he could handle snakes. He used to carry a little garter snake around in his pocket and frighten the girls at school with it. He always fell in love with the snake-charmer when a circus or carnival company came to town. The other boys could have their trapeze performers and bareback riders, but Dennis always felt a little pang in his heart when he saw a snake-charmer, even if she did have a mouthful of gold teeth.

All the threshing hands crowded around the writhing rattler and began stabbing it with pitchforks and beating it with the steel prongs until its head was a bloody pulp. Now and then its tail would make a feeble *hutr-r-r-r,* but everyone conceded that a snake's tail couldn't die until sundown anyway. They decided to leave the snake alone and to go on back to work, just as Mr. Kuykendall kept yelling at them to do.

Abe McInnis, the man who had found the snake, left his pitchfork sticking through its body as he had first thrown it. He wouldn't touch the handle to pull it out himself, nor would he let anyone else touch it, because he knew that the snake had sprayed some of its venom on the handle, and that it would be fatal to get fresh rattlesnake venom on one's hands. So they left the pitchfork sticking and Abe took baling-wire and fixed up one with a cracked handle to pitch bundles with the rest of the day.

It was a warm afternoon and Dennis had been feeling pretty sluggish with all that heavy cabbage in him, so he lay down in the wheat stubble and propped his chin up on his elbows. He picked up a clean yellow straw and began chewing on it, glancing now and then at the bloody snake.

After a while he began to be moved by an irresistible desire to poke one of the snake's torn, bleeding eyes the rest of the way out with the stiff wheat straw he was chewing. He knew that he didn't want to do that, really, and he kept trying to keep himself from doing it, but it was like trying to keep yourself from yawning when you want to yawn.

So as he was lying there prone he began moving out one hand very slowly and nervously until the yellow straw actually touched the flat, bloody head. As soon as Dennis felt the contact, he jerked the straw back quickly, but the snake hadn't even made a whirr with its rattler. It gave not a sign of life, so Dennis moved the straw out again. This time he was more courageous and quickly jabbed deep in the bloody socket.

It happened suddenly, but in Dennis' memory it was like a slow motion moving picture. He saw the snake's strong, vibrant coils twine themselves, saw the flat, blind head outthrust, saw the coils melt as the rattlesnake lashed out at him.

He saw the hollow, streaming sockets staring into his own eyes and he felt the dank breath on his cheeks. Had he been an inch closer, the rattlesnake's fangs would have struck him full in the face. The pitchfork held. The poisonous mouth spread wide and closed. The brutal head snapped back.

Dennis glared with wide, hard eyes at the heaving mass of bloody scales before him. He felt the short hairs on the back of his neck prick up. His breath began coming in short, dry, racking gasps.

The pitchfork was quivering as the tortuous body of the rattlesnake, strong in its death agonies, rose and fell in grotesque curves about the steel prongs. Gouts of blood oozed afresh in the dull, lacerated curves.

Dennis felt the skin on his body pimpling, pushing him closer, and he gripped the wheat stubble, pressing his nails into the baked earth. He stared so hard at the dying snake that tears started in his eyes.

It seemed a long time before he could get to his feet, pushing himself up with his knees. He was giddy. Suddenly he could feel the fetid breath of the snake in his own nostrils again. The dark sockets danced in bloody little burrs before his eyes. His stomach swelled and the greasy cabbage came slithering up.

Dennis clasped his gray, wet forehead with both hands. He moaned weakly.

Pretty soon he felt better. He stood there gazing sickishly at the ground. Then he began feeling strong, strong. A fantastic anger, like some marvelous elixir, flooded his arteries, and he felt the strength of savage centuries moving in him.

His bile-flecked jaw jutted and his knuckles bulged white. The fronds of stone-age forests swept about his head. The killing hunger was in him.

There was a rock in a near-by furrow. It was half-buried in the hard-baked soil. He wrenched it from its setting with one mighty tug. He held it above his head. A grown man could not have done it easily.

The motionless coils of the snake spattered under the force of the heavy stone.

Again and again he crushed the lifeless body. At last the snake was a crimson-gray smear there in the golden stubble.

When the farm hands came up to him, Dennis was

sitting on the big rock sobbing horribly. He wept in the way a strong man weeps.

Mr. Kuykendall hitched up the phaëton and took him home.

Dennis was a very sick boy that night.

10

PILGRIM'S PROGRESS

One day early last June I and Mr. Harpending was driving home from New York City in the Pierce. He goes in about once a week to contact his publishers and the movie people and salve the "book-club" judges, etc. More than likely he will take in a party if his Mrs. is not along with him. But I guess she is just as bad, and would do the same to a certain extent.

We was almost to Mamaroneck when we see this hitch-hiker standing beside the highway giving us the thumb. The cars was all going right on past him continuous without stopping and, as Mr. Harpending never has had me stop for hitch-hikers before or since, I did not even slow up. All of a sudden I feel him poking at me with his cane.

"Hold on, Spicer," he says. "Let us stop and pick this lad up."

So I eases out to one side and stops. Here this guy comes running as hard as he can. He has all this gear hung on his back. He opens the door panting hard and climbs into the back seat beside Mr. Harpending. He was not a bad-looking young man, albeit he was dressed in a funny-looking way. I presume that the way he was dressed was what attracted Mr. Harpending to have me stop the Pierce and pick him up. He was a slim, dark-complected youth. I would estimate him between five and one-half or six foot tall. He had on leather riding boots and "khaki" riding breeches and a short sleeved silk shirt with collar open at the neck. Also on his head one of these little caps like artists wear, set over on one side of his head. He had a blanket roll and "knapsack" fastened on to his back with shoulder straps and he was carrying a leather brief case in his hand. I could see him in the mirror and he appeared to be a nice-looking kid in the respect of everything except his upper teeth, which was set forwards quite a bit.

Mr. Harpending give him one of those cold, fish-eyed looks which he can give you and make you feel like you have got "something" hanging out of your nose. "Where are you headed for, young man?" he inquired coldly.

"Westport, Conn.," the hitch-hiker said, very polite.

"Well! And how did you come to be going to Westport, Conn.?"

"Sir, I am on a 'literary pilgrimage,'" the youth rejoindered. "I am going to Westport to call on Oliver Harpending, the great American novelist, whom I am informed lives in that vicinity. I have traveled two thousand miles to see him."

"Ah!" quoth Mr. Harpending, evicting considerable interest, but no surprise. "You can drive on now, Spicer!"

"Is this Harpending expecting you?" queried Mr. Harpending with a slight smile playing upon his lips.

"No, sir, he is not," the young man admitted, "but

I think when I tell him that I have come two thousand miles to see him, he will be interested in seeing me."

"Two thousand miles!" exclaimed Mr. Harpending, all pleasant and nice by now. "How did you happen to take the notion?"

"Why, you see, Mr.—, Mr.—? I do not believe I caught the name."

"Pardon me," Mr. Harpending said hastily with a twinkling eye. "The name is, uh, Simms,—Addison Simms."

"Pleased to make your acquaintance, Mr. Simms," said the youth, shaking hands without catching on for an instance. "Here is *my* card."

Mr. Harpending took the card and read it:

J. ELBERT LAMB
OXFORD UNIVERSITY
POET & AUTHOR

Opuses:	*Address:*
Purple Vignettes	Overseas Adviser,
The Wine of Life	Oxford University,
The Jesting Jongleur	Oxford, England

"Well, well," observed Mr. Harpending. "What sort of poetry is it that you write, Mr. Lamb? Inspirational poetry?"

J. Elbert Lamb nodded. "Yes, sir; I guess a person would call it inspirational poetry. It's all written by inspiration, anyhow. Here is a copy of my latest opus, *The Wine of Life*. If you are a lover of good poetry, Mr. Simms, I do not doubt but what you would enjoy *The Wine of Life*."

Saying which, he reached into his brief case and handed Mr. Harpending a little paper-backed book.

"Well; uh, tell me this," haltingly resumed Mr. Harpending. "Something here on your card puzzles me. Would you mind explaining what this 'overseas adviser' means? Does that mean that you are this country's adviser to Oxford University?"

Mr. Lamb laughed hale and hearty. "Oh, no, not at all, Mr. Simms! That is funny. A lot of people do not understand about that address at first. I guess it does look a little peculiar. Several newspaper reporters who wrote me up misunderstood about it, also. I have to be careful and explain it, or else they get all mixed up on that point."

"Oh, do the newspapers write you up?" said Mr. Harpending. "Well, well! It looks like we have a real celebrity in our midst!"

"Aw, no, I do not claim that, Mr. Simms," blushed the poet, "because I cannot say that I have 'arrived,' as the expression is among we writers. Not 'arrived' in the fullest sense of the word, anyhow.

"But let me explain about the address. All that 'overseas adviser' means is, that is my address at Oxford U. You see, I am an Oxford U. student, and for the time being I have my mail sent care of 'the adviser to overseas students' at Oxford University, Oxford, Eng. That is what they call him 'over there.' I did not mean for it to look like *I* was the overseas adviser, though it gives some folks that impression."

"I see. Then how do you happen to be hitch-hiking

in this country if you are a university student in England?"

"Well, Mr. Simms, just to tell you the truth,—technically I am not actually a real Oxford student right at this time. All I have to do to be, though, is get over to England. Just as soon as I get there I am going to be an Oxford student. Meantime I just give Oxford as my forwarding address."

"But whatever gave you the idea of entering Oxford University?"

"Mr. Simms," J. Elbert Lamb said earnestly, "I will try and give you the main details of how I happened to get this inspiration to attend Oxford U. Also how I come to be on this 'literary pilgrimage' of mine. Also why I have to either become a student at Oxford U., or else continue to wander, an exile in my native land."

II

Right in here I would like to pause and put in a few words of my own. Now I did not mean to say anything about this, and have never approached Mr. Harpending in regards to the matter, because I did not see where I would stand to gain by registering a kick. But I might as well explain that it is on account of a certain little incidence that I am writing the following story just to beat Mr. Harpending to it. What I allude to is how Mr. Harpending managed to get me strung out one night over a year ago. I so happened to let drop a few details concerning my own career. At the time, thinking that the conversation was just man to man, it never dawned on me that Mr. Harpending, unbeknownst to me, might take and use what I told him. So I opens up and gives him the details of my experience hacking for Yellow out in Chicago, Ill., also about how women was always my particular poison. They never would leave me be. Also about the little unpleasantness I had with the wife when I fallen for a little "dame" in a jitney dance hall, etc. Well, about a year later the wife calls my attention to Mr. Harpending's latest opus, *Centaur on Wheels*.

Perhaps you may of read *Centaur on Wheels*. The character of Monty Roebuck, the taxi driver, is supposed to be me. Whereas the fact of the matter is, I am nothing like that character. But the more my Mrs. read of *Centaur on Wheels*, the more familiar sounding it become to her, and, needless to say, things of that kind put into print will have a tendency to create unrest in the home. What I mean is, there in *Centaur on Wheels* Mr. Harpending used everything that I had told him concerning myself along with a pack of lies I never told him.

Now I always thought from what they learned me back in ward school that an author was supposed to be a person of fine imagination and make up all his stories by inspiration. You take these stories about the people living on Mars: it takes more imagination than I have got to think up that kind of a story. But that certainly is not the way Mr. Harpending gets his stories. So that is how I come to know what Mr. Harpending was up to that morning when he started in to ask that hitch-hiker one thousand questions. And a little something that happened later on practically convinced me that

Mr. Harpending was figuring to get himself another story by "pumping" that poet.

Whereas I am fully aware that when this story is published it is liable to cost me my job. But I do not much care, owing to the fact that I am considering breaking into the writing game myself. If Mr. Harpending can gyp readers in this way I do not see why I cannot do the same. So now let us return to J. Elbert Lamb.

III

"I was born," reminisced J. Elbert Lamb, "on a farm about two miles from the town of Red Arrow, Okla., in the east part of the State. I am now twenty-six years of age, and up until a little over a year ago I had spent most of my life on my father's farm. My father and mother are good people, but they never did understand me. But as time went on the farm became more and more unbearable to me, because I was not built for farm work."

"You appear to be a fairly husky lad," put in Mr. Harpending.

"Yes, sir, I know I *look* to be. My stalwart 'physique' has always worked a hindrance to my poetic career. My folks thought I ought to make a farm hand. They could not get it through their head that I was cut out for a literary career. For instance, I used to have to milk cows when it seemed to me like my wrists was so weak that they would give out before I could get one cow stripped. Also my father made me plow. But my mind would get to wandering off into 'the vasty realms of thought' and my furrows would get crooked. Then my father would come over from the next field and get aggravated and use rough language toward me. He did not understand my temperament.

"Meanwhile I graduated from the eighth grade of country school and my father sent we children to high-school in Red Arrow. I will admit that he was in favor of us getting high-school educations, but nevertheless he could not comprehend my poetic complex and that made him harsh towards me. My mother was a kind woman, too, but she was just as much worried and provoked as my father was. They did not have any conception of how a poet is supposed to act.

"My high-school teachers all told me that I showed real genius. I was appointed class poet of the senior class, and when we graduated from high-school I wrote a poem that made all the names of my twenty-three class mates rhyme with something. This poem was published in the Red Arrow *Weekly* paper. Afterward a number of folks come to me and said that I certainly would miss my calling if I did not become a poet. I had a feeling of my own that I was not 'born to blush unseen.'

"But my father made me go back to work on the farm, having his head set on making me an ordinary plow hand whether I could plow a straight furrow or not. Yet this did not prevent me from dreaming my dreams and studying about my poetry. As you probably realize, Mr. Simms, a poet is no good as a plow hand."

"Of course not," agreed Mr. Harpending, "but could you not make your parents see that? Did you not read your poems to them? I'd think they would of been proud to of had a genius in their midst."

Now it was easy for me to see that he was just stringing this J. Elbert Lamb along, but the poet did not get it. Without cracking a smile, he continued on just as serious, "There it is, Mr. Simms! My parents should of been proud. I thought myself that they should of been proud of me instead of acting like I had something wrong with my head. But they worried about me and oftentimes cross words would be exchanged. When I would sit up nights trying to write my poems they would try to break me to their will. They wanted me to get to bed so that I could arise the next morning early and go out and milk the cows.

"Well, this went on for several years after I got out of high-school. And I was feeling smothered all the time. I wanted to go to college where I could receive critical attention and embark upon my 'literary career.' Seemingly it was not to be. But one morning when we was just getting started on the Fall plowing, it all come over me. I finished the field I was plowing right on down to the meanest part to plow, 'the dead furrow,' and then I unhitched—"

"The *dead* furrow?" inquired Mr. Harpending. "What is a *dead* furrow? I don't think I ever heard of a *dead* furrow."

"No, sir, I don't guess you have unless you have worked on the farm. I will try and make clear to you what the dead furrow is. Now say you start plowing on a twenty-acre field. You begin and plow along the edge, up one side, across, down the other side, across, then up the first side again, and so on, around and around. So every time you make a round your square of unplowed land in the center gets smaller and your furrows shorter. Until you have a little place in the middle of the field covered by furrows on both sides of it, but still unplowed. You call that your 'dead furrow.' It has to be plowed, and there's where your skill as a plowman comes in."

"Skill as a plowman? Does it take any skill to plow?"

"Oh, sure, Mr. Simms. It takes plenty of skill to plow. There is a knack to plowing just like there is a knack to anything, even writing poetry. You take my father: he was a skillful plowman. He could plow a field and make it come out so as every inch of it would be broken. You have to be plenty good to do that. If a person will lay his furrows straight and even from the first beginning, why the dead furrow will not trouble him much. But anyone like me, I let my plow get out of line and I would always have a dead furrow to plague me."

"Why did you not just leave it go?" asked Mr. Harpending. "It looks to me like a little patch of ground would not make much difference anyway."

"Mr. Simms, that's the way I looked at it myself. But a good *farmer* likes to look at a field and know that every inch of it is plowed. My father always used to say that you could tell the difference between a first-class farmer and a shiftless farmer by the way he had plowed out his dead furrow. He claimed that anybody can plow, but it takes a good man to come out right on the dead furrow.

"Like I was telling you, though, I unhitched the two old white horses and drove them off toward the barn. I watered them and shook down hay for them. Then I went on up to the house and put water to heat on the kitchen range for my bath. I begin taking off my overalls.

"Mother come running in. 'What's the matter, son?' she says. 'Are you feeling bad?' 'No,' I replies, 'I am feeling O.K. But I have just decided to break away from it all and go to Tulsa and enter college. I cannot delay my literary career any longer.' 'Oh, son!' she cries, 'you can't go off like this and leave your pa and the boys here in the middle of the Fall plowing!' 'I can, too,' I says. 'It all come over me in the field while ago that opportunity knocks but once. Now is the time for me to embark on my career if I ever am going to. Tomorrow might be too late!'

"Well, I got all cleaned up and put on my good suit. By then it was dinner time and my father had come in from the field. Mother must of told him what I was up to, but he did not say one word all through dinner. When we got up from the table he pulled out his wallet and took out the money he always kept with him. He peeled off five ten dollar bills. 'Here is your wages and your share in them hogs you been slopping,' he says. 'When you get ready to come back, your home will be here for you.' That was all he said. He was a kind man, but we lived in two different worlds.

"I walked over to the highway and thumbed a ride into Tulsa. That same afternoon, without wasting any time, I enrolled at the University of Tulsa. I procured me a job as a delivery boy for a near-by drug store, and that paid me a dollar an afternoon and tips. I was able to live on that. Soon after this my first book of poems, *Purple Vignettes*, was published."

"The money you made on your book must have helped out some, too," gently suggested Mr. Harpending.

"No, Mr. Simms, I am sorry to say that I was doomed to disappointment on *Purple Vignettes*. It cost me every cent of the fifty dollars my father give me when I left home, and I still owed the printer fifty dollars more after it came out. I did not sell only but about ten copies at fifty cents a copy, and give away some more. So you can see that I profited ill on my first book.

IV

"For a while there," continued J. Elbert Lamb, "fortune smiled on me and it certainly seemed that I had made no mistake in starting to college when I did. The other boys in the men's dorm where I was rooming all seemed to take a real keen interest in my poetry. They kept after me to favor them with selections from my book. Lots of times when I would come in from work at night almost too tired out to read my poems with the proper feeling, nothing would do those boys but that I bring a copy of *Purple Vignettes* down to the main hall and read to them. I was always glad to oblige, though there was nights when I would rather of gone straight to bed.

"What is more, the editor of the student paper accepted a number of my poems for publication. There was no money in it for me, but I was more than glad to help out with my literary efforts. So I seemed to be getting off to a good start on my literary career.

"Well, as the saying goes, it never rains but what it pours. Right at the time when it seemed like I was getting along the finest kind, and even the columnists of the local daily newspapers was commencing to publish my work and give me considerable notoriety, why everything seemed to blow up on me. It all happened at once.

"One night I arrived back at the dormitory from my job at the drug store. I was not feeling very good, because that afternoon I had had an accident and had lost my job at the drug store."

"Accident?" asked Mr. Harpending. "What kind of an accident?"

"Not a serious accident, Mr. Simms. That is, I only got a little skinned up. The way it was, I was making a delivery for the drug store on a bicycle and I accidentally hit a street car. I guess I was thinking about a poem or something, and did not see the street car stop. My bicycle got all bent up and a prescription dropped out of the basket and the bottle broke. It so happened that the customer was in a hurry for the prescription. So when I got back the drug store proprietor, my boss, would not listen to any explanations, but got mad and flew off the handle and fired me.

"I was feeling low in my mind over that when I came in that night. Now I had 487 copies of *Purple Vignettes*, which I had not yet sold, packed in a box up in my room. When I came into the main hall of the dorm that night, what did I see but those boys with all my books of poems, wadding each one of them up just as fast as they could. Mr. Simms, I could not hardly believe my own eyes. When I rushed over to try and save my books, they begin pelting me with wadded copies, hollering and laughing. Nearly every last one of *Purple Vignettes* was ruined by them before it was over.

"It seemed that I had been mistaken about those boys. They did not actually care for poetry as much as they had been pretending they did when they kept after me to favor them with selections from my work. They had been mocking me behind my back all the time. Of course I went the next morning and complained to the college president. He called the boys up on the carpet for destroying my books, but nothing was ever done about paying me for them in any way. So far as I know none of the boys received the punishment they so justly deserved.

"Another thing, too: when the next issue of the student paper came out, the editor of it felt privileged to print a number of crazy imitations of my poetry. It was easy to see that the student paper was just making fun of me, and that the editor had not appreciated the poems of mine he published. That was a real disappointment to me.

"By this time I was beginning to get good and sore. There is a limit to what a person's patience can stand. When the student paper turned on me like that, I got plenty mad. I just sat down and wrote a hot letter to the editor about the injustice which had been worked upon me. I don't know what all I said, I was so mad. I know I come right out and said that all the students I had come into contact with there was just a bunch of ignoramuses. But the most influential thing I said was that the next year I was going to England and enter Oxford U., where poets and their work are better appreciated than in a little one-horse Oklahoma college. I was so mad I did not know what I was getting myself into.

"When the student paper come out with my letter, of course, the students all started in roasting me. For a while my life was made miserable. The girl I had asked to marry me even turned on me. The suffering I went through with at that college beggars description. It was not enough that all the students was razzing me, but the profs begin picking on me in class to make me appear comical.

"I packed up and went back home. Now it so happened that the story about my trouble at college and also about my accident was played up in the Tulsa newspapers. They reported that I had tried to knock a street car off the track with my bicycle. Which was not the facts in the case. As I say, in the short while I was there in college, I had managed to make myself quite a well-known personage in Tulsa. The people in Red Arrow and vicinity all read the Tulsa papers and they knew all about my threat to go off to an English university even before I arrived back home. So I soon found that some people in Red Arrow took the same attitude towards me that I had encountered at college. I don't know, but I always seemed different from other boys in Red Arrow, and when they got wind of my ambitions to attend Oxford U., they begin making fun of me, too. It got to the place where I could not walk down Main Street without the sidewalk loafers making wise cracks about me. So I knew then that it was up to me to go ahead and make good my brags. Or else never hold my head up again.

"The problem was how to finance myself. Once I had read a newspaper article where some fellow in Michigan incorporated himself and sold shares in his future and thus put himself through college. So I decided to try the same stunt. There was a good many people around Red Arrow who had been following my career and had faith in me and my future, despite the things which the local smart alecks said. I persuaded the printer who published *Purple Vignettes* for me to run off 4,000 coupons, each representing one share in my future and selling for one dollar each. This would possess me of $4,000, which would be plenty to get me to England and put me through Oxford U.

"Well, it was a tougher proposition than I had anticipated. I worked like a dog that Winter trying to put it across, talking myself hoarse and walking miles to see people. I had my sales talk all lined out, and what I had to do each time was sell myself to the prospect. I would start off by showing them the letter I had from the Oxford U. adviser to overseas students, which showed that I was not bluffing.

"I soon discovered that I was doing well when I sold a prospect even one share in my career. It was not that people did not have faith in me. They just did not have the money. Some people, of course, had more faith in me than others. For instance, the printer started me off by taking twenty-five shares the first crack out of the box. Also the baker in Red Arrow was a man of liberal ideas and had always appreciated my talents and he bought twenty shares. Also I sold a Red Arrow barber twenty shares. None of these folks was well-fixed, and it certainly does make me proud to think of their confidence in me. That is why I absolutely cannot disappoint them. When I went to the baker to collect the final payment on the block of shares he took, he told me that he was handing me the last dollar he had in his till. It was confidence like that that made me realize that I absolutely had to go ahead and get to Oxford U. some way.

"Early last Spring I could see that I was not going to sell much more stock in myself around Red Arrow. I had sold only 386 shares, and I had to pay $100 on what was owing to my publisher, because my second book, *The Wine of Life,* which you hold in your hand, was ready to come out. So I decided to leave with what I had. I had already been in correspondence with a steamship coöperation about buying a ticket to England, and they had give me to understand that I could buy a ticket on the easy payment plan. So I started out, hitch-hiking to New York City.

"I carried my blanket roll as now and nights I would sleep behind billboards. I had a brief case packed with copies of *The Wine of Life* and every time I caught a ride I would try and sell the fellow who picked me up an autographed copy of my book. They would nearly always buy. I was a week on the road and I arrived in New York City with $4.95 more money than I left Red Arrow with.

V

"When I arrived in New York City I looked up the steamship coöperation that had been writing to me. But I guess I made the mistake of going in there without dolling up or anything, because when they saw my dusty clothes, they refused to sell me a ticket on the easy payment plan. I did not let this get me down, however, because I had the money to buy a ticket in full if I had to. So I went to see about getting my passport.

"They told me at the passport office that you have to have permission to get into England. Which they call it a visa. So when I went to the British counsel's office to get my visa, he would not issue me one. It seems that he was scared that I would get over there and become a beggar. On account of my dusty clothes, I guess. Anyway he passed several remarks about 'these foreign beggars who become public charges in England.' I showed him my two letters from the Oxford U. adviser to overseas students and also a copy of my book. It seemed like nothing made any impression on him. All I could get out of him was that when I could show that I was backed by $1,000 in cash, he would grant me permission to enter England. So I found that I lacked about $700 of being able to go to Oxford U.

"Well, there I was staying at that hotel the Y.M.C.A. runs, and my money was playing out fast. There was no such thing as going back home, because a number of people had bought shares in my future and I could not go back and tell them that their money was gone and that I had not gone to Oxford yet. I had traveled half-way across the U. S. towards what I aimed to do, and if I went back some folks in Red Arrow would have been nastier than ever. So I realized that I absolutely *had* to get to Oxford, England, even if I did not do anything but mail home a bunch of post cards with the Oxford postmark on them. So I was confronted with the problem of accumulating $1,000 in order to get myself admitted into England. Which I'll do it yet! I sure will!"

"The sum of the whole thing seems to be," said Mr. Harpending, shooting the youth a piercing glance, "you have come to another dead furrow. You were able to get just so far, and then you struck one of those dead furrows that you never could get past. Is not that right?"

"Dead furrow?" said the poet. "I do not get it, Mr. Simms."

Mr. Harpending shrugged and waved one hand. 'Oh, just a little figure of speech that happened to strike my fancy. The dead furrow seems to me to offer a pretty good symbol for a type of person who finds it easy enough to get ambitions, but who never has quite what it takes to put himself across and finish the job."

"I guess I don't get it, Mr. Simms," the poet said, puzzled.

"No matter!" said Mr. Harpending. "But this still does not explain that 'literary pilgrimage' to Harpending that you mentioned."

"I was coming to that, Mr. Simms," J. Elbert Lamb resumed. "That is what I have been specializing in ever since I learned that I could not get into England without I could show the British counsel one thousand dollars."

"Specializing in what?" asked Mr. Harpending.

"Literary pilgrimages," said J. Elbert Lamb.

"What do you mean?" said Mr. Harpending impatiently. "Is not this pilgrimage to Harpending your first?"

"Oh, no, Mr. Simms, this is by no means my first literary pilgrimage. I have been making literary pilgrimages for several months now. I have been to see nearly every writing man of any prominence in the Eastern part of this country. Mr. Harpending is just one of the celebrities I have on my list. I am only catching up on some of the ones I have missed heretofore."

Mr. Harpending's face does not look like the photos his publishers send out at best, but now it looked like someone had dropped a brick upon him. He grumbled, "But I do not see where all this roaming around is getting you any closer to Oxford. Have you not just about used up your $286 you had toward going to Oxford?"

"Oh, that $286. I meant to tell you about that, Mr. Simms. I paid all but $36 of that to a New York book publisher for getting out *The Jesting Jongleur*, my next book of poems. It is due to come out next week. That is why I'm waiting around in the East right now. I have to pay the publisher $150 more when he delivers the books."

"Humph!" grunted Mr. Harpending. "You're certainly optimistic! How do you expect to live now that your money is all gone?"

"My money is not all gone, Mr. Simms. I hope I did not give the impression that because I am hitch-hiking I am a pauper. It is true that I hitch-hike to save on traveling expenses. But I also like it because I can contact new fresh viewpoints. And every time I ride with a person, it enlarges my audience just that much."

It was easy to see that Mr. Harpending was about to lose his temper. "Yes, yes!" he sputtered, fairly red in the face, "but what I want to know is, where is all this getting you?"

"Why, let me make my activities clear, Mr. Simms. You see, my stunt is this: when I find myself in a small town or city, I go around to the local newspaper office and show my credentials, letters, autographed photos, etc., and then the newspaper gives me a write-up as a vagabond poet who has rubbed elbows with all these famous people. Then I contact the head of the local ladies' literary club, and arrange to give them a talk on the famous personalities I have visited. My talk always goes over big, because you take women, they seem to be more interested in literature than most men are. I take a free-will offering and also sell autographed copies of *The Wine of Life* after each talk. So I'm bound to make. I can't lose."

"So you find this—er—'lecturing' profitable, do you?"

"Oh, my, yes! My expenses are light, and if I keep on doing as well as I have been, I figure that by next Fall I ought to have the $1,000 I need to get to Oxford U. And, just between you and I, my next book, *The Jesting Jongleur*, does not have only but three or four new poems different from what I already have in *The Wine of Life*. It seems like I do not get much chance to write new poems here lately. But I think the title is going to put this book over. Also the cloth binding. So I will be able to ask $1.50 for *The Jesting Jongleur*. Whereas I am only getting a dollar a copy for *The Wine of Life*."

"But I would think that these writers would resent your intrusion on their time in this way. Don't you meet with rebuffs? Don't they get mad when you break in on them?"

"Well, if they do, Mr. Simms, that makes just as good stuff for my talk before the ladies' literary clubs as if they had welcome me with opened arms. Now, for example, I went to see Mr. ——, the famous novelist who lives in Pennsylvania, I learned that he has a little house around back of his residence for a workroom. I knocked on the door, but got no answer. But I heard him in there. So I pushes open the door and steps in. He jumps up from his typewriter in a rage and yells, 'Get out of here!' I stood my ground and said firmly, 'I won't get out, because I have traveled two thousand miles to see you.' 'The heck you have!' he shouts, 'I have traveled two thousand miles to *keep from* seeing you!' Now that little antidote is one of the best ones I have in my talk. It always gives the literary clubs a hearty laugh.

"But it is only very seldom when I tell an author that I have come two thousand miles to see him that it does not flatter him. He usually asks me to stay to dinner, and sometimes even to stay the night."

You could see that Mr. Harpending was having a hard time to keep a grip on himself. He was breathing hard and looking daggers.

The poet did not catch on and went on talking cheerfully. "Well, I figure that as soon as I sell out this edition of *The Jesting Jongleur* I'll be able to show that British counsel the $1,000 all right. When I get to England, I aim to pull the same stunt over there."

"Yes, I would if I was in your place," Mr. Harpending said sarcastically, but it was over J. Elbert Lamb's head.

"But I've still got several big writers to call on in this country before I'll be ready for the English 'men of letters.' As soon as I've seen Mr. Harpending I will of got about all of any prominence in the East."

"You won't have to wait long," Mr. Harpending said drily, "because we are right at Westport now."

"Oh, is that right?" exclaimed the poet. "Then, before I let it slip my mind, that book of poems you took will be one dollar. I throw in my personal autograph free of charge."

Now you might not believe it, but I don't figure to write a story *exactly* like Mr. Harpending does, and I can assure you that everything I write here actually happened. But I certainly could not hardly believe it myself when Mr. Harpending just said, "Why, yes! Yes! To be sure!" hastily pulling out his billfold and handing over a dollar. J. Elbert Lamb took the money calmly and got out his fountain pen to write in the book.

"I don't suppose you have any idea of just where Mr. Harpending lives in this vicinity, do you?" he queried as I stopped the car.

"No, I do not!" Mr. Harpending snapped. "I am a total stranger in these parts myself." We drove off and left the poet standing there.

VI

"Spicer," said Mr. Harpending, peering back to see which way J. Elbert Lamb had started walking, "drive fast and get this car in the garage out of sight before that pest gets out there and recognizes it. I am going to give him the slip and I do not wish him camping on my trail."

As soon as we got in I drove the car into the garage and closed the doors as per instructions. Pretty soon I looks out a window and sees this J. Elbert Lamb and all his gear come plugging up the drive. I kept watching and it was not long before I see him go walking off down the drive again. About thirty minutes later Mr. Harpending comes out to the garage and starts poking around in the back seat of the Pierce. I knew what he was looking for, all right.

"Did you lose something, sir?" I asks.

"Why, yes, Spicer. Did you see anything of a little white card? It was a card that crazy hitch-hiker handed me. I seem to of lost it."

"I did not see anything of it, sir," I says, playing innocent. I had the card in my pocket all the time, but

I guess I can still tell Mr. Harpending a few lies and not be even with him yet.

"It must of fell out of the car when he got out. D—m it, Spicer, I wanted particularly to save that card. It was amusing."

I had half a notion to say, yeah, amusing enough to work into your next story along with a lot of lies, just like what I told you about my own career was amusing. But all I said out loud was, "In case I see anything of it, I'll certainly let you know, sir."

A little later on I happened to be up at the house and I met Marie in the back hall. "What did that funny-looking kid that rang this afternoon say?" I asked her.

"He wanted to see Mr. Harpending," Marie said. "But Mr. Harpending had told me that if any stranger came asking for him to say that he was in Hollywood, Cal."

"Yeah, I know," I said. "And what did the kid say when you told him Mr. Harpending was in Hollywood, Cal.?"

"Why, he said that was all right. He said that he was going out to Hollywood next week to call on Will Rogers anyway and that he would try and look Mr. Harpending up. Why didn't Mr. Harpending want to see him?"

"Search me," I said. "I guess Mr. Harpending was scared that the kid was liable to pull him into a dead furrow."

"What do you mean, a dead furrow?" Marie said.

"You ask Mr. Harpending," I said. "He can tell you all about dead furrows."

11

THE DRUMMER'S SHOES

Mrs. Esterbrook, the mayor's wife, was the kind of woman who couldn't do her own housework. She had to have a hired girl all the time. But she always called her hired girl the maid, and Mrs. Esterbrook's putting on airs like that was the reason she had such a hard time getting anybody to stay and work for her. A country girl who had come to town to get a kitchen job would be insulted when she heard Mrs. Esterbrook calling her the maid in front of visitors and when she found that she was expected to eat alone in the kitchen. Then she would quit the job.

None of them liked the way Mrs. Esterbrook called her attic the servants' quarters, either. It wasn't that they minded sleeping up there in that barren, dusty place with the sharp-pitched underside of shingles for a ceiling and only enough loose flooring laid over the rafters to set an iron cot and a washstand on. That was as good as they had been used to at home in the country. But what they couldn't get used to was the way Mrs. Esterbrook had of calling things by stuck-up names. So none of the hired girls stayed at the Esterbrooks long, and Mrs. Esterbrook's favorite topic of conversation was the servant problem.

She never did get over it about Lois Schaefer, because

she thought that Lois was the best maid she had ever had. She stayed blind about Lois long after everyone else in town knew that the hired girl was flighty. But it was a long time before Mrs. Esterbrook would listen to any of the stories about the way Lois had been carrying on. And then she acted as if she were more deeply shocked and hurt than anybody.

Lois came to work for the Esterbrooks one Spring. She was a tall, heavy-hipped farm girl with satchel cheeks and a throat full of braying laughter. The attic room was like an oven on the long Summer evenings, and after the supper dishes were done, Lois would put on her drop-stitch stockings and paint the full sides of her face with orange rouge and walk out. She would stroll past the Kentucky Colonel Hotel where, usually, two or three drummers would be sitting on the porch, propped back in rocking chairs with their feet up on the railing, taking the evening's cool. Lois would wag her hips under her tight skirt and stare at them boldly. The next time she came past, sometimes a traveling man would get up and follow her off in the dusk.

That went on all Summer. People went to Mrs. Esterbrook and to Mayor Esterbrook, too, and tried to tell them what a shameless girl they had staying with them. But Lois was a hard worker and she was more respectful to Mrs. Esterbrook than any of the other hired girls had been, so the Esterbrooks never would listen to anything against her.

It was along at the beginning of Winter that Lois picked up a big shoe drummer. Bad weather was coming on then. Lois came past the hotel just as the shoe drummer was coming down the front steps.

He said, "Uh oh, there!"

And Lois said, "Uh oh, yourself, kid!" and gave a blast of laughter.

The shoe drummer came on down the walk, and said, "Which way you going, baby?"

Lois said, "Which way does it look like I'm going, smartie?"

The shoe drummer said, "Well, looky here, sweetie, I sure do like your type. I could care a whole lot for somebody like you. How far ahead you dated up?"

Lois said, "Aw, well, I've got some groceries here I've got to get on to the house with, but if you want to walk with me, I'll show you whur I live."

So the big shoe drummer walked on as far as the Esterbrooks' with Lois, and she made a date with him for eleven o'clock that night.

Of course the Esterbrooks were all in bed when eleven o'clock came, and Lois crept down the back stairs to meet the shoe drummer. It had been looking stormy all day, and it was beginning to spit sleet a little. The shoe drummer was waiting out in front of the house, leaning against a tree.

Lois told him, "It's going to sleet, and we ain't got no place to go."

The drummer, all fire, said, "What's the matter with your room?"

Lois said, "Oh, gosh, no! The people I live with would hear us coming in, and then I'd get canned."

"Aw, no they wouldn't," the shoe drummer said.

"I'll take off my shoes and carry them and step so soft they won't even hear me come in."

So Lois said, all right, and when they got to the foot of the back stairs he stooped over and unbuttoned his shoes and took them off. He carried them in one hand. He had a small flash light in his other hand, and they went creeping up to her attic room. They stepped tiptoe, sly and cautious in the way that only lumbering big people can be.

"Now you want to watch out up here at the top," Lois whispered, "because the boards on this floor is loose, and they ain't no floor laid on part of it, and if you ain't keerful, you're liable to step off on the laths and go right on through the plaster. And the man and woman I'm working for has their bedroom right below. They're sleeping down there."

As soon as they got to the top of the back stairs and opened the attic door, the first thing the big shoe drummer did, of course, was step on a loose board. It flipped up and he lost his balance. He landed over on the unfloored part of the attic. He floundered a moment trying to get back his footing, the great, heavy man, and then he went crashing through.

He fell, with a shower of plaster and splinters, in the center of the Esterbrooks' large bed on the floor below. They were both sound asleep, but they were awakened suddenly by the frightful noise. Both of them leaped out of bed, terrified, and as of one mind made for the door. The shoe drummer still clutched his flash light, and he saw the door, too. They all reached it at the same time. All three of them were big, stomachy people, and they jammed tight and unyielding in the bedroom doorway.

Lois Schaefer peered over the edge of the jagged hole in the bedroom ceiling, shrieking, "I told the big boob to watch out for them there loose boards! No, he wouldn't listen to me, the big old slob! But I sure told the big boob to watch out for them there loose boards!"

Almost silently there in the dark the big-bellied three twisted and grunted. They were caught fast in the doorway. But finally the drummer tore loose, and, bearing shreds of Mr. and Mrs. Esterbrooks' nightgowns, he went thudding out through the parlor to the front door, and was gone.

The Esterbrooks told Lois Schaefer to pack up and get out that very night.

The next morning they found the drummer's shoes in the bedroom where he had dropped them. They were fancy, button shoes, a pale yellow leather, with hard-knobbed toes, all pinked at the seams. They seemed to be an expensive pair of shoes.

Mayor Esterbrook tried to wear them for a while, but they were so tight on his feet that he traded them to Paperhanger Birchett for plastering up the hole that the shoe drummer had left in the bedroom ceiling.

12

BIOGRAPHY OF A PROPHET

An aunt of mine, who had literary leanings and kept among her souvenirs a letter written to her by Ella Wheeler Wilcox with violet ink, once gave me a piece of advice about this craft. "My boy," she said, "every person's life, no matter how insignificant it may appear on the surface, is worth a book." Her precept later passed around among other writers, and, more important, the publishers took it up, and it got to be all the rage for a while. As for myself, I never did hold to it very strongly, and the older I get the more dubious about it I grow. Maybe I'm wrong, but it seems to me that one life is hardly ever worth a book. Still I am convinced that even in the dullest life there is usually some bright episode to be uncovered, lopped out, and set into an interesting tale.

Now there was Goldstein. There are people, I suppose, who would insist that his life is just as much worth writing a book about as Paul Gauguin's or Ambrose Bierce's, but I doubt it. I was young when I knew him and I may have missed a good deal, but I feel that I was fortunate in knowing him at that time and no other, because I witnessed his crisis. A year or so later no one would have suspected that anything had ever happened to ruffle the mediocrity of his existence.

The first time I ever laid eyes on Goldstein was in the eight o'clock section of English 51 when I was a sophomore attending a Summer session of the State university. I saw him sitting there in the front row the first day I came in, a swart man with black hair merging into baldness and mild brown eyes behind rimless spectacles. He was dressed neatly in a gray business suit, a stocky, middle-aged man, looking bewildered and out of place in the classroom. I remember wondering momentarily about him.

One morning, a few weeks later, the professor selected my essay on "How the Salmon Spawns" to read before the class. I felt that it was really an improvement on the article I had found in the encyclopedia, and I was proud to have him read out my name as the author.

When we were leaving at the end of the hour Goldstein waited by the door and clutched my arm. He introduced himself to me and explained hurriedly that he was trying to learn how to write, because he had some ideas that he wanted to put before the world. He said that he wasn't getting along as well as he had expected to, and that he was eager to talk with someone who could give him a few pointers.

"Do you have this next hour off?" he said. "Maybe we could go somewheres and have a cold drink together." Then he added hastily, "This will be on me, see? I'm paying for it."

"Sure," I said, somewhat flattered, "let's go over to the Varsity Shoppe and get a coke. I've got a nine o'clock, but its geology under Bumgarner, and I like to have an excuse to cut it."

By the time our cokes were served I realized that Goldstein did not want any advice from me about expository writing, but that he did want me to listen while he talked about himself. He wanted to tell me what had happened to his life, his drab, commonplace life that had always been so smooth and well-ordered, and that he himself, looking soberly back on it now, was shocked to find broken and hopelessly jumbled.

I felt the vague embarrassment that a youth often feels with an older man who wants to meet him on his own level. There is always a question as to whether the boy should be forward and thus come up to the older man in age, or whether he should refrain from letting it out that he also knows a thing or two and thus give the other an opportunity to talk down and be instructive according to the experience that goes with his years. This indecision never failed to disturb me.

I was confused, and at the moment he was prefacing his story over the empty glasses, I bit down on my pipe stem and it cracked. He stopped talking suddenly with a blank look in his soft, moist eyes. His mouth stayed open and all the expression went out of his sweat-shiny face.

"What was that?" he said after a moment.

"Only the mouthpiece on my pipe," I said. "I bit down on it too hard and it cracked. It was almost worn through, anyway."

I grinned at him stupidly, and he craned across the table, his narrowed eyes intent on my mouth.

"Boy!" he said, speaking with confidence for the first time, "that's a fine set of teeth you got there. Good strong teeth. But you should ought to take better care of them. What kind of toothpaste do you use?"

II

Dr. Goldstein told me repeatedly how he happened to become a prophet, but he was as much mystified about *why* as anyone. His revelation did not extend that far. He would attempt to explain it and he would end in a maze of half-finished sentences, completely baffled.

He had been a "painless" dentist in Houston, Texas, and after twenty-four years in the profession he had built up a very profitable practice. He had a good many Jewish patients, although he welcomed all creeds and races, excepting the black. He kept his suite of offices on the second floor of a small, somewhat run-down office building which he owned himself, because, as he explained to me, many of the patients he was after would have been intimidated by fast elevators and sumptuous fixtures. His equipment, however, was the best that money could buy. He spoke enough Spanish to get along with the Mexicans who came to him.

Every afternoon, as punctually at five o'clock as possible, he left the office and went around to an auto park, where he got into his Chrysler sedan and drove out to his seven-roomed Dutch Colonial house in one of the earlier real estate additions. His wife had a canary in an ornate brass cage and six gold fish in a glass urn on an imitation marble pedestal, and she kept the overstuffed purple velours parlor furniture covered with awning-striped linen slipovers the year 'round. They had three children, the oldest of whom was fourteen. Up until the time of his trouble, he told me, he had never spoken a harsh word to his wife, although she had been cross with him perhaps five or six times in the twenty years that they had been married.

They went to the reformed synagogue and belonged to a Jewish community club. He voted the Democratic ticket straight and was a 32° Mason. There were not many things that he was opposed to, but he was opposed to Zionism, just as he was opposed to Communism and the Ku Klux Klan, because it struck him as being un-American.

His opposition to the movement at the beginning, however, was very mild. Dr. Goldstein was a mild-mannered man. Years of ministering to human pain had made him so, a person of soothing voice and consoling countenance. No one had ever suspected the spark that glowed in the good dentist, and no one could have predicted the proportions of the flame to which it was presently fanned.

He permitted his wife to coax him into going with her one night to hear the speech of a man just returned from Palestine. All of their friends and relatives were going, and Dr. Goldstein accompanied his wife docilely enough. But in the course of the speech on Zionism some very pointed questions occurred to him.

"I don't know why it was," he told me, his bland face twisted with puzzlement, "but these questions just kept bothering my mind. I never had made much study of the Zionist proposition; wasn't especially interested.

But I knew just as well as I knew anything that I was going to speak out in meeting that night. I never had done anything like that before, always found it a good business to keep my mouth shut, but it seemed to me that I never could rest easy until I had gotten some kind of an answer to these questions that popped into my mind that night."

So as soon as discussion was called for at the end of the speech the mild dentist rose to his feet and, rather apologetically, put his questions. He didn't pretend to be an expert on Zionism. But what about the Arabs in Palestine? How did they feel about the Jews moving back? What about the area and productivity of Palestine as compared with the number of Jews in the world? How about the British? Couldn't you count on the British having some strings tied to that protectorate somewhere? And the U.S.A.? Weren't American Jews satisfied with the U.S.A.?

The speaker was very sarcastic in his replies and ended by calling Dr. Goldstein a Babbitt. Dr. Goldstein didn't know at that time exactly what a Babbitt was, but he had seen the word and he didn't like it. It made him angry.

"Seems like it just all came over me in a flash," he told me. "I never was much of a man for getting mad about anything, but, believe me, I started in right there, and I got that fellow told. I showed him that I could give just as good as I could take, all right. And I don't know how I happened to, either, because any other time or any other place, likely as not, I would of been scared to death to say anything."

It was on that occasion, then, that Dr. Goldstein tasted the first heady delights of public appearance. He saw all the faces turned toward him, stretching up to get a look at him, and once there was a ripple of laughter at some snappy comeback he had made to the speaker. The following day he was further gratified by having several patients mention the affair to him at the office and by having Rabbi Roth stop him on the street to remonstrate with him.

Those were the little puffs that set off the spark in Dr. Goldstein. He began attending every Zionist meeting that he could get around to, and he got around to almost as many as he could find announced in that part of Texas. At the end of each meeting, just when everyone was feeling happy about *Eretz Ysroel*, the Promised Land, and warm and well-disposed toward the rehabilitation of Palestine and proud to have a chance to take part in the wonderful work by making financial contributions, at the crucial instant when the pledge blanks were being passed around, Dr. Goldstein, like the specter at the wedding feast, would rise up, his nostrils dilated, his lips trembling, a fanatic gleam in his mild, brown eyes, and he would fix the speaker with a rigid, horizontal right arm. Dr. Goldstein had no more perplexing questions now. He had a little speech of his own to make about the realities of the Zionist movement.

He told them that this whole business of getting the Jews to set up a national home in Palestine was just another scurvy trick of British imperialism, no more; that the Jews were being used as catspaws in the Near East; that Palestine was already occupied by the Arabs and that anyway it was a worn-out land; that only a sentimental bum would leave America to go back: altogether a very fiery and disturbing summing-up. And, even though he were cried down before he had said all that he had in mind to say, he always brought his peroration to a close in the same way, most effectively, by shouting an ominous prediction.

"The Arabs will cut your throats!" he would yell hoarsely. "They'll-cut-your-throats!" he would repeat gutturally. His large brown eyes would bulge and he would draw a stubby index finger across his own distended throat two or three times very rapidly, making the while a series of sharp little sibilants by sucking his breath through his teeth. It was a very disheartening and appalling gesture. It never failed to send an apprehensive shiver through the wrought-up audience at the very moment when everyone should have been in beatific contemplation of the march onward to Zion. Everyone would have been feeling most cordial toward the world at large before Dr. Goldstein got up, but by the time he had got in his two cents' worth the place would be in a riot. The chairman of the meeting would often wish (audibly, too) that Dr. Goldstein would draw something across his throat less soft and blunt than his own forefinger.

The dentist continued to haunt and to hound every Zionist meeting that he could reach, and he soon became a familiar figure not only in Houston but in several near-by cities. Pudgy and respectable-looking though he was, and pleasant and suave and with a cheerful word for all though he had been, he grew to be as sinister a man as one could wish for. He became so well-known that the Zionists used to post a couple of strong men at the door just to exclude him when he showed up for the meeting. Usually, however, he devised cunning ways of eluding the guards, and he would be in there for the finish.

While his obsession increased, his dental practice fell off. It was not only that he was neglecting it. His Jewish patients were angry. His Mexican patients were frightened by his dire mutterings while he had them helpless in the chair. Things had come to such a pass that he had let the office girl and the young man who worked in the laboratory go. He spent most of his time at the reception room desk writing letters about Zionism to the newspapers. He had become a pariah by this time. His friends ducked down alleys when they saw him on the street. He had insulted the rabbi. His own relatives shunned him and his wife's relatives berated him.

One night, in a frenzy brought on by Mrs. Goldstein's advancing some of the arguments she had heard from her brother, R. D. Froelich, the fur man, he shouted that he would slap her face off, and then proceeded to slap her face so hard that he feared for a moment that he had done it. So Mrs. Goldstein gathered the three children to her and went away to live with the Froelichs. Dr. Goldstein closed up the Dutch Colonial house and slept on the wicker sofa in his outer office, taking his meals at a *kosher* cafeteria down the street.

All this time the obsessed man had been conducting

an untiring (to himself, at least) correspondence with the "Letters from the People" departments of various daily newspapers. Sometimes the editors would append short comments, flippant notes and smart-aleck headings that indicated they had not the slightest understanding of, or sympathy with, what Dr. Goldstein was writing about. This distracted him all the more, because no one ever made any mistake about what he meant when he spoke at a Zionist meeting. Nevertheless, he clipped all his published letters carefully and filed them away in his billfold. He still had them when I knew him, yellowed and gray-creased and frayed, and he was fond of bringing them out while he was talking.

The newspapers' indifference to the Zionist menace, meanwhile, troubled him more and more. He began to suspect his limitations in the use of written language. It seemed impossible, at length, for him to write what he wanted to say forcefully enough. He could speak in a convincing manner, but when he tried to get his thoughts and warnings down on paper the words he wanted often would not come. Sometimes he would sit for hours thinking of just how he wanted to phrase a single sentence of his message. He noticed, too, that changes were always made in his letters, and he carefully marked these in on the clippings with a pencil. It got to the place where there would be whole pages left out, and his letters would not be half the length they had been when he had mailed them.

He still met his Jewish friends and patients of more prosperous days on the street, but not when they could help it. Even when they could not avoid him altogether, they would not stop to talk with him. So, seeing them a block away, Dr. Goldstein would start making that portentous throat-cutting gesture, and as they hurried past he would let go with his weird hissing noise, just to keep his prophecy fresh in their minds. "They'll cut your throats!" he would exclaim fiendishly to any unwary Jew who got within earshot.

Then the newspapers stopped publishing his letters. Dr. Goldstein hinted that strong influence had been brought to bear on the editors, although he was never confident about this. It was inconceivable to him that the editors could have decided that the question was no longer moot. Always he was worried by the misgiving that his own inadequacy might be to blame, that his writing was defective in some way. He did not doubt for an instant that if he could only get his message across in writing it would make page one. It was in his literary composition that he finally lost confidence, not in the potency of his oracle.

One morning in June, 1929, he received notice of an overdraft from his bank. That was when Dr. Goldstein, aged forty-nine years, made a courageous decision. He would learn how to write. He would learn to write so compellingly that every magazine and newspaper in the country would awaken to the menace of Zionism, and Jews everywhere would be warned in time.

Dentists have a custom of removing a faulty gold bridge or a crown and tossing it carelessly into a cuspidor without bothering to call the patient's attention to it. It is one of the profession's legitimate and most lucrative sources of revenue. Dr. Goldstein had an accumulation of this discarded scrap gold on hand. The morning of his great decision he bagged it and sold it. He arranged with his bank for the collection of his office rentals. Then he locked up his own office, put the key in his pocket, and took train for the State university.

There, after making a careful study of the university's Summer school bulletin, he enrolled in the School of Journalism. But the catalogue description of English 51, an expository writing course, fitted his desire so precisely that he entered that class also, determined not to spare himself in improving the quality of his written discourse.

III

The Summer progressed and we got to know each other pretty well. It was a strange relationship. It was not that we were close friends or anything of the sort, yet I must have been closer to him than anyone else at the university. I am sure that he did not confide in any other person there. The professors treated him with the coolness and suspicion that one monomaniac has for another. And the students, lank school-ma'ms working out their masters' degrees and dumb co-eds making up flunked courses, had nothing in common with him.

He would single me out at eating places, and if I were alone he would come over to my table. If I were eating with someone he would wave and pass on to take his meal in solitude. He had a certain shyness about him that I thought paradoxical in one whose very blatancy had brought him there.

Indeed, that was one of the things that puzzled me most about Goldstein. The longer I knew him and the more I talked with him, the incredibility of what he had done increased. Bit by bit I came to understand that no one could have been more firmly settled in his groove than he had been. He had lived in a comfortable home, he was deeply attached to his wife and children, it had been years since money matters had troubled him, his disposition was, if anything, a shade too meek and complacent; and then, in the midst of this tranquil happiness, for no very powerful reason, he had deliberately wrenched himself out of it and had plunged into a new and uncertain life. It was almost enough to convince one that his was a call to soothsaying over which there was no mortal control.

Our conversations, of course, always came around to that one subject. However, he no longer gave the impression of being fanatical about it. Sometimes he spoke feverishly, when he had whipped himself into it, but more often he was simply dogged in his attitude. His original warning ran through his talk in a constant refrain: "So I told them, 'The Arabs'll cut your throats,' I said," but there was seldom any passion in his voice. It was more often weary and full of vast resignation. I used to look on him as a ruined and beaten man, but later I knew that I had been mistaken. He was simply waiting for the inevitable.

One night in July I went with him after dinner to his room, a squalid hole in a cheap dormitory, barren and forbidding and smelling of lysol. He showed me some of the letters his wife had written to him. They were pathetic letters, all questions and puzzled apologies. Her humbleness was abject. She said that she was sorry for everything that she had said, although it was apparent that she was bewildered by what had happened to their life. She told of the difficulties that are unavoidable when one is quartered with one's relatives. She was miserable. There was absolutely no recrimination in what she wrote, and I was touched by her humility.

Goldstein sat on the swayed iron bed with its cracked white enamel and its ragged quilt, his head bowed and clasped in his hands while I read.

I looked up from one of the letters and said to him, "Why don't you forget it and go back and start all over again?"

He flinched as if I had struck him. He turned his mild, sad eyes at me and looked at me for a moment before he answered. "Oh, I couldn't do that!" he exclaimed in a shocked voice.

"Why couldn't you?"

"Oh, I just couldn't! You don't understand. You don't know how it is with the Jews. They all think I'm crazy. If I was to go back now, I never would be respected again. They think that I went out of my head there, but they'll see. They'll see I wasn't lying to them. I couldn't go back there until they did see."

It was along in August before I saw Goldstein again, and the Summer school session was almost over. His attendance in the expository writing class had become more and more irregular, and I had supposed that he had dropped out altogether. I didn't even know that he was still in town.

Then one sweltering evening I came into a small café near the campus where I usually ate dinner. Goldstein hailed me from a side booth. I didn't want to hear about the Zionist menace again. I didn't want to hear him repeat his dreadful prophecy. I didn't want to re-read his newspaper clippings and the latest letter he was composing for the press. I was sweaty and tired and I was looking for cooler companionship. But he seemed so forlorn there, I sat down opposite him.

While we were waiting for the waiter to bring our orders, a newsboy came by, and Goldstein bought a paper. He always bought a paper and searched through it hurriedly to see whether one of his letters had been published. He turned directly to the "Letters to the Editor" column without looking at the front page. After a few moments he put the paper down with a disappointed grunt.

"What are the headlines?" I asked.

"Let's see," he said, picking up the shuffled wad that the newspaper had become and fingering through it. I saw him look at the front page, holding it over by the shaded wall light. He was silent.

"What does it say?"

"Well," he said quite calmly, "they done it. They finally done it." Then his hands began trembling violently and he repeated again, "They done it!" in a voice so loud and quavering that people began sticking their heads out of booths to see what was going on.

"Who done what?" I said.

Goldstein shoved the newspaper, a late peach-colored edition, toward me with a palsied hand. Spread across the top of the front page was a headline:

MANY DEAD IN HOLY LAND MASSACRES

"Jesus!" I said, "this is terrible, isn't it?"

"Terrible? Terrible? What's so terrible? Not so terrible!" he said popping his hands together and chuckling exultantly. It occurred to me that that was the first time I had ever heard him laugh. He picked up his hat and started sliding out of the booth.

"What're you going to do?"

"I have to be going," he said.

"Aren't you going to eat dinner?"

"No. I have to find out what time I can get a train out for Houston, Texas."

He walked away. I thought I had seen the last of him but when I glanced up he was back again. He leaned over in the booth and clapped me on the shoulder, smiling broadly.

"They sure enough done it, didn't they, son?" he said jovially. "I guess old Doc Goldstein wasn't so looney, after all. I kept telling them that the Arabs would cut their throats, and, by God, the Arabs sure enough *did* cut their throats! If you're ever in Houston, Texas, son, you be sure and give me a ring. Doctor Irving A. Goldstein. You'll find me in the 'phone book."

He clucked suavely, gripped my hand in a sticky farewell clasp, and was gone.

IV

When I saw Houston for the first time I was a great deal older in experience, if not in years. I was on my way to Galveston. I was with a geologist who had some business to transact in Houston before driving on. I decided to walk around and have a look at the town while I was waiting.

Houston has not distinguished itself from any other American city: a cluster of tall buildings rising up suddenly above the plain for no reason at all. I paused on a street corner a few blocks away from the business canyons, half-determined to go back to the automobile and wait. And then I glanced up and saw the Neon sign on a corner opposite: Dr. Goldstein—Painless Dentist.

It was as exciting as catching a glimpse of a familiar face in a foreign throng. The possibility of there being more than one painless dentist named Goldstein in Houston, Texas, did not occur to me for an instant. I hurried across the street and found the stairway entrance around the corner. Beside the door an electrically-lighted glass case gleamed with its rows of pink-and-white dentures. There was in it, too, a tray, labeled "Poison Distributors," heaped with yellowed canines and root-tufted molars, proud harvest, I felt sure, of Dr. Goldstein's many years in the profession. I turned and mounted the worn, tobacco-spattered stairs.

Down a shady hall with resounding wooden floors and red streaks of floor sweep along the base-boards, following the brown pointing fists painted on the plaster walls and lettered with Dr. Goldstein's name, I came to the glass-paneled door of his outer office. The office girl, plump and pretty, with a gold-rimmed smile that assured me that she was one of Dr. Goldstein's jobs herself, asked me if I had an appointment when I told her that I should like to see Dr. Goldstein for a few minutes. I told her, a bit impatiently, that I didn't have, but that he'd want to see me anyway.

As soon as he came walking out in his soiled surgeon's gown, I knew that I was meeting a stranger. It was Dr. Goldstein, all right: but Dr. Goldstein the painless dentist and not Dr. Goldstein the indomitable prophet.

He shook hands with me very casually and kept saying in a slow voice, "Well, well, well, what are *you* doing in town? Well, well, well. I see you still have a fine set of teeth on you there." He spoke as if my teeth were a piece of his work.

I sensed that he was ill at ease, and I was about to make some excuse about my just hurrying through Houston and thinking that I would stick my head in and say hello before going on. He gave me a furtive glance and circled my shoulders with his arm.

"Come on in the laboratory," he said. "I want to show you some equipment that's the very last word in dentistry."

He ushered me in and closed the door carefully behind us. There was a fat Mexican woman sitting in the dental chair with a rubber gag across her mouth.

"I didn't want to say much out there," he said, "because Rose Blatt, that's the office girl, is liable to run and tell, and I don't want to stir up anything again. But I didn't want you to get away without talking over old times." We were college chums together again. I glanced toward the Mexican woman. "Oh, she won't make any difference," he said quickly. "She don't *sabe* nothing except Mex anyway."

"Well, how are you getting along?" I said.

"Just fine. First-rate. Collections are slow, but I did better than $500 worth of cash business alone last month. I'm thinking about getting me a new Neon sign."

"That's a good one you have there now. It has a delicate pink color that reminds me of an artificial gum."

"Oh, I know, but I've been thinking about putting up a better one. A bigger one. I'm going to get one that spells out 'We Give Gas' on it."

"Everything came out all right, then?"

"Sure. All's well that ends well. Oh, I had to go easy there for a while. It took time. Time and patience. I just let that other business drop. They were all pretty suspicious for a while, but when they saw that I wasn't going to crow about it, they were ready to agree that I was right in the first place. Then the Depression put a crimp in that Zionist business anyway."

I felt vaguely uneasy with the calm, efficient man there in the soiled white smock, so composed and well-satisfied. Was this what a prophet came home to?

He selected a tiny bit and fitted it into his electric drill. The drill began whirring and he bent over the fat Mexican woman. Then he glanced up at me with a flicker of the old light in his eyes and he grinned proudly.

"But I sure told 'em that the Arabs would cut their throats," he said, his voice quivering with delight, "and, by God, the Arabs *did* cut their throats! Eh, didn't they? I sure told them, plenty of time before it happened, didn't I, son!"

13

WHITE MEAT

ALL SUMMER long they sat rocking. They rocked and they talked and they never took any decisive action about their rights in the white meat at Mrs. Nettleton's board. Nearly all of them had come to spend the entire season. Every time there was a vacancy they would see Mrs. Nettleton's small advertisement reappear in the country board columns of the Sunday *Times:*

> PINE CREST MANSION, LAKE TRIAD, N. Y.—Mountain scenery, broad piazza, Southern cooking. $18 wk & up. Christians only. No invalids accepted.

They sat rocking and their rockers thrummed a hollow undertone on the broad, screened-in piazza of Pine Crest Mansion. Over on the other side of the lake, where the pine crest really was, carded clouds browsed on the ridge like sleepy fowls. Long black lines of traffic fried continuously over the concrete at the foot of the barren slope, and sometimes an outboard motor moved a dab of frosting across the cool bright surface of the lake. This they did not see or hear. They leaned toward one another over the arms of their rocking chairs, very discreetly, talking in subdued voices about the white meat.

Each of them had lived wisely enough to have acquired a competence and all of them had lived long enough to have learned the aptness of platitudes. Even if it had occurred to them that they were carrying out a hackneyed theme with their unrest about the white meat, it would have made no difference. Daily the subject grew more vital, not more banal, and daily their interest in it was excited and renewed.

Usually, along in the afternoon, four of them would get up a table of contract, but they had a hard time keeping their minds on their cards, because the white meat was always on their minds. Who dealt? They were moved by indignation about the white meat, although they concealed their true feelings before Mrs. Nettleton. Their indignation was strong and furtive when they were alone together on the broad, shady piazza. Who dealt? But they did not know what they could do about it. They were not sure what their rights in the white meat actually were. Who took that last trick? Even testy old Judge Leftwich, the boldest of them, a retired surrogate occupying one of the $30-a-week-bedrooms, never did anything more than to exclaim hoarsely that by Jupiter they were paying for the white meat and they ought to be getting the white meat, and to champ and glare when the others on the broad piazza shushed him and glanced nervously over their shoulders to see whether Mrs. Nettleton was within earshot.

She was not a woman who could be approached on such a subject, because she had given them to understand that she was a Southern lady who had been reduced. The loss of her husband had brought her to taking in Summer boarders. Before her paying guests Mrs. Nettleton was always very genteel and gracious, but she did not permit them any illusions about her charity, taking them in like that and accepting their paltry $18-a-week-and-up. They were all Northerners, so they could appreciate her attitude. Mrs. Nettleton made her large mouth rather small when she talked and she often prefaced her remarks with a soft little *oo-wup-uh!* and, while she did not use a lorgnette, she had a way of holding her eyebrows high and her neck arched that always made her guests feel as if she were looking at them through a lorgnette. So they would have no more complained to Mrs. Nettleton about the white meat than they would have suggested to her that she shave off her sparse, colorless whiskers. Mrs. Nettleton was not a woman with whom one could be impulsive. But for all that there was dissatisfaction among the boarders, even though it always remained a velleity.

And they rocked and they talked and there was only one topic of moment. The only thing that broke the monotony of the long bright Summer days was the arrival of the mail, or, at infrequent intervals, the arrival of a new guest from the city, a spinster school-teacher or a mother-in-law shipped off for vacation. The initiation was usually accomplished in a day or two of guarded conversation, and the routine would be scarcely ruffled.

Soon after lunch Oscar, the house boy, would climb into the station wagon and coast off down the crunching drive. Thirty minutes later the train whistle would echo mournfully through the valley and Oscar would come jouncing back up the hill in a spray of gravel, bearing the mail. Mrs. Nettleton subscribed privately for the New York *Times* and the Atlanta *Constitution*, and she would retire to her bedroom with her newspapers. When tea-time came she would come back out on the broad piazza, twiddling her spectacles and rustling her crumpled newspapers, ready with her comment on current events. This digest of the day's news was an office that Mrs. Nettleton performed with a full sense of her responsibility and she made her opinions unequivocal and absolute.

"Oo-wup-uh!" Mrs. Nettleton would say, putting down her spectacles and the untidy roll of newspapers and assuming her pouring position by the tea table. "Ah see by the *Constitution* whuh they attended to anothuh negrah in Miss'ippi last Sad'dy. Lemon, Mis' Chambahs? Well, it wouldn' bothah me none if they wiped them all out, the black scounduls. Is it *you* that don' take sugah, Judge Leftwich?"

Mrs. Nettleton was obsessed with a great bitterness toward the entire black race, and she was fond of introducing racial news at these informal little afternoon discussions. When the cool breezes were blowing at Pine Crest Mansion the dog days were wearing on in the Southland, and Mrs. Nettleton's newspaper kept her supplied with brief reports of the current nigger hunts. These were items about which Mrs. Nettleton could be most voluble.

She often reported, with a trilling little laugh, a conversation she had once had in New York City. "And he says to me, 'How do you stand on the negrah question, Mis' Nettleton?' and Ah laughs and says to him, 'Mah deah suh, Ah didn' know they *was* a negrah question until Ah come Nawth and seen negrah bucks ridin' settin' down in the subway when white ladies was standin' up!' "

Southerners did not come to Pine Crest Mansion. Her guests were New Yorkers, the firmest respecters of the Southern tradition. Occasionally, of course, there arrived one of those intrepid Yankees who would be pleased to flout Southern womanhood by taking issue with Mrs. Nettleton. But these regrettable encounters were rare and Mrs. Nettleton always acted with great calm and dispatch. Then the other boarders would anticipate seeing her small advertisement reappear in the Sunday *Times* and the amicable atmosphere of Pine Crest Mansion would be restored.

The Summer boarders were not puzzled by Mrs. Nettleton's unusual virulence against Negroes. They had their own explanation for it. It was whispered among them that her husband had been murdered by a Negro. The boarders' rumors described Mrs. Nettleton's husband as having been removed in a variety of ways, but it was always accomplished by a Negro. They sympathized with her even when, among themselves, they did not feel that they could go all the way with her in her attitude toward colored folks. But when one has suffered, they agreed, it makes a difference.

II

Mrs. Nettleton talked about her husband at great length, but she confirmed none of these rumors about the manner of his death. All of the boarders, however, were convinced that he had met it at the hands of a Negro, even though Mrs. Nettleton had never told them so. The reverent tone in which she spoke of him, at least, made him a man definitely and remotely dead.

"Why!" she told some favored female guests one day, rolling her eyes and talking back of her hand, "when Mr. Nettleton was alive Ah nevah so much as touched a slop-jah!"

She liked to recount the manly virtues that had shone in Mr. Nettleton as they can shine only in a Southern gentleman. True, he had been a gambling man and he had gambled all around, but Mr. Nettleton had been a sportsman, never a sport. Mrs. Nettleton made that distinction quite clear to her boarders. He had been a man of wealth, an owner of race horses. She often related how Mr. Nettleton had won Pine Crest Mansion on the turn of a single card one night at Saratoga. Easy come, easy go. After the gambling debts were paid in the best Southern tradition, and after the stables were sold, all that Mrs. Nettleton had left to her were her diamonds and Pine Crest Mansion and two small daughters.

Nowadays the daughters attended Barnard, finishing their educations. They always arrived at Pine Crest in June, not long after the first paying guests. They were two pretty brunettes, silent and well-behaved. They seldom smiled and they spoke only when spoken to. If their Summer isolation from other young people made them unhappy, they never complained to the boarders. They appeared only at luncheon and dinner, and they maintained a bland aloofness that rather awed the elderly cliéntèle at Pine Crest. In the Winter the three of them, the mother and her daughters, all lived together in a female residential club in West One Hundred and Twenty-Second Street. Then in May Mrs. Nettleton, harbinger of Southern cooking and Summer ease, would set forth to reopen Pine Crest Mansion for another season.

Mrs. Nettleton usually talked on one or another of four topics when she presided at the dinner table. She liked to talk about her lamented husband, that handsome, dashing Southern gentleman from Atlanta. She liked to describe the opulence from which she and her two daughters had fallen when Mr. Nettleton had passed away. She enjoyed talking about the black race, talking very bitterly about the filthy, lustful brutes, expressing her hatred and scorn in the strongest words of abuse a Southern lady is permitted. But most of all Mrs. Nettleton liked to brag on her two daughters.

Agnes sat at Mrs. Nettleton's right and Irene sat at Mrs. Nettleton's left and all the paying guests sat ranged around the table listening to Mrs. Nettleton venerate Mr. Nettleton and regret her reduction and loathe negrahs and praise her two lovely daughters to their faces. Of all the girls at Barnard, Agnes and Irene were the most popular. Of all the girls at Barnard, Agnes and Irene made the highest grades, unless the professor happened to be partial. Agnes and Irene danced wonderfully. Agnes and Irene sang beautifully. Agnes and Irene had been remarkable babies and extraordinary small girls. Agnes and Irene wrote better themes than any of this stuff that gets published. Agnes and Irene were clever. Sometimes they got off the cutest things. In New York the suitors waited on Agnes and Irene single file.

Agnes and Irene sat looking down modestly at their untouched plates, two plump, pretty girls, sloe-eyed and shy. They never interrupted while their mother was talking, and they neither affirmed nor denied what she said about them. They sat toying delicately with their food. They ate very little at the table.

"Oo-wup-uh! Ah simply cain't get mah guls to eat hahty!" Mrs. Nettleton would say, beaming on Agnes and Irene and then toward her guests assembled. "Sometimes Ah think they'll just swivel up and blow away, not eatin' any mo' than they do. Ah always like to see a puhson eat hahty, but mah guls nevah did. Ah guess Ah haven't got much right to complain mah ownse'f, though!"

Then the paying guests would all exchange secret, meaningful glances. Mrs. Nettleton wasn't fooling them at all. They knew that she and her daughters filled up in the kitchen before the waitress sounded the chimes to call *them* in from the broad piazza. Filled up on the choicest white meat, too. So when the fried chicken, crisp and tawny, cut up and cooked Southern style under Mrs. Nettleton's supervision, was passed around there were never more than three or four teasing pieces of white meat on the platter. There were drumsticks and necks and backs and even thighs aplenty, but the breasts were missing,—devoured, the boarders were convinced, by Mrs. Nettleton and her two daughters before the meal.

"Oo-wup-uh!" Mrs. Nettleton would say. "It seems lak mah daughtahs don' eat enough to keep a buhd alive!" And Mrs. Nettleton's two pretty daughters, one on her right hand and one on her left hand, stuffed with white meat before the paying guests ever had a chance at it, would flutter their long, dark eyelashes and dabble languidly at the food on their plates.

That was what disturbed the boarders so much. They felt that Mrs. Nettleton wasn't doing right, having deprived them of the white meat, to remind them of their deprivation. But Agnes and Irene, so placid and beautiful, and with their patrician aloofness, seemed beyond reproach and the boarders found it difficult to imagine them in the kitchen gobbling up the white meat. And yet they knew it must be so.

Then one night at dinner Agnes, the youngest and prettiest daughter, astounded them all, her mother included. Mrs. Nettleton had been describing a particularly luscious lynching that she said she had once had the pleasure of attending in Georgia. She was a madcap young girl at the time. A most irregular thing for a Southern girl to do, but just for the lark, they understood. Youth, just youth! It was one of Mrs. Nettleton's favorite anecdotes and it was too familiar to everyone there to be harrowing to anyone. She had scarcely got going good on the details of the torture when Agnes looked up and interrupted sharply. "Mother," she said, "you ought to be ashamed, telling that disgraceful story at the table!"

Mrs. Nettleton rared back in her chair with an equine gesture and she gasped, "Ashamed? Ashamed! Well, Ah nevah!"

"Yes, ashamed!" said Agnes. "You don't seem to realize that a real *lady* would never gloat over such horrible things. The upper classes do not hate the Negro. It's only the whites who are in economic conflict with the Negro who—"

"Aggie! Hush yo' mouth! Stop talkin' to yo' mothah in that disrespectful mannuh!" Mrs. Nettleton exclaimed harshly.

Agnes stared straight into her mother's eyes for a moment and her lips were pressed together in the same way that Mrs. Nettleton's were pressed and her chin was tilted at the same angle that Mrs. Nettleton's chins were tilted. At last she looked down at her plate again, but her hands were trembling so violently that her fork rattled against her plate. Irene did not even glance up. The boarders ate in silence for a few minutes while Mrs. Nettleton glared at her youngest daughter, still as much in surprise as in anger. After a while Mrs. Nettleton changed her expression, simpered, and said with frigid sarcasm, "Ah reckon the next thing Ah know you'll up and tell folks that you'd just as leave *marry* a negrah!"

Agnes pushed back her chair suddenly and stood up. "If I loved him I certainly would," she said firmly. Then she tossed down her napkin and thudded flat-heeled out of the room.

The blood came back to Mrs. Nettleton's face darkly

and bright sweat stippled her forehead and she strained to breathe. Old Judge Leftwich jumped up quickly and, wetting his napkin with drinking water, began to make passes at Mrs. Nettleton's face. But she waved him back haughtily and groaned that she would be all right. She sat with one hand pressed against her bosom, drawing deep breaths for several minutes and then she looked toward her electrified guests.

"Some fool college professuh has put that notion into that child's head," Mrs. Nettleton panted apologetically. "Ah swan, it's just a question whethuh a body is doing right these days to try and give they childun a college education. So many infidels and bolsheviks and negrah-lovuhs and I don' know what all teaching in the colleges now'days. That's the kind of stuff childun gets in college now'days. That's whuh Aggie got that notion. Aggie nevah got no notion lak *that* at home!"

III

After dinner the boarders all filed out on the broad piazza, leaving Mrs. Nettleton alone in the dining-room. They hadn't quite got their bearings yet. They were puzzled and distressed. It was all so extremely unusual. As they rocked they could hear murmurs of a protracted battle filtering through the walls of the Nettleton suite overhead.

Presently old Judge Leftwich clicked his false teeth and chuckled low. He said, back of his hand, "That kid's a chip off of the old block, all right. The old lady's going to have a hard time quelling *that* kid, let me tell you."

"It's all so *very* unusual," breathed Miss Ernestine Watts, the school-teacher from Brooklyn.

"I feel so *sorry* for Mrs. Nettleton," Mrs. Traylor whispered. "I always say a person slaves and cares for a child, bringing them up, and then what thanks does a person get? I know what it is to suffer from a child's ingratitude myself."

The following day there was a persistent coolness between Mrs. Nettleton and Agnes. Irene seemed not to be taking sides, one way or the other. Agnes sat gazing sullenly down at her plate without even picking up her fork. Mrs. Nettleton avoided the controversial subject at meals, but she redoubled her laudatory comment on Irene and she did not mention Agnes at all.

This went on for a week. The boarders carefully pretended not to notice that anything had gone wrong. They kept up this pretense before Mrs. Nettleton and her two daughters. But as soon as they were alone together on the broad piazza they resumed their murmured discussion of the family rift. The tension was growing unbearable to them. Their excitement would take their minds off the indignity of the white meat for hours at a time.

One noon they came in to lunch and found that both of Mrs. Nettleton's daughters were absent from the table. Agnes and Irene had never come down for breakfast, so they had not been missed earlier in the day. Mrs. Nettleton's face was fixed in a grim smile and she explained nervously that the girls had gone away the night before for a short visit to their cousins in Syracuse.

It was obvious to the boarders that she was telling a falsehood.

IV

Day by day they saw Mrs. Nettleton's fleshy, complacent face go haggard with the little gullies of care and fear. She kept her face set in a languishing smile, but she fell into strange silences and whole meals would pass without her having uttered more than a dozen words. She no longer appeared at tea time.

One afternoon, not long after the mail had come up, the time of the siesta, Mrs. Nettleton came plunging forth on to the broad piazza, her yellowish-white hair disheveled, her eyes blurred red, hysterical sobs billowing her bosom. She bore a crumpled, tear-splotched letter, and she wailed out a report of its contents. It was from Agnes and Irene. The postmark showed that they were in East Orange, N. J. They had jobs selling Real Silk hosiery from house to house. They weren't ever going to live with their mother again. They were sick and tired of Summer boarders, fried chicken and Negro baiting. They were both of age and they were going to be their own bosses from now on.

Mrs. Nettleton's paying guests, clucking and murmuring, rallied with their sympathy. Mrs. Chambers chattered endlessly about how her niece, Helen, her sister Ella's child, had done the very same thing. Ran off with a vaudeville team and then wrote exactly the same sort of letter home to her mother. And Mrs. Traylor kept asking everyone whether her son, Clarence, had not been just as heartless, marrying a young snip and sending his mother off to spend the Summer alone, the first time they had been separated in thirty-five years.

Meanwhile Mrs. Nettleton's hysteria had risen to a point terrifying to behold. The others stood around, aimlessly trying to comfort her. But every time one of them would lay hands on her, her sobs would become shrieks and she would fling herself about the porch like a mad woman.

"God knows Ah did evuhthing Ah could foh mah guls! God knows Ah tried to give mah guls evuh advantage! God knows Ah did!" And her insane cries echoed against the mountain and came trailing back across the lake. All of a sudden she yelled, "It's the low-down Nettleton in them! None of mah folks would evuh have done a trashy thing lak this! That low-down Nettleton tribe *was paht niggah!* Evahbody knowed that was why he left the place he was from. But Ah nevah knowed it! Ah nevah knowed it till Ah'd had two babies by they daddy. Befo' God, Ah left him the day Ah found it out. As God is mah witness Ah left they daddy when Ah found out what he was!"

Her gaping guests no longer tried to subdue her. They stood back as frightened and embarrassed by her revelation as they would have been if she had stripped off her clothing. They stood helpless while her hysteria ran its course. She began wailing again, "Ah tried to do foh mah guls! God knows Ah tried!" Soon she collapsed on a porch swing, moaning in sing-song, "Mah guls! Mah po' li'l guls!"

It was a touching thing to see a woman once so proud now so humble. The boarders finally got her off to her chamber upstairs and they deposited her on her bed, a sodden, miserable old woman. She was all alone in the world and they felt a great wave of pity for her.

That evening at dinner there was fried chicken again, the first that had been served since Agnes and Irene ran away. There was plenty of white meat for everyone. They ate their fill of white meat.

Somewhat sluggish from overeating, they moved back out onto the broad piazza. They sat rocking and they were silent for a while. A butter-colored moon bobbled against the pine crest across the lake. Someone belched softly in the dark. Occasionally a throat was cleared with abrupt garrumps.

Once or twice they made uneasy attempts to start a conversation. Mrs. Traylor stopped rocking for a moment and leaned over an arm of her chair and said, "Well, I always say you can't make a silk purse out of a sow's ear!" But no one had any interest in recalling the frightful things that had happened that afternoon. They searched for something else to talk about, but they were unable to find a subject of common interest. Presently the only sound was that of the rocking chairs muttering on in the darkness.

The hovering, vague discontent gradually settled over them. None of them knew the reason for their discontent. They had the white meat now. But there was something lacking. Something that they had had before was gone. One by one the rocking-chairs went quiet. One by one the boarders stood up, mumbled, and went off to bed. There was really nothing left to talk about.

14

INQUIRE WITHIN

Yes, it's a right pretty little place, all right. It'd be just the thing for a young married couple. I like it fine, but I feel like a young married couple would be more happier in it, where an old woman like me feels out of place in it.

I'm getting on in my sixties now, you see. No, I know I don't look it, but I am.

It's up-to-date from cellar to attic. Hardwood floors, electric lights, city water piped in, and all. And let me take you and show you the bathroom. It's the prettiest little bathroom you ever did see. All in lavender tile. You see them water lilies, that little fringe around the top of the tub. They're hand-painted.

Oh, it's a real bargain at what I'm asking for it—thirty-five dollars a month. Although that does seem quite a bit, too. Now don't it? But you won't find nothing in town any nicer, and I doubt if there's anything as nice. Not a house this size, anyhow.

You-all like flowers in the yard, don't you? I wouldn't want anybody in here that wouldn't take good care of the flowers.

I guess I ought to have a stick took to me for wanting to tear up and leave it. My, my! A shame, that's what it is. But I've already got my mind made up about it.

The children all act like they think I'm ungrateful. I don't aim to be, but I guess maybe I am ungrateful. In fact, Nettie—that's Mrs. Carlock, she's my oldest married daughter, married to Mr. C. B. Carlock, president of the Fidelity National Bank. Mr. Carlock is my son-in-law. My daughter, Nettie, she just come right out here the other day and said, "Mamma, you're just plain old ungrateful, that's all you are. You don't even appreciate your children's thoughtfulness."

Well, Nettie was wrong about that, because I do love my children, and I wouldn't hurt their feelings for a pretty. But Nettie always was an outspoken child. Been that way ever since she was a little thing.

I guess I actually don't show my gratitude enough, though. I'm just set in my ways, I reckon. But I'm getting on toward seventy years of age, now, my three-score-and-ten, and you can't teach an old dog new tricks. You've heard that old saying, haven't you? And you can't, neither.

Goodness knows, though, I didn't want to seem hard-headed and stubborn about it. I just couldn't help myself from feeling the way I did.

Here I am, though, rattling on like an old fool, and you-all haven't got any idea under the sun what I'm talking about, have you? I guess I ought to start right in with the beginning, and tell you the whole business, now that I've got started.

When Mr. Harmon was alive,—that was my husband, Mr. G. W. Harmon. Mr. Harmon passed away of complications three years ago last January. We had a hospital room, and a trained nurse, and two doctors with him, but complications set in, and we lost him.

Well, Mr. Harmon used to always say to me when he was alive, "Ellen," (My first name is Ellen. Yes, I always thought Ellen was a right pretty name.) "Ellen," Mr. Harmon would say to me, "for the land's sake, when you start to tell a thing begin with the beginning, and tell it right straight on through so as a body can make head or tail of what you're trying to say."

But I always used to say to Mr. Harmon, "Well, Papa," I would say, "the longest way around is the shortest way home."

I guess you've heard that old saying, haven't you? "The longest way around is the shortest way home?" It works out pretty often that way, too, when you stop to think about it.

But I guess I did used to aggravate Mr. Harmon, the helter-skelter way I always had of telling anything. He used to just get mad and slam down his paper. That rocker right over there is the chair he used to set in, reading his paper. We had a base-burner instead of the gas-logs then, and Mr. Harmon would set by the stove in his stocking-feet, reading. I never could get him to keep his shoes on in the house.

I remember just like it was yesterday, him saying, "Ellen," he says, "you're just like some old jay bird," he says. "You just chatter on without nobody having any idea of what you're talking about. And sometimes I don't think you know your own self," he says.

Mr. Harmon could be very plain-spoken when he was a mind to. Nettie, my oldest daughter, took after him. When Nettie takes it into her head to say a thing, why she just comes right on out with it, and nobody's going to stop her. She was always like her papa in that.

But he's passed on to his last reward, dear man. And I want to tell you, last August, when I come back from a visit to my married daughter's that lives in Fort Madison, Iowa, I thought for a minute there I was ready to join him. I never got such a shock in all my life before.

But I certainly am putting the cart before the horse, as the saying goes. Let me start right in from the first. I can tell a pretty straight story when I set my head to. You see if I don't.

Well, to start where I should of at first, after Mr. Harmon passed away my children all got after me to go off somewheres and take a visit. They just kept after me, and kept after me, and for two years there that was all I heard.

"Mamma, you need a rest! Mamma, you need a rest! Why don't you go out and visit the Collinses, out in Pasadena, California? The Collinses used to be former next-door neighbors of ours. Lived right here next door to us for twenty-five years. But Mr. Collins got the moving bug, and sold out and moved to Pasadena, California. Never a Christmas goes by but what Mrs. Collins don't send me a picture postcard showing some scene in sunny California.

And Melvin, that's my married son here in town, says, "Mamma, why don't you let us pick you out a nice, quiet hotel somewheres in Florida, and you could go down there and spend a nice, mild Winter in Florida."

"Mamma, why don't you go here?" And, "Mamma, why don't you go there?"

They just kept ding-donging after me, trying to get me to go off on a vacation. But I just says to them, "No, thank you! I'd just as leave die of old age right here in my own home, with all my belongings around me, as to go off somewheres and get swallowed up in an earthquake, or get blowed off by a hurricane."

"No, thank you!" I says, "I'll just stay right here in my own home, where Papa and me spent ever' winter for the last forty-seven years, and got along all right."

Mr. Harmon passed away only two years and eight months before we was to have celebrated our golden wedding. September 12, last year, that would of been. We had already talked about having our picture took for the newspaper.

I want to tell you, though, my children always stick right with a thing when they get their heads set. That's the way I am, too. They take after their mother in that, all right.

They're scattered all over the country, but two of them is living right here in town. Nettie, she's my oldest daughter, is Mrs. C. B. Carlock, the banker's wife, and Melvin, that's my second son, owns a wholesale grocery company. You've seen that big electric sign on the right hand side of the railroad tracks as you come into town from the north—Harmon's Wholesale Grocery Company? Well, that's my son's, Melvin's. He owns that big building, and the wholesale grocery company, too. That big sign advertises his business.

Then I've got a married daughter in Fort Madison,

Iowa, and two married sons in Chicago, and Henry, my oldest boy, he's an old, bald-headed bachelor, and he lives in Detroit, Michigan.

One of the things that seemed to worry the children most was that they was afraid that I would go around the house brooding over Mr. Harmon's death. I guess they was scared that I was going to get moony and lose my mind, or something like that. But I had my house and garden to take care of. A sensible woman's always got plenty to do without going around pulling a long face.

So I just says to Nettie and Melvin, both of them, I says, "Now looky here, you kids. Looky here: I kept my right mind living with your papa for forty-seven years, didn't I? And I'm not apt to lose it living without him, am I?"

But they kept on about my house. It was the house that Mr. Harmon had helped build for us to live in. He built it the year of 1880, and we was married September 12, of that year. I was sixteen years old when I married Mr. Harmon. Now, if you'll use your arithmetic, maybe you can figure out how old I am now.

Well, it was a big fine house. All the children was raised in it. Of course it was big. It had to be. But it was a good one. It had walnut floor sills. And, of course, we had always kept it in good repair.

But the children kept making out like it was too much for me to take care of, after Mr. Harmon passed away. They wouldn't any more than set foot in the house before I could begin to see them casting their eyes around to make some complaint about me living on in it.

"Mamma," they said, "it's too much for you to take care of this big house, climb these stairs and all. Supposing you was to get sick all of a sudden, living here all alone. Or fell down the stairs, or on the back-porch steps, or something like that, and broke your limb?"

I told them that I'd been taking care of that house before any of them ever seen the light of day, and that it was funny anybody should get anxious about me over-working myself this late in the day. I must say, though, that Mr. Harmon was always after me to get a hired girl. But I never could put up with an outsider messing around among my things. Do you blame me? I've got certain places of keeping things. I know right where to go and find them, and I never did want to pitch in and try to teach some hired girl to think like I do.

But there wasn't any putting Melvin and Nettie off. Not them children of mine. Finally, here last Spring it's a year ago, I got a letter from Margaret, that's my other married daughter, Mrs. Ed Means of Fort Madison, Iowa. My son-in-law is in the grain business there, and is doing right well. Margaret invited me in her letter to come up there and spend the Summer with them.

Well, I thought, now that's sweet of Margaret, but I didn't have no idea of going. I told Nettie at the time: an old mother-in-law going around visiting among her married sons and daughters! You couldn't of hired me to then. Like that time Mrs. Means, that's Margaret's mother-in-law, come there and made such a big row about naming the baby. I used to say to myself, "What's all these jokes about mother-in-laws for, it there's not some truth in them?" Did you ever stop to think about that? Well, I have, and ever since the first of them got married, twenty-five years ago this coming June (Nettie was the first one to go), I never had gone to spend a night in the homes of any of my children, unless some of them, or one of my grandchildren was bad sick. I always said to myself, "No, sir. I've got a house of my own to stay in and take care of, and that's job enough for anybody. So I'll just tend to my own business."

So I was going to write to Margaret, and thank her very kindly for the invitation, like I always have any of my children when they asked me. But the idea of going up there to spend the Summer never come into my head. Somehow, though, Nettie and Melvin, my two children living here in town, got hold of it that Margaret had invited me up to Fort Madison, Iowa. Just as soon as they got wind of it, they was after me to get ready and go.

I held out for quite a while. "What do I want to go traipsing off to Iowa for?" I asked them. "Here I've got my garden set out, and my flower beds in and all. And who'll keep the lawn watered? And what about the vegetables out there?" Why, I had tomato vines out there with green tomatoes on them as big as your fist, that early in the year. The finest stand of tomatoes I had since 1910.

That was one time, though, that Nettie and Melvin

couldn't be put off. They just wouldn't take no for an answer.

I kept delaying as long as I could. Finally, what it amounted to, they just marched right in one day and started packing my things for me. Was going to get me on the train whether or no. Melvin went out and bought me a solid cowhide leather suitcase. Which I'll bet it cost him ever' cent of twenty-five dollars. And Nettie went down to Madansky Brothers and bought me a black satin dress for $39.75. Oh, those kids of mine never was ones to skimp.

Well, when I saw how things stood, I give in. Because, of course, I couldn't let those children do my packing for me. How would they of known what I wanted to put in? I hadn't had a chance to do any sewing, or anything, which naturally I would of done if I had been figuring on taking a trip that year. But I never was any hand to let anybody else monkey with my personal belongings.

I got up and said, "No, thank you: if you're bound to move me right out of my own house, at least have the consideration to let me take the things with me I want to take." So they did.

II

Well, Melvin bought me my ticket, and him and Nettie took me to the depot the next morning. I caught the 7.25 A.M. passenger train out of here the morning of May 17, and we didn't pull into Kansas City until that evening at 7.15 P.M. My lunch give out before we got there. Riding on the train just wears me out anyway.

I had made up my mind to one thing, anyhow: that I absolutely was not going to do any traveling at night in that Pullman coach. Stripping off your clothes right there on a railroad train, and going to bed! I knew I wouldn't be able to get any sleep on one of the things, anyhow. And what if there was a wreck, or something, then where would a body be? There in a night gown! So I had decided about that, and nobody was going to argue me out of it.

There was a little lay-over there at Kansas City anyway, and while I could of gone on and got out of there at 7.55 that night, that would of throwed me into Fort Madison at two A.M. in the morning, and I certainly wasn't going to get anybody out of bed to meet me at that hour of night.

So Melvin had telegraphed on ahead to a third-cousin of ours, Elmer Blinn, of Bonner Springs, Kansas, to meet me there in the Union Station at Kansas City. Bonner Springs is just a few miles from Kansas City, across over in Kansas.

Elmer got mixed up about the train-time somehow, though, and he missed me downstairs where the train stopped. So there was a man with a red cap on picked up my handbag, and showed me the way up to the matron's office in the Union Station, and I set down there to wait for this third cousin of ours.

I got very well acquainted with the matron there, a Mrs. Winslow,—or Kinslow, I believe she said her name was. Now that I come to think about it I believe she did say Winslow. Well, we got to talking; she was an elderly lady, and do you know that we hadn't been talking there five minutes before we found out that we was both members of the Presbyterian Church, and that she had a married daughter living in Tiffin, Ohio, which is just 18 miles away from where Mr. Harmon was born and lived till he was quite a good-sized boy. The world certainly is a small place. You find that out when you begin traveling.

Well, finally this third-cousin, Elmer Blinn, come along. He had been looking all over the place for me, and he had about give up all hope of ever finding me, when this man with the red cap on brought him right up to where I was setting talking to Mrs. Kinslow.

Elmer drove me right on out to his home at Bonner Springs, and put me up for the night. Elmer's not real well-fixed, but he drives a new Ford coop. He has a wife and one little baby, and they certainly have a pretty little place there in Bonner Springs. It's not anything extra, but it's homey.

The next morning bright and early we got up and had breakfast, and Elmer drove me on back to the Kansas City Union Station to catch my train. The train left around eight o'clock, so we had to get up early to make it. Him and his wife was after me to stay with them awhile, but I was already sick and tired of this visiting business. If I had of had my way about it, I would of just caught the next train headed on back home, and been done with it. When I think about it now, I'm sorry I didn't. But what's done's done, and maybe it's all for the best. I try to think it is, anyhow.

Well, I caught the eight o'clock passenger train out of Kansas City, and that put me right on into Fort

Madison at 1.45 P.M. that afternoon without any more lay-overs. Margaret and Ed, that's my son-in-law, was at the train to meet me, and they drove me on out to their house in their Buick automobile.

I will say one thing: Margaret and Ed certainly do have a fine big home there in Fort Madison. They have two of the sweetest little children you ever did see. My grandchildren. Right there on that whatnot is a picture of them. Standing there in that plush frame. Those are my grandchildren. Now this one here is Edwin, Junior. He's the boy, and he's the oldest one. He'll be eight this coming September. And this here is little Jane Ellen. She was five the fourteenth day of this month.

She was named after me at first, just Ellen. Then Mrs. Means, that's my son-in-law's mother, the child's other grandma, come for a visit, and raised such a rumpus about being left out, they had to go on and name her Jane, too, after Mrs. Means. Jane was her name. It was all right, I guess, but I never did care much about double names for children, myself. I always think it's such a burden to a child. But an old lady like Mrs. Means gets cranky spells, and there wasn't anything to do but humor her.

But ain't those two the sweetest little things you ever set your eyes on? And smart! My, my! They called me Granny, and they would just put their little arms around my neck and hug me until I couldn't hardly draw my breath.

Oh, everything was mighty nice at Margaret and Ed's, and I enjoyed my visit with them and my little grandchildren. But I kept worrying about my garden, and whether the boy that my son had hired to keep the things watered and the lawn mowed was tending to his business, or whether he was laying down on his job, like they *will* do, unless there's somebody around to keep their eye on them.

Of course there was a lot of functions, and it just seemed like we was on the go all the time. We drove ever'where in their Buick car, down to Keokuk to see the big dam, and all around there. But I want to tell you, I never had the days to drag for me before like they did last Summer in Fort Madison, Iowa. I don't mean that just like it sounds. Margaret and Ed was both fine, and I was glad to be there with them and my little grandchildren. But I just had a feeling, I don't know how to describe it, that something was wrong at home, and that that was where my place was, and not off gallavanting around in Iowa.

I would have regular nightmares at night, dreaming about things happening to my house, the first dreams I remember of having since I was a young married woman. Nearly ever' night I would dream that burglars had broke in through the kitchen window, and was in carting ever'thing out. Or, if it wasn't that, the place had caught on fire, and there wasn't anyone to find it out and turn in the alarm.

But I didn't open my head about going back until I had been there two weeks. It seemed to me like two years. Then, on the second day of June, I says to Margaret, my daughter, I says to her that I was going to have to be starting back pretty soon.

Well, sir, I want to tell you that Margaret just went perfectly white. She turned as white as a leghorn pullet, and her voice kind of trembled, and she says, "Oh, Mamma, I thought you came to stay all Summer."

Then I thought to myself, "Now you've done it, you've gone and hurt her feelings." I wouldn't of done that for anything in the world, because Margaret and Ed was both being perfectly wonderful to me. They wouldn't let me turn my hand to do a thing, and they had a darky girl at my beck and call. But I don't know, I just never was used to being waited on. I've got to be up and doing things for myself. And I wanted to be back home working with my flowers so much I could taste it.

I got to worrying about all sorts of little things. Whether anyone would think to train the morning-glory vines up on the side-porch, or whether they would fall down and choke out the sweet peas. And whether I had left a pan under the leak in the north bedroom. And whether the younguns had been around there with air rifles, shooting my mocking birds and breaking windows. Nobody there to chase them off.

Still and all, I didn't want to hurt Margaret's feelings. I tried to explain to her why I had to be getting back, and that it wasn't that I hadn't had a grand visit. But she always made out like she didn't understand why I wanted to leave so soon.

She must of wrote to Melvin and Nettie about it ever' time I brought up the subject of leaving, because it would just be a few days, and then these letters would come in from both of them, telling me to go on and have my visit out, and not to worry about things at home, that ever'thing was being taken care of.

Well, sir, that would happen ever' week while I was there. I would hint to Margaret that I had ought to be getting back, and then several days later, in would come these letters from Nettie and Melvin, begging me to stay there. I *am* an old fool, or else I would of made out right away that something mighty peculiar was going on.

I wish I had those letters to show you. I saved all of them, but I guess I must of left them back at Margaret and Ed's when I was getting ready to come home. Anyhow, some of them was the craziest things you ever read. They just said the same things, over and over: stay there, stay there, ever'thing's all right here. Sometimes they pled with me, and sometimes they bossed me, and sometimes they wrote sweet letters, and sometimes they was right cross and cranky, especially Nettie.

III

Well, the days drug on. June passed, and the Fourth of July come. Ed brought home a whole box of fireworks, and the night of the Fourth he put on the prettiest display of fireworks for his little boy and girl I ever did see anywhere.

But I just couldn't enjoy myself any more. It wasn't that I was homesick. It was just that I wanted to get back to my home, because I felt like something was going wrong. It was a strange feeling. I can't explain it exactly.

How I ever pulled through that month of July, I

don't know. I was pretty near crazy. Melvin and Nettie had both made such a big to-do over me living all alone in my house, saying that I would mope around through it, remembering Papa with ever'thing I saw, and that I was liable to lose my mind. But staying away from it was worse than anything ever I'd had to go through with before. And Margaret and Ed treating me so nice only made it worse instead of better. I just couldn't come right out and say that I was going to pick up and leave. I couldn't hurt their feelings after they had been so nice.

When the first of August come, I just decided that I wasn't going to try and stand it any longer. I was helping the colored girl dry the dishes in the kitchen that morning. Margaret had got to where she would let me do that. And I made up my mind right then and there.

Without saying nothing to nobody, I went to my bedroom. They had give me a room downstairs instead of upstairs like I had always been used to. And I started packing my clothes. When I had got ever'thing in, I put on my black satin dress, and picked up my suitcase, and come on out. Margaret was in the parlor. She saw me come out.

"Why, Mamma," she said, looking scared, "what on earth are you getting ready to do."

I says to her, "Margaret," I said, "I can't hold out no longer. I'm catching the next train home. I love you and Ed and little Edwin Junior and little Jane Ellen better than anybody in the world, excepting my other children, and just as good as any of them, but I can't stay away from my own home any longer. I've been feeling for a long time that it needed my attention."

Well, I guess it was the tone of voice I used. Anyhow, Margaret saw that I had my mind made up, and she didn't try to argue with me any more. She only said, "Well, Mamma, if you must go, I suppose you must. But let me call Ed, and get him to see about the train and ticket and things."

Her voice was so weak and trembly, I thought she was going to cry. I actually was ashamed of myself to act like that, but I had to do it.

So Margaret called Ed at his office, and he got in his Buick car, and come right on out to the house. I was setting there in the front room with all my things on, ready to start. Ed and Margaret went off in another room, and I could hear them talking low, but I couldn't catch what they was saying.

After while they both came back in the parlor, and my son-in-law begin trying to persuade me to stay a little longer.

"Mother," he says, "just stay one week more, and we'll wire to Melvin and tell him you're coming. You don't want to start off on a long trip like this right here in August, the hottest time of year. Just wait one week more and maybe we'll have a little cool spell that'll make traveling more comfortable. Don't start off right here at the beginning of August," he says.

But when I get my mind sure enough set to do a thing, nothing in the world can shake me.

"No, children," I says, "I've had a wonderful visit with you, and I love you all, and I hate to take my leave of you, but it all come over me this morning that my visit was at an end. I'm leaving for home this very day."

When they saw how I was, they give in. They was very nice about it. Ed sent a telegram to Melvin that I was starting, and they took me to the train right after we had had a little bite to eat.

IV

I made the trip all right, excepting that it was awful hot, just like an oven, in that steel coach. I thought I would melt. And riding on the train always did make me a little sick.

Then I had that lay-over at Kansas City, but I got that Mrs. Kinslow, or Winslow, maybe her name was, the matron at the Union Station to direct me to a good, reasonable-priced hotel. I didn't stop to bother Elmer Blinn, our third-cousin in Bonner Springs, Kansas, on the return trip.

The next day, when the train started getting close to home, I was so glad that I forgot all about being tired and wore out.

When the train pulled in here at 5.50 P.M. that afternoon, Nettie and Melvin was there to meet me. Nettie was driving her big closed car. When I kissed them, I noticed that they both looked a little peculiar.

As soon as she said anything, Nettie was right sharp. "What's the matter, Mamma?" she says, "Can't you go any place and stay until your visit is out?"

"My visit was out, Nettie," I says.

"Well, I'll bet Margaret and Ed thought you didn't

enjoy yourself," she says, "the sudden way you picked up and left."

I lost my temper there for a minute, I'll admit. "Goodness' sakes alive, child," I says, "haven't I got a great big house of my own to live in, without living off of other people?" And then I shut right up and didn't say any more.

But Melvin was nice and pleasant about it, and he told Nettie to hush up, that that wasn't any way to welcome her Mamma home. He says, "Does it feel good to be back, Mamma?"

And when I told him it did, I was so glad to be back I was just sick with it, and I pretty near broke down and cried right there in the car.

When we got to the street I live on, Melvin reached over quick and put his hands over my eyes, and said, "Now, Mamma, prepare yourself for a big surprise."

And then I felt the car stop, and Melvin took his hands away, and said, "Well, Mother, here we are home again. Welcome back."

I looked out and says, "Ah, we're not. Quit your joking me, and hurry up and drive me on home, you kids."

And Melvin says, "Yes, here we are. You just don't know the old place. You come on such quick notice that we just barely had time to get the scantlings cleared away, and the lawn and flower beds is still in pretty bad shape. And there's still some paint work to be done," he said.

And then Nettie said, "But you *would* come ahead of time, Mamma. The men had to work like dogs yesterday, one of the hottest days so far, moving the furniture back and straightening it around."

Well, sir, I looked out and saw this little brick cottage with its green shutters and its brass knocker on the white front door, and no front porch at all, setting here just as pretty as you please. I still couldn't make out but what it was some kind of a joke. And then I looked a little closer, and I could see that Mr. Mizner's house was there on one side, and D. R. Jones' house on the other side, both just the same they had been when I left, the seventeenth day of May.

You know, while I was gone to Iowa, those children of mine had all chipped in and built this little brick house for me. They had tore down my old two-story house, and hauled off the lumber, and there wasn't a smidgeon of it left. Only this new little brick one in its place.

As soon as it dawned on me that my old house was gone, the bottom of my heart just seemed to drop out. I thought for a minute there I was going to faint. And then I happened to notice that Melvin and Nettie was watching me, expecting me to tell them how much I liked the new little house. But I couldn't trust myself to speak. I didn't say anything. I walked up the front walk with them, and how I ever kept from breaking down and crying is more than I can tell. I was trembling so much, Melvin almost had to hold me up.

My old home was gone! I kept thinking that it was one of those nightmares I always woke up from, and it was two or three days before I got out of the notion that it wasn't just a bad dream.

But listen to me talking like that! My, my! I ought to be whipped. I wouldn't have the children know I took it like that for anything in the world. I know they meant well, and I don't hold it against them. But I couldn't bring myself to thank them. And because I never have said anything, one way or the other, that's what give Nettie the idea I was ungrateful.

"Mamma," Nettie says to me, "I don't believe you appreciate this wonderful little house your children built for you."

"Why, what makes you think that, child?" I says.

"Well, you don't, now do you?" Nettie says.

And maybe I don't. I guess maybe I am ungrateful.

Oh, it's a wonderful little place, all right. I haven't got no criticism to make. But I had lived the biggest part of my life in the old house, and me coming into this new one to live was just like me going off somewhere and getting married again, at my age.

I know the children's intentions was good. I don't think anybody has got more wonderful children than I've got, and I love them all. They thought it would be better for me to have all my rooms on one floor, and to have a pretty bathroom with the smooth enamel tub, instead of the old copper one with the wooden rim. Faucets and city water piped in is a big improvement over the old hand pump I had at the kitchen sink, too, and I guess a cement basement has a lot of advantages over a cave in the back yard. But somehow I never do feel right in the place, and I don't believe I ever would.

So I've decided to rent it out. What I'm going to do now is visit around among my children. They're so nice to me—well, you can just imagine what kind of children they are, to take money out of their own pockets and build a whole new house for me!—they're so nice to me, I can't think of a better way to spend the rest of my days, than visiting around among them. I'll spend a few months with one, and then move on to the next one. That will show them that I'm not ungrateful.

And if I space my visits out far enough, the rent on this house will be enough to keep me in traveling expenses.

15

LOVE SONG

VIRGIL CLAY had never been loved by anybody. There wasn't any reason for it. It was even strange that no woman had ever loved him. He was as pathetic as a spaniel, and women are more often attracted by pathetic men than they are by strong men.

He remembered his mother as a harsh, gravid woman, strident-tongued and over-worked. She had too many babies to bury to pay much attention to any of her children who had been weaned. She had no affection for any of them, and, since Virgil was the oldest one living, she had called him a mangy brat and had cracked him hard every time he came within arm's reach.

Virgil's father had been a drunken carpenter who had satisfied a youthful ambition to have the most imposing house in town by building a two-story house with a turret and bay windows and a great deal of jig-saw gingerbread on the porches. Snickering townspeople had named the place "Clay's Pride." Fortunately the elder Clay had never had the money to furnish the place, and inside it was barren and lofty, with scabrous wallpaper and carpetless floors, the baseboards splashed with scrub water. Thin squalls and the loud rasp of the scolding mother's voice echoed through the half-empty rooms, and the air was heavy with the sour odor of many babies.

The rickets left Virgil a bandy-legged, dish-faced youngster with great, protruding ears and a thin mat of colorless hair. He was cowed and dull, but from some unknown source he had drawn a spark of ambition. Even as a small boy he plied any number of odd jobs. He washed dishes at the Broadway Café, and his pinched, skinned-rabbit face gleamed above the tubs, as red as the chilli skum on the dishwater. He shined shoes at the Luxor Barber Shop, and he learned to make a kind of tune, popping the rags and brushes. He peddled the Chicago *Blade and Ledger* on the street every week, and he had a smutty, flippant reply for farmers who put him off with a good-natured, "No, sonnie, I ain't got no use for a paper. I cain't read." He repeated his smart rejoinder each time without variation, just as he had learned it, until his old man heard him one day, and belted him a good one, and sent him blubbering home.

Virgil did everything he could to make money. He was not bright in his books, and he left school when he was promoted to the eighth grade. His father appropriated his earnings, and Virgil was too faithful, or too slow-witted, to save out any money before he came home. The old man had grown sodden with whiskey, and he did not work at carpentry often. D. C. Giles, the undertaker, sometimes gave him work digging graves. Virgil helped his father with that work.

One night the old man came home at supper time, reeling drunk. His wife locked him out of the house. He went back to the grocery store and bought a dime's worth of cheese and crackers. The next morning they found him dead in the street, the empty paper bag clutched in his hand.

After his father died Virgil dug the graves alone. His mother died the next winter, and D. C. Giles offered to let the youth work out the funeral expenses as a helper around his furniture and undertaking shop. The four smaller children were sent to an orphans' home, but Virgil stayed on in town, living alone in Clay's Pride, the big, hollow house, skimping to pay up the back taxes.

Virgil was conscientious and dependable. He was showing an unusual aptitude for the work, and Old Man Giles told him that if he would stick around he would teach him the embalming trade.

The wage the undertaker paid him was small, so Virgil got a job as janitor at the Farmers' and Merchants' Bank. When there were no burial preparations going on at the furniture store, he stayed around the bank to carry the mail to the post office, and to run other errands, and along in the afternoon he swept the floors and mopped the tile.

One of the wags at the Sanitary Barber Shop made a joke about it: "Say, have you heard about Virge Clay getting a job as teller in the Farmers' and Merchants' Bank?"

"Naw, sure enough, has he? How did he get to know anything about banking?"

"He don't have to know nothing about banking. He *tells* the customers to stand over a little so as he can sweep there." Everyone thought that was a good joke.

Virgil, nevertheless, was doing all he could to win the esteem of the community. He retrieved the house, Clay's Pride, from a sheriff's tax sale, and he went to work alone painting the place over. He kept himself neat and respectable-looking, and he had a savings account at the bank. He was handling nearly all the embalming work for Old Man Giles, the undertaker. He still had a beaten, hang-dog manner on the street, but when he assisted at funerals he assumed something very much like an officious air. Giles had already broached the subject of his buying into the business.

II

Virgil Clay was twenty-three years old when Minnie Flynn came to town. She came from her parents' farm in western Kansas, ostensibly to visit her brother and his wife, but really to help with the housework while Mrs. Flynn had her first baby. Clarence Flynn at that time couldn't afford to hire a woman for the confinement, so he sent for his younger sister. She was eighteen, and eager to get away from the drudgery and monotony of the farm.

One afternoon Virgil Clay was coming out of the Farmers' and Merchants' Bank, after finishing his sweeping job. He was always careful to keep a pair of overalls in the closet with his brooms and floorsweep; he wore them while he was sweeping, and then took them off as soon as he got through. He looked very neat when he came out of the bank that afternoon.

Clarence Flynn came walking up from the depot

with his sister Minnie, who had come in on the 4.45 train. They were passing the bank just as Virgil Clay came out.

Clarence spoke to him, and Virgil said, "Howdy, Clarence," and then, with the frank curiosity of the small town, but with a boldness so unusual in him as to be astounding, even to himself, he said, "Having visitors at your house, Clarence?"

Minnie Flynn, at eighteen, was a dumpy, thick-ankled farm girl, with gopher cheeks, but fresh, and even in her ill-fitting store dress, not at all unattractive.

"Sure thing, Virge," Clarence said. "Minnie, let me make you acquainted with Virgil Clay. She's my sister," he added to Virgil.

Virgil's rufous moon face went a deeper red, but he put out his hand and waggled the girl's arm. "I sure am glad to make your acquaintance," he squeaked in confusion.

Later it came to him suddenly that that was the first time in his life he had even been introduced to a girl.

Clarence and Minnie walked on.

"Who was that?" she asked as soon as they had got out of hearing distance.

"That was Old Lady Clay's son, Virgil."

"I mean, what does he do for a living?"

"What does he do for a living? Why, why—" Clarence remembered the waggish barber's pun, which had delighted him when he had first heard it. He said quickly, "Why, Virge is a teller in the Farmers' and Merchants' Bank." He turned his face back and rattled laughter in his throat.

"What's so funny? What're you laughing at?" Minnie was flustered.

"Oh, was I laughing?" he asked, making his face very straight. And then, slowly, "What did you get so intrusted in little Virgil Clay all of a sudden for?"

Minnie's rough face turned brick-color. "Why, I'm not intrusted in him. I was only just asking. You interduced him to me yourse'f."

After that Virgil Clay met Minnie Flynn on the street two or three times. He always tipped his hat, but his tongue would get thick, and his greetings would be incoherent. Minnie always smiled pleasantly, even encouragingly, at him, and spoke and went on by.

Minnie was disappointed about the kind of time she was having on her visit to town. She was kept too busy drudging at her brother's house to get to come down town more often than she had while she was on the farm. She had met scarcely anyone, and she had made no friends. Virgil was the only young man she had been introduced to. She thought Mrs. Flynn a queer fool, and she had no feminine confidantes. She had been happy over the prospect of living in town, with parties and dances and people to talk to, but now she found that she had to work so hard she seldom had a moment to set her foot out of the house.

III

Four months passed before Virgil Clay finally dared to write Minnie Flynn a letter, asking her to go to church with him the following Sunday night. Minnie was overjoyed. She immediately wrote a note back to Virgil, saying that she would be glad to go to church with him.

The Flynns' baby had been delivered six weeks before, and Mrs. Flynn was able to be up and about doing her housework again. Already Clarence was making plans to send Minnie back to her farm home in Kansas. She hated the dreary prospect, and she was doing everything she could to delay it. Much as she detested washing diapers, her only excuse now for staying, she had suggested to her brother that she stay on and work there. She hated the diapers bitterly. They gave her such a feeling of degradation that she would weep over the washboard. But she was desperate.

When Clarence heard that his sister had a date with Virgil Clay, he chanted, "A teller in the bank is coming here to spark Minnie! A teller in the bank, he come sparkin' Minnie." He kept repeating it. He roared with laughter.

Mrs. Flynn, the silent, secretive woman, was too engrossed in her new baby to pay any attention to the proceedings. She was a little resentful about Minnie's continued presence in her house, as much as a woman of her mild disposition could be.

"What's so funny about a teller in the bank?" Minnie would ask huffily. She knew that her brother was trying to ridicule Virgil Clay.

But Clarence whooped with derisive laughter, and he wouldn't explain. He was very vain about his sense of humor, and he was pleased with what he considered one of the best practical jokes he had ever pulled.

Virgil began taking Minnie to church regularly, and

two or three times he hired a rig at the livery stable, and they went buggy riding.

The townspeople, many of whom knew about the joke, tittered over the strange courtship, but none of them could see that Virgil was any worse catch than Minnie.

Clarence sometimes thought of telling Minnie that Virge's family had been good-for-nothing poor white trash, and that she ought not to get serious with him. But he liked Virgil very well. He could be patronizing toward the little man, and it was gratifying to his belief in democracy to have one of humble origin around. And Flynn was growing somewhat uneasy about Minnie, too, because every time anything was said about her going back to their parents' Kansas farm, she would weep and make a big scene and end up by getting very vicious. She was a terror when she got started, and not even Clarence's hoarse bellow could silence her. So he began to see a way out.

Virgil, very likely, never would have proposed to Minnie. It was not that he didn't want to. It was that he would never have had the courage. She was the only girl he had ever sat close to.

He always sat, very stiff and speechless, while she did most of the talking. He would have liked telling her about his embalming work, of which he was very proud and which he could have discussed by the hour, but he was too much intimidated by having a woman near him. He thought of many things to say to her, he lay awake nights thinking of things to say to her, but when he felt her near him, his throat tightened and his glowing face sprouted sweat and unintelligible noises lolled on his tongue.

If he hadn't been her only hope, Minnie would have thought him an awful fool.

One night they went buggy riding. The moon was a glaucous golden plum, low-hanging. Minnie began telling Virgil about how she hated living on the prairie farm. The wind, blowing all day long, would finally drive her crazy, she said. Going to bed after dark and getting up at dawn. The monotonous clank of the windmill pump. Scrubbing the hired men's filthy overalls. The endless preparation of heavy, greasy meals in a torrid lean-to kitchen. Living from Saturday until Saturday without seeing a strange face.

Finally she said, "I'm going to have to go back to Kansas next Monday."

Virgil was startled. His dry, constricted throat loosened, and he croaked, "Aw, Minnie, no, you're not!"

"Yes, I've got to," Minnie whispered in a frantic voice. "Clarence don't want to keep me no longer, and Papa keeps writing that he needs me there to he'p with the work. And, oh, Virgil, I'd rather take a killing than go back now."

She began sobbing heavily.

That was Virgil's cue, and he thought of proposing, but he could not make his lips form the words. He could only stammer, "Shucks, Minnie, I sure wisht you didn't have to go."

He touched her cautiously on her clasped, writhing hands. Minnie stopped weeping at that, and said, "There's one way I *could* stay, Virgil."

"How would that be?" Virgil said eagerly.

"As your wife," Minnie said, simply and directly. Then she began weeping more violently than before.

Virgil's heart was a plunger in his throat. He strained at speech. "Why, why, Minnie, you wouldn't want *me* for a man. I might do all right just to keep company with, but—well, you'd want somebody with enough money to keep you right."

"Well, Virgil, you've got your place at the bank."

"Yes, sure, I've got that. And I pick up other money, too. But do you think you would be satisfied to live on what I make? It's not—"

Minnie's tears stopped flowing, and she began laughing loudly, interrupting Virgil. A banker's wife! She had dreamed of it, and now it was going to come true. Living in town on a banker's salary!

As soon as she could control her laughter, she said quickly, before the agitated little man could protest more, "You old sugar, you! You just try me, and see if I can't get along on your salary."

Minnie couldn't wait to be married. She wasn't sure what her brother would say, and she knew that her deserted father would be furious. She urged Virgil on, fearful that he might escape her. They drove immediately to a justice of the peace, and they were married that night.

IV

They set up housekeeping in the big Clay house the next day. Virgil had bought a few pieces from the furniture store, living there as a bachelor, and Old Man Giles let him have a bedroom suite and some chairs and carpets on time. Minnie, used to the squalor of a farm house, and to her brother's small, sparsely furnished cottage, thought the place a banker's mansion. She was delighted. She was prepared to take her proper station in town as a banker's wife.

They had been married a week before she discovered that her husband was a janitor, not an official, at the Farmers' and Merchants' Bank. She came in to surprise him at work one afternoon, and she found him sweeping the floor.

She was surprised, but she laughed pleasantly. "Do you have to do that, too?" she exclaimed. "Why don't you get you a man to do that, Hon?"

Virgil was bewildered. "Get a man to?" he said. "They got me h'ard for it. How did you mean, get a man to, Minnie?"

Then Minnie was puzzled. "You mean you *have* to do the *sweeping out?*" she said, incredulously.

"Sure. That's my job."

"Aw, Virge, you're guying me. I know. You're the teller."

Virgil turned his distracted, cow-like gaze on her, utterly baffled.

"The teller?" he repeated absently. Then his dished face curved deeper in a slow grin. "Oh, I know, that's that old joke that Ote Fellows, down at the Sanitary Barber Shop, got out on me. It's just a joke."

"A joke?" Minnie faltered.

"Yes, it's a joke a smart aleck got up."

"But you *are* the teller in this bank. Clarence said that you was a teller in the bank the first day I came to town.

And he said it other times, too, when you was sparking me."

"Yes, sure, but it's a joke," Virgil explained patiently. "It goes like this: I'm a teller in the bank. I *tell* the customers to stand over a little so as I can sweep there. It's just a joke them barbers got out on me, see."

Minnie turned very pale. She seemed ready to faint. Virgil let his broom clatter to the floor when she swayed, and jumped forward to catch her, but she pushed him from her. Then she turned and stumped pudgily out of the bank, swollen with venom, the titters of the bank clerks in her ears.

Virgil Clay stared moodily after her. Then he picked up his broom and started sweeping again.

Minnie, livid with rage, marched up to Flynn's Pharmacy, and turned a tirade of abuse on her brother. Clarence roared with laughter. Then he tried to console her, telling her that Virge was a good man. But she flung out of the place. She did get reconciled after a time, and, since she didn't make new friends readily, she sometimes made afternoon calls at the Flynns', and Mrs. Flynn came to her house. But Minnie's rancor was a worm in her heart. She never set foot in the bank again.

Her child was born less than a year later. It was a boy, and she named it Harold, after a hired hand in Kansas who had been her first sweetheart.

Virgil was fond of the baby, but every time he went over to shake its carriage, or stooped to pick the child up, Minnie would shriek, "Don't you lay hand on that baby! Don't you touch it!" And she would rush across the room to snatch the child up, hugging it to her, glaring at her husband. He would sit, chin in hand, his sad, vacant stare on the mother and child. Minnie would rock, and coo and cluck, and the baby would gurgle. But if Virgil got up and approached the two, the little one's face would wrinkle and twist, and it would burst into strangled whoops.

"Get back yonder and sit down!" Minnie would shout, and then, consoling the baby, she would say, "Now, now, don't you fret. Mamma's not going to let no one get Mamma's own child. Don't you cry like that, or you might get your face to looking like your daddy's."

Virgil was still perplexed about his wife's sudden change in attitude toward him, after that one week of happiness. It was more than he could understand, and he went about his work more cringing and like a beaten small dog than ever.

Eight years passed, and then Old Man Flynn died on his wheat farm in western Kansas. The old man died a widower. His wheat lands had increased in value, wheat prices were good, and he had a small fortune when he died. He left each of his four sons, among them Clarence, a quarter-section of land and $15,000. But he had never forgiven Minnie, and he left her only $4,000.

Clarence Flynn immediately remodeled his house and bought a new marble soda fountain for his drug store and a large electric sign to hang out in front.

V

Minnie Clay was bloated with hatred. She had one giddy moment of telling her hot-air artist of a brother and his sappy wife what she thought of them. She got them told, and then flounced out of the Flynn house forever.

The Clay household, too, was torn with her tantrums. She declared violently that she would sue to break the will. But her distrust of lawyers and her fear of losing the sum that had been allotted her kept her from going ahead with such an attempt.

Virgil, after an interval of calm, dared suggest that she combine her legacy with his savings to buy the furniture store and undertaking parlor from Old Man Giles. Virgil had been a licensed embalmer for some time, and he had been managing the undertaking part of the business for years. Old Man Giles wanted to sell out and go to California. He was willing to let the place go at a sacrifice.

Minnie consented to invest her money in the business with surprisingly little protest. She had long been eager to escape the humiliation of being a bank janitor's wife. The thought of her boy, Harold, growing up with the stigma of being an odd-job man's son frenzied her. So she consented to change Giles's Furniture and Undertaking Store into Clay's Furniture Company and Funeral Chapel. Virgil Clay put aside his brooms and brushes and overalls at the Farmers' and Merchants' Bank, and assumed the dignity of a business man and a sole proprietor in the community.

He felt his increase in position, and, his lashless eyelids blinking rapidly, his red moon face beaming, he talked sagely about business conditions. He began attending Chamber of Commerce luncheons. There the other merchants accepted him, somewhat dubiously, as an equal, lately arrived.

But he paid dearly for his change in status. His life at home had been wretched since that unhappy day Minnie had discovered the truth about his work. At first she had expended her fury on her brother, but the more she brooded about the deception, the more she turned her hate on her abject husband. The innocent part he had played in the fraud did not soften her resentment toward him. That only convinced her that she had married a fool.

She hid from him the reason for her bitterness for several years, glaring down all his piteous questions about what was wrong. But one day she sneered at him, "You poor sap! You don't think I'd ever of married you if I'd of had any idea what you was, do you?"

Virgil gazed back at her with the hurt look in his eyes, and his lips quivered, but he did not say anything.

At last she locked the bedroom door against him, and Virgil, uncomplaining, brought a second-hand cot from the furniture store, and set it up in the shed-room off the kitchen.

Harold, his small son, whom Virgil would have turned to for companionship, accustomed since babyhood to hear his mother yell and to have her clutch him when the red-faced little man came near, was frightened by his appearance, and would scurry away the moment he came into the house. The boy could scarcely be coaxed into the same room with his father. This was Virgil's sorest wound, but he had never charged Minnie with it, even in his own mind. Gropingly, he decided that there was something about him that frightened the child.

Now the undertaker's misery sounded the depths. Minnie, having used her money to elevate him, did not let him forget it for an instant. Her recriminations became more violent than ever, and she would go screeching through the house:

"Yes, you! Yes, you! If it hadn't of been for *my* money, where would you been? You'd still been an undertaker's flunkey and a janitor in the bank, that's where you'd been. Yes, sir, a flunkey and a janitor the rest of your days, that's where you'd been. You ain't got no more pride nor git-up-and-go about you than an arnery cur. No, you ain't! And don't you say nothing to me."

Virgil cowered before her. Hunched in a kitchen chair, he would hear her through, his warped beet-face framed in his hands.

It is doubtful whether the thought of separation or divorce ever entered his mind, except the times when Minnie suggested it herself. And she, raging, would assure him that she would have put him off long ago if it hadn't been for the disgrace it would bring on Harold, her darling son.

Virgil had the profound terror of public opinion that a person of humble beginnings who has reached a respectable status always has. He would plead, with tears starting in his eyes, "Now, Minnie, don't talk like that! Please, Minnie, don't carry on like that!"

His greatest anxiety was that something would happen to bring public disgrace on his home. He bore Minnie's shrewish diatribes the more patiently because of his fear that some day her rage might prompt her to physical violence, and that his misery would then be bared before the town. He did not seem to realize that the neighbors could hear nearly everything his wife said. As long as the scenes were confined by the walls of their home he supposed them private. But he lived in constant horror of the day when the community would learn the truth about his home life. He would have suffered death more gladly. Indeed, death, in comparison, was a happy and simple matter. But even if Virgil had been imaginative enough to consider suicide, he would have rejected it, thinking of how people would talk.

Having acquired the furniture store, he soon showed that he would never make a fortune as a business man and his own boss. He was adept at odd jobs, and at working for other people. He had been able to save doing that. But having a business of his own confused him. Their living came from the slender profits of the furniture store without his ever knowing how it did.

He grew more and more moon-struck, and he walked aimlessly up and down the aisles of his store with a feather duster, unable to believe that it was all his property. His head was filled with fantastic schemes for bringing in business, ideas gleaned from trade publications. He was easily fetched by any glib salesman who came along with a novel "trade stimulator." He was attracted by bizarre and faddish furniture, and he soon had his place filled with geegaws. His stock of staple goods ran down. He knew nothing about furniture display, and the pieces were stacked about in a varnished jungle of disorder.

He had the agency for Edison phonographs, and he kept several in stock. One of his advertising schemes was to set an Edison on a table out in the front entrance of his store, and play it with the horn directed toward the street. He said that he believed music attracted business.

"Yes, sir, I'll tell you men," he said solemnly and impressively at Chamber of Commerce luncheons, "it's a proved psychological fact that music is a big trade stimulator. That's why I use the phonograph."

But buyers were strangely immune to the charm. He would pull out a comfortable chair on long summer afternoons, and sit by his phonograph, his ruddy, beaming face in his hands, staring moonily into the tin horn, painted to resemble a purple morning-glory. He played the same record, over and over. Out of the tin horn issued a sweet contralto, singing,

> Let me call you "Sweetheart,"
> I'm in love with you—
> Let me hear you whisper
> That you love me, too.

Virgil Clay's lips would move.

> Keep the love-light glowing
> In your eyes so true;
> Let me call you "Sweetheart,"
> I'm in love with you—

Virgil dreamt she sang to him.

16

A POSITION ON THE STAFF

WHEN Paul Stuart came out of his father's house that morning he was leaving his home forever. He was going only the distance of a trip he had been taking every school day for four years, and he would come back many times. But he would always come back a stranger and he would never come back to stay.

Daylight was commencing to broaden. Darkness clung to the hollows like old snow in Spring. The neat rank of poplars along the side of the cow lot nearest the house made a black grid against the glowing east.

Paul came out at the front door stretching his long, sleep-stiffened legs. He set his new three-dollar panama carefully upon his dank pompadour, tilted the brim, and stalked down the flagstone path. June was only a few days off and he was dressed for a scorcher. The early air felt cool and tonic on his scraped pink cheeks.

He opened the ornamental wire gate at the foot of the lawn, and stood hesitating by the small blackboard on the gatepost. The blackboard was trimly stenciled, "Farm Home of Jas. A. Stuart," and chalked "Fresh Country Butter & Eggs For Sale Here." Ford trucks, stacked high with egg crates and squirming chicken coops, wheezed past on the concrete slab. He stood with his hands pressed against the lean wedge of his face, waking himself more. If he had still been a high school student he could have hitched a ride into town. For that matter, if he had cared to wait an hour, he could have ridden in as far as the creamery with Buck, the hired man.

He turned his gaze toward the city's skyline. It jutted up from the dun prairie, as colorful and preposterous as a pile of toy blocks. The first rays of an unseen sun were washing in golden light the limestone spires of the Choteau Building, the chromium mast of the Drovers and Drillers Trust Company, the colored-tile turret of Petroleum Tower. Paul regarded the distant city with solemn wonder. It was always as if it had not been there the night before. Year by year, all through his boyhood, he had seen those peaks rise marvelously out of the barren earth.

"The magic city!" he murmured, "The magic city!"

This was no day for him to go thumbing a ride into town like an ordinary school boy. Resolutely he clanged the gate shut, strode out onto the concrete, skipped in front of a coughing flivver, and jumped the broad ditch on the other side. Careful of his crisp seersucker suit, he climbed the fence that enclosed the municipal airport. Down in front of the corrugated iron hangars a red Lockheed was warming up, but Paul did not swerve from his diagonal march across the landing field, lately a neighbor's cow pasture. On the other side there were uncleared hillocks thickly covered with scrub oak. He pushed along a faint trail and presently came to a broad street cut through the wilderness. The cement-encrusted board forms had not yet been taken away from the curbing and the fresh pavement was heavily coated with loose sand. White lot markers, regularly set, showed through the brush. Paul crossed a quaint stone bridge that the real estate people had built across the creek and came out into open country again through two rustic stone columns arched with a cut-out iron sign, "Wildwood Heights."

Half a mile down the road, as he was nearing the Fair Grounds, he passed a great red-brick building. For all its well-kept lawns and shrubbery, there was a barren look to the place. Its shadeless windows were stained red by the rising sun. It was the county poor house; in local euphemism, "the county farm." It was Paul's symbol of success.

He peered toward Outlaw Hill, a mile away, curving high and smooth above the plain. There at its top they had found Elisha Birdsong's body. When they turned out his thin pockets they got a piece of twine and a rusty barlow and nothing else. Old Man Birdsong, half-blood Creek pauper, crept away from the poor house at midnight. He faltered across the prairie and climbed to the highest hilltop for a dying look at his ranch. Birdsong's Ranch in 1900: two thousand acres of fine grazing land watered by the murky Arkansas. Elisha Birdsong, honest and respected cattleman, expert at making bull calves into steers, but no hand at making pastures into subdivisions. Statehood came and the boomers came. Elisha's sons and daughters were eager cat's-paws. Parcel by parcel, quarter-section by quarter-section, shysters and bankers and lease hounds and gamblers nibbled away at the Birdsong allotment. Wiser men than old Elisha poked holes in pastures that were his no more and up spouted their millions. Men of superior vision raised twenty-story skyscrapers where his ranch house had been and they built serried bungalows where his corral had been. So no real booster dared say how many millions that land was now worth, because it was sure to be worth a great deal more the next day. One midnight Elisha Birdsong, with the phlegm of death upon his eyes, looked down upon the fabulous wealth that had once been his but had never been his. The old Indian pauper, dead of exposure and eighty years, had a wisp of twine and a broken jackknife and nothing more in his thin pockets.

Oh, it made a whizz of a feature! It had been published under Paul's by-line in the following week's *Tatler*, the high school paper. "One Time Owner of Site of City Died in Poverty." Paul had the nose for news all right. Neither of the city dailies had carried a word on Elisha Birdsong's death. Paul had scooped the world. The editor of the morning *Enterprise* admitted that he had and regretted that there was no opening on the staff. But the evening *Star* had for its subtitle, "The Newspaper with a Soul." Oh, it was a peach of a yarn! Mr. Lytle, the *Star's* managing editor, told Paul that it was. Mr. Lytle was the greatest newspaper man in the State. After he read the story of Old Man Birdsong's death he promised Paul a position on the staff.

II

He saw the Fairgrounds car pull up at the end of the line. He broke into a run and came up breathless just as the motorman had finished changing the trolley. He dropped in his token before the surly motorman carried the coin box up to the other end of the car. Paul stood close to the open windows at the rear and lighted a cigarette. Smoking was still a mild adventure for him, especially smoking on a street car. He did not enjoy it very much, but it was part of a newspaper man's equipment. The smoke rolled sharp and sweet across his tongue. It gave his head a large, light feeling. He took a few more drags and flipped the butt away.

The empty car, running at top speed, careered along cool shadowed streets. Paul wrinkled his thin high nose to catch the pleasant smells of dewy lawns, bacon smoke, warm linen on sleeping porches, and gasoline from early motors that raced by with the sound of adhesive tape unreeling.

He was glad that he had caught this car. The motorman was sure enough balling the jack. If he had not caught this car he would have had to wait at the end of the line for another hour. Before six o'clock in the morning the Fairgrounds car ran on an hourly schedule. Now there was no danger of his being late the first day.

He was sorry that the motorman had not made some comment on his being out so early. Then he could have told him that he was a reporter for the *Star*. He strolled up toward the front, thinking he would begin a conversation with the motorman. Maybe he could let it slip that it would be a long time before he'd drop another token in the coin box; from now on he'd be riding dead head. He had a position on the staff. But at the next corner several passengers got on, and he decided not to talk to the motorman.

The street car filled gradually. Many of the passengers were carrying copies of the morning *Enterprise*, and they opened their papers and began to read. Paul had already developed the loathing for the *Enterprise* requisite to a loyal member of the *Star's* staff. He felt strongly tempted to move over beside one of the *Enterprise* readers and tell him what a lousy sheet it was.

The car, turning on Washington Avenue, came suddenly into an area of stark desolation. The empty streets were long, charred rows of ruin. Niggertown, Paul reflected proudly, stood as a perfect reminder of the *Star's* motto "First with the News." The *Star* had scooped the *Enterprise* on the rape story. The *Star* had scooped the *Enterprise* on the mob's forming and the riot's beginning. And later the *Star* had been the first to come forth with a civic plan for white reclamation of the burned Negro section and for segregating the Negroes in a new real estate addition. Stubborn Negro property owners had started a court fight and it was this, not lack of progressiveness, that had kept these streets standing waste since last July.

But what a scoop the race riot had been! What if he could pull a big scoop like that the very first day! He had a fleeting, delicious day dream of the second morning he came to work being called into the managing editor's office for a raise in salary. Not that he had made the scoop with any thought of getting better pay. He had done it to give the *Star* a day of triumph and because he was a natural-born newspaper man who chanced always to be near by when the big news broke. His first big scoop would prove to Mr. Lytle, the managing editor, that he had made no mistake in giving Paul Stuart a position on the staff.

III

He transferred at Main and Broadway, the center of town, and rode the North Broadway car as far as the Santa Fé tracks, where a long train of tank cars was snaking onto the main line, blocking thoroughfare. He left the street car, swung on one of the slow-moving tankers, and, emerging on the other side, hopped off at the alley that led to the *Star* building. When he came out on Third Street, around to the front, he saw the great press of the *Star*, so tall that it was on a level with the street although it was set in the basement. Its brass fittings gleamed faintly through the plate-glass window. It was silent now and Paul did not linger. When he walked into the new building's foyer he saw that the two elevator cages were still dark. As he clanged up the metal stairs the Senior Class motto ran in his head: "The Elevator to Success Is Not Running—Take-the-Stairs."

The second floor was the composing room. There was no light showing on the long black row of linotype machines and in the early morning dusk the clank of a thermostat turning on heat for a metal pot made a ghostly echo in the silent room. He paused only a moment and climbed the second flight of stairs to the large editorial room. He looked through the round windows in the swinging doors before he went in. No one was there. The place looked much more orderly than it had the day Mr. Lytle promised him the job. Western Union time showed five o'clock, straight up.

He walked over to the head of the big U-shaped table where Mr. Darling, the city editor, would sit. There, to his amazement, he saw a stack of morning *Enterprises*, moist from the press. Shocked and incredulous, his first thought was that this must be some scurvy trick played by the *Enterprise*. But how could they dare invade a sanctum where paper was never sullied with that hated name? Any conscientious reader of the *Star* knew that hostilities between the two newspapers were so bitter that the *Star* never permitted the name *Enterprise* to appear in its columns. Moreover, the *Enterprise* never mentioned the *Star* except in terms of the vilest abuse. When acknowledgment of the morning paper's existence was unavoidable the *Star*, with admirable restraint, called it the city's "second paper." Now the *Enterprise* had resorted to this sneaking insult! Paul restrained an impulse to chuck the whole batch into the wastepaper basket. He picked up a copy to look at the latest AP reports. Time was passing slowly, so he turned to the syndicate stuff. Then he glanced at the *Enterprise* editorials and read a few of its local stories.

He began wondering whether the *Star* expected to get out a paper that day. He finished sports and turned to the *Enterprise* woman's page. At a quarter to seven, when he was starting on the *Enterprise* want ad section, Mr. Darling, the lank city editor, came in. Paul tossed the *Enterprise* down hastily and guiltily, but Mr. Darling's greeting was cordial. He was glad to see that Paul was an early bird. It took early birds to get out an afternoon newspaper.

Paul felt encouraged. He was about to call Mr. Darling's attention to the taunting pile of *Enterprises* on his table when the city editor said, "Well, Paul, I can see that you catch on fast,—reading the morning paper the first thing. Good work! Read it all the way through?"

Paul stammered, "Why, no, sir, not *all* the way through. That is, I just sort of skimmed through, reading the headlines while I was waiting."

"Well, from now on read it all. Best thing is to get an *Enterprise* on the way to work and read it on the car coming down. Then you'll be all set to follow up the night's developments from the moment you reach the office."

The city editor seated himself and fell upon the pile of morning papers with long bright shears. Soon he called Paul over and handed him a sheaf of clippings. "Give me three or four lines on each of these. Simply reduce each story to the fewest possible words. It's for our news briefs column, 'Star Points.' "

Paul, puzzled and sheepish about lifting the *Enterprise's* stories, took the clippings over to the typewriter bench. While he labored, making quarter-column pieces into short paragraphs, the rest of the staff drifted in. A pimply office boy, yawning and picking his nose, distributed the *Enterprise*, a copy to each desk, and examined paste pots. Men, all of whom looked either very young or very old, came in one by one and snapped on lights over desks. They sat down wearily and fed copy paper into typewriters and leaned back, reading the *Enterprise*. A pretty girl with stodgy ankles plopped a large purse down on a near-by desk. Paul recognized her as Dixie Dawn, the *Star's* sob sister, because he had seen her picture in the *Star* so often. A horse-faced woman breezed through with a glint of eyeglass and a trilling "Cheerio, everybody!" and disappeared behind the frosted-glass door marked "Mrs. Caperton, Society." The office quickened when Mr. Lytle, the managing editor, bulged through the doors with his palm beach coat over one arm, fanning himself with his stiff straw hat. Mr. Lytle, a short, plump man, was already sweating hard.

Someone at Paul's elbow said in a peevish, squeaky voice, "Would you mind moving to some other typewriter? I'd like to use mine now." Paul looked up and saw a sharp, freckled man with pink hair. Hard brown eyes centered on him with all the intensity of a burning glass. He hopped up quickly, ripped his paper out of the machine, and apologized for having ignored the grimy label above the keys: "Fowler's Personal Mill. All Others Lay Off."

Paul moved to another typewriter. The long bench was banked with half-a-dozen machines set in wells so that their platens were on a level with the table top.

Soon Mr. Lytle came out of his glassed-in office. He strolled past, patting with a handkerchief his boiled, beaded forehead. He paused in front of Fowler's typewriter.

"How's that bribery yarn coming, Steve?" he said, low-voiced.

Paul pricked his ears. It dawned on him suddenly that he was actually sitting at the same bench with Steve Fowler, the greatest newspaper reporter in town, author of the sensational "Secret Agent No. 13" series of exposés on the city's narcotic and white slave traffic. Six feet away from him Steve Fowler was writing today's headliners! He must have been blind, not to have recognized at once the name on that typewriter label. Steve Fowler!

Fowler jerked his peaked face upward and gave Mr. Lytle a preoccupied glare. After a moment he said crankily, "Didn't I tell you I'd turn that story in by noon today?"

"That's not the point!" Mr. Lytle said in a vexed undertone. "The *Star* can't afford to go off at half-cock on a yarn like that. If necessary, you'd better take another day or two and check the evidence."

"Listen, Lytle, are you trying to impugn my accuracy? I'm not accustomed to turning in stuff I can't back up, am I?"

"No, I'm not questioning your accuracy, Steve," Mr. Lytle said fretfully. "I'm just telling you to check every angle before—"

"Say, do you want the story, or don't you? If you don't, to hell with it. If we don't break it tonight, it's a hundred to one the *Enterprise* will have it spread all over their front page tomorrow morning. Then watch the *Star* try to climb on the bandwagon!"

"Well, all right, Steve," Mr. Lytle panted, moving away. "But I was just cautioning you against the danger of libel."

It was hell, having to brief piddling little items with *news* simmering six feet away. But what a load of the inside stuff a man got when he had a position on the staff!

IV

At the end of a tortured hour Paul had finished the briefing. He carried his copy over to Mr. Darling with a sick hope that he would be rewarded with something on which he could unleash his originality. He wanted something about Steve Fowler's speed.

The city editor droned, "All through? That'll be your first job every morning. You'll have to get so you can do it more quickly. Now let's see what I've got for you this morning." He studied the assignment sheet.

"Here's a good yarn for you. August Schmidt, who runs a butcher shop over on the corner of Fifteenth and Cortez, is being sued for $10,000 breach of promise by Minerva Lovett, a madam residing at the La Plaza Rooms, 412½ South Broadway. Schmidt has been living with his legal wife all the time and still is. The *Enterprise* carried the story this morning, so take this clipping. Now go tell Schmidt that the *Enterprise* only played up Minerva Lovett's side of the story, and that we're anxious to see that he gets a fair deal. Get him to talk and explain how he got himself into this mess. Then go to the La Plaza Rooms and give Minerva Lovett the same line. The *Enterprise* beat us on the story, because it was a late filing. But what we want to do is get the human slant into it. Play up the humor of the situation.

"Now what else? Yeah. Twila Jean Frisbee, 19, attempted suicide by taking poison in the Dreamland Theatre lobby last night. Probably some publicity hunting little tart. It doesn't matter. Go over to Morningside Hospital and ask her why she did it. Get the love angle in it if you can, but don't give it much if she was out of work. The *Enterprise* didn't have but a paragraph on it, but here's a clip of what they had. The human slant is what the *Star* wants.

"That ought to hold you. Don't forget the noon edition deadline. You ought to be back in the office a little after ten. Wait a minute, though! On the way back, drop in and see Colonel Osborne K. Biggers, 1401 Petroleum Tower, and ask him how work is progressing on the new 25-story Coronada Hotel. Ask him how soon they expect to finish the steel work. Ask him whether he thinks the Coronada will be ready for occupancy in time for the Elks' Convention. That's all now. When you get back I'll have a luncheon assignment for you. A free feed; that'll help out. And here's your street car pass book."

Paul walked buoyantly out through the swinging doors. He rang for the elevator in the hall. When he reached the street the presses had started, grinding out the bulldog edition. A line of small boys and loafers stood with their faces flattened against the plate glass, watching the papers cataract out of the folder.

Paul hurried along Third Street toward Cortez Avenue with prancing steps. He held his head up, flushed with pride. This was the day! It had come at last!

He pitied the people he passed because they had no way of knowing that they had brushed elbows with a newspaper man. He was the proudest, happiest, luckiest guy in the whole city. He had a position on the staff.

V

He found Schmidt's Market on the corner of Fifteenth Street and Cortez Avenue. It was a neat butcher shop gleaming with white enamel and polished refrigerator display cases, but the floor, old-fashionedly, was carpeted with clean, fragrant sawdust. August Schmidt, with white, close-cropped hair, moustache, scrubbed red face, smooth-aproned belly, looked like a man in a Liederkranz ad. As soon as Paul explained that, as a reporter for the *Star*, he thought that the story in the morning paper had given Mr. Schmidt a rotten deal and that the *Star* wanted to present Schmidt's side of the story, the butcher grew garrulous with a strong German accent. The only other person in the store was a pleasant-faced, rather pretty woman, not so old as Schmidt, but middle-aged, neatly dressed and slight. She did not speak. Paul assumed from her worried expression that she was Mrs. Schmidt. The old man bellowed that he was being blackmailed.

When Paul left the shop he halted at a high brick terrace on Cortez Avenue to jot down notes of what Schmidt had said. While he was scribbling on his pad of folded copy paper he was startled to hear someone call, "Hello!" He turned and saw at his side the woman who had been in the meat market. She was crying.

"Please give August the best of it, son," she begged. "It was not all his fault. He is so simple, like a child. I was away to my sister's on a visit in the country, or he never would have got into this terrible trouble. Every thing we have in the world is tied up in our shop, and our business this scandal will ruin. So won't you treat him as fair as you can? That is all I ask, so little."

"I sure will, Mrs. Schmidt," Paul said fervently. "I'm going to see to it that your husband gets a square deal before the public. That *Enterprise* story was mean and malicious, and we're going to try and counteract the damage it did in the next issue of the *Star*. You just remember that the *Star* is 'the newspaper with a soul,' and don't you worry."

The woman grasped his hand. "Bless your heart!" she said, smiling with the tears on her cheeks. She turned and walked away. Paul, with a powerful feeling of virtue and justice, boarded a street car.

The entrance to the La Plaza Rooms was marked by a small electric sign at 412½ South Broadway, next door to a second-hand furniture dealer's. He took the rubber-treaded stairs three steps at a time. On the second floor he came to a small anteroom filled with a short counter, a set of pigeon holes, and a few rocking chairs. He saw no one about. He walked over to the counter and banged the plunger on a large call bell. There was a sound of a door opening down the hall and he heard the approaching shuffle of slovenly feet. A slattern wearing a pink boudoir cap and a dingy bathrobe appeared and went behind the desk. Her belly, round as a friar's, bulged away from the bathrobe cord. Hanks of hennaed hair escaped her lacey boudoir cap.

Paul said politely, "I wanted to see Miss Minerva Lovett."

The woman opened her mouth and with the tip of her tongue deliberately pressed her gray teeth into place. "I'm Minerva Lovett," she said, her swimming leaden eyes intent upon him.

"Oh!" Paul said in surprise. "Well, Miss Lovett, I'm from the *Star*, and—"

"Yeah, I know!" the woman barked. "Well, I ain't got no statement to make, see. My lawyers is taking care of that. I do all my talking in court, see?" She came around the counter with her arms out, as if she were going to shove him. Paul backed toward the stairs, tongue-tied. "Get on out! See? Get on out!" she yelled, grasping him by the shoulders and shoving him toward the stairs.

Paul came out onto the bright street feeling cowardly and humiliated. After all though, he reflected, a newspaper man must be prepared to come into contact with all sorts of people. People who wouldn't even know what 'a position on the staff' meant. He shrugged his shoulders. He thought of how splendidly he was going to champion the cause of old August Schmidt. The thought restored his dignity. He set out for Morningside Hospital.

He had to wheedle several minutes before the head nurse would admit him to the ward where Twila Jean Frisbee lay. "Nothing wrong with her," the head nurse, a crag of a woman, kept snorting. "I wouldn't give her the satisfaction. That's all she done it for, just to get the publicity. She's not hurt. We're getting her out of here this afternoon. Don't quote *me,* though!" The head nurse softened only when Paul explained that it was his first day on a newspaper and that he had to make a good showing.

Twila Jean Frisbee was a pretty girl with attractions that hospital sheets accentuated rather than concealed. Her brunette corkscrew curls were carefully fanned out on her pillow. The splotches of orange rouge on her cheeks and the two pinkish acid burns trailing down from the corners of her mouth gave her pallid face a curious clownish appearance. Oh, yes; she had a job; or hoped she still had. Car hop for the Puritan Fountain, Veronica and Twenty-third. Her boy friend, one of the soda jerks, had started trifling on her. That had made her tired of life. But she seemed quite cheerful about her bitter experience. She brought out a photograph of herself from her vanity case. She thought that the *Star* might like to use it. She spoke with all the perkiness of a street urchin. Soon she was interviewing Paul. Tall boys with blue eyes had always been just her type. She borrowed his pencil and paper to take down his 'phone number. Paul, discomfited and secretly doubtful as to whether a newspaper man should permit himself to be compromised in this fashion, edged away from her bedside. But he said, sure, he'd be glad to have her give him a ring as soon as she got well. Twila Jean Frisbee clasped her hands and rolled her narrow dark eyes and exclaimed that now she really and truly had something to live for.

Paul made for the door. She called after him, "Just tell your readers that I done it for love, dearie! But say that I'm going to get well and live, 'cause I've already found me another sweetie. Hot cha! Boo-pa-doop! I'll see you in my dreams!"

Paul grinned and blushed and his voice sounded faint when he tried to make it pert. "What kind of dreams?" he asked.

"Oh, boy!" cried Twila Jean Frisbee. "That's for a certain party to find out!" The sheeted curves wriggled.

As he left the hospital, Paul felt that he was retreating again. He strove to regain his composure. But he was still thinking of Twila Jean Frisbee when a Petroleum Tower elevator was carrying him aloft to the fourteenth floor and the renowned building promoter, Colonel Osborne K. Biggers. Impersonal thoughts of her, however, because above all he was a newspaper man.

"That lead is ready-made," he was thinking. " 'Please tell your readers that my desperate step was prompted by love for a man,' moaned beautiful Twila Jean Frisbee, 18-year-old car hop, of 1476½ Railroad Ave., as she lay on her bed of pain in Morningside Hospital today after having swallowed two ounces of carbolic acid in the Dreamland Theatre lobby at 11.15 last night.'

"Yes, sir," he murmured, "there's my lead, ready-made."

VI

When he got back to the office, he wrote Twila Jean Frisbee's story first, because the lead paragraph was ready-made. He saved the Schmidt interview until last, because he wanted to give that everything he had. It was going to take skill and careful thought to get that Schmidt story just the way he wanted it. He aimed to pack a lot of humanity into that Schmidt story. He had a vision of justifying poor old August Schmidt, the honest butcher, before a cynical world, and of saving the Schmidt home and business. A lump came into his throat while he was thinking about it.

He wrote three hundred words on Twila Jean Frisbee's misadventure in love, putting a lot of humanity into that, too. But he was not really lavish with the humanity, because he was conserving it for the Schmidt story.

The Frisbee girl's story off to the slot, he turned to the mimeographed press release that Colonel Biggers had urged on him at the close of the interview. Every smidgeon of news about the new 25-story Coronada Hotel had been printed and reprinted in a hundred elaborate articles, but it was still spot news for civic-minded readers. It was a routine booster story, however, and Paul was eager to have it out of the way before he started his day's masterpiece. He gave the Coronada Hotel developments a couple of pages.

As he was feeding paper into his typewriter, all ready to knock out a shotgun lead on the blackmail plot that was wrecking the life of August Schmidt, the hands of the Western Union clock were creeping close to eleven, deadline for the noon edition. He stared at the crisp gray copy paper in a panic. Every adjective, every noun, every word that he had ever known had vanished from his mind as utterly as if he had slipped back to babyhood. He rattled the space bar. He rubbed his forehead so hard that it ached.

Mr. Lytle, the roly-poly managing editor, spanked-bottom face gleaming, dead cigar pasted on his rolling under lip, loomed in front of him. "Having trouble, Stuart? Trying to meet this deadline?" he asked, sympathetically.

"Yes, sir," Paul said, too miserable to be awed.

Mr. Lytle gave him a fatherly, understanding smile. "Let me have your chair. Now what's your story, son?"

Paul outlined it to him with sinking heart. He could not summon courage to tell Mr. Lytle that he had the story all planned. He read his notes tremulously.

"Hah! This is rich!" Mr. Lytle said with a pontifical belch that displaced his dead cigar. He began a furious pecking of the keys, reading aloud as he wrote: " 'While wifie is away hubby will play. This is the philosophy of August Schmidt, 62, butcher, Cortez Av. and Fifteenth St., if allegations set forth in a $10,000 heart balm suit brought late yesterday by winsome Miss Minerva Lovett, proprietor of the La Plaza Rooms, 412½ South Broadway, are true. 'Dot voman iss blackmailing me!' cried August, slashing murderously at a beef quarter with his huge butcher knife, when informed of the suit by a *Star* reporter this morning. This charge, however, does not extricate the irate butcher from the unique situation of having allegedly plighted his troth to another woman while yet married to and living with his legal spouse. 'August never would have got into this vampire's toils had I not been out of the city on a visit,' sobbed Mrs. Schmidt . . . !"

The managing editor typed "30," ripped the last page out of the typewriter, and glanced at the clock. "See there!" he exclaimed triumphantly. "Four minutes till eleven and all through! I just wanted to give you a little demonstration of how to meet a deadline, son. You'll get the swing of it pretty soon. We took only ten minutes on that, and we've got a corking good story here, Stuart. It's got what it takes to make a good news yarn,—that human element."

VII

Paul lunched in the Venetian Grill of the Hotel Planters with the Kiwanis Club. Feeling well-filled with varnished buns, red-oiled lettuce, chicken-fried steak, and a thirty-minute sermon, "The Kiwanism of Christ," by the Rev. Herman Roscoe Cartwright, the militant modern minister from Washington Avenue Baptist Church, he 'phoned in a short report of the luncheon. Mr. Crosby, the re-write man, switched him over to Mr. Darling, the city editor.

Over the 'phone Mr. Darling said, "Go over to the court house and report to Steve Fowler. You'll find Steve in Judge McClaren's court, where Matt Cline, head of the Cline outfit, is on trial for bank robbery. We're putting you on the court house run under Fowler now. We'll expect you to take a great deal of the routine stuff off his hands. Steve'll explain your duties to you and 'll introduce you around. Come in around three o'clock so that you can catch the home edition deadline. Call in if you get anything hot."

His heart thumped high in his chest while he walked six blocks over to the county court house. He must have made a good impression after all. His deadline ague had not given Mr. Lytle a bad opinion of him; else he would not have been put on a run with Steve Fowler, the best reporter in town. Landing a position on the staff had seemed pretty good. Sharing a run with Steve Fowler made it perfect.

He picked Fowler out in the crowded court room. The freckled, sharp-faced man was sitting over at the press table within the enclosure. Fowler greeted him with a friendly whisper, his morning pettishness forgotten, and beckoned Paul to follow him out of the court room. Paul noticed with deep shame that he was a head taller than the great man. His own height seemed an impropriety.

"Nothing going on in there, anyway," Fowler said in his high, waspish voice when they were out in the marble hall. "I'll take you around and introduce you to the common pleas judges and the humane officer and the sheriff and some of your other news sources here. Most of it's simply routine,—covering petty arraignments, getting the marriage licenses, divorce petitions, damage suit filings from the county clerk's office every afternoon, and so on. But keep your eyes open for anything hot. Lots of times an item that seems insignificant will cover a big news break. And watch out for Bryan Rogers, the *Enterprise* man on this run. He's a double-crossing bastard."

They made the rounds of the county offices. On Fowler's introduction Paul shook hands with judges, clerks, county politicians, lawyers, bondsmen, and stenographers. Some of the names he heard were often in print and locally famous. Steve Fowler spoke to these great men with easy familiarity. Paul saw in him the ideal newspaper man, and he was dazed with hero-worship. They took the elevator to the county jail on the top floor and the county jailor pumped Paul's hand and conducted them down a reeking corridor to the cell where the Cline outlaw band was behind bars. They descended to the third floor and Steve Fowler delayed a marriage ceremony while Paul shook hands with Judge Carroll, who held the State record of having united in holy wedlock more than one thousand couples.

Between offices Paul thought up questions about the craft and put them to Fowler timorously. He drank in the dogmatic replies. No, Fowler didn't believe that shorthand gave a reporter any advantage. He'd never seen a newspaperman of any account who could write shorthand. Nor touch-typewriting, for that matter. Lytle? Lytle was a son of a bitch; still it took a son of a bitch to make a good managing editor. But Steve Fowler said that he hated Lytle's guts and he said it with a thin savagery that left Paul awestruck and speechless for a few moments.

"Lytle's been riding me for two years. I don't know whether it's jealousy, or what it is. He knows I wouldn't go over to the *Enterprise*, because I hate old Breckenridge over there even worse. And he knows I can't leave town, because I've got an invalid child who's too frail to travel. So he thinks he's got me. But some day he's going to ride me once too often, and I'm going to coldcock the bastard with a pastepot.

"Now I'm taking you in to meet Sheriff Blodgett. He's dumb as hell, but he's honest and good-hearted and he's too dumb to be scared of anything. He's the man who captured Matt Cline single-handed. He's in a position to give you plenty of tips, so keep on good terms with him. The *Star* elected him, so he's under plenty of obligation to us."

VIII

Paul left the court house in time to catch the home edition with the vital statistics.

When he had turned in his copy, Mr. Darling, the city editor, said, "Now, I've got a feature for you to write. When you get through with it you'll be done for today. What I want is a good human-interest yarn for Decoration Day. Take a South Broadway car to the end of the line and walk out to the new Angelus Memorial Park. Here a while back the United Daughters of the Confederacy had sixteen Civil War veterans dug up from Oaklawn Cemetery and re-interred out in Memorial Park. Work in some good description of the beauties of these old heroes' new final resting place. Tell about the beautiful drives and shrubs. Mention the new modernistic monument to World War veterans in the center of the burial park. How peaceful and quiet and modernly arranged the new Memorial Park is. This is to tie up with a burial lot sale they're starting on Decoration Day, and they've got a big advertising appropriation. So you see the importance.

"After you've visited the burial park and stood at the graves of these old Confederates, call up Mrs. Mainwairing Johnston, president of the local U.D.C.; and get a statement from her about her organization's Decoration Day plans. Have her tell you about the descendants of Confederate soldiers who are living here in the city. Bring in the fact, young as it is, this city has already developed a deep social and cultural background. Remember your human slant. That's what we want for the *Star*."

IX

It was after five o'clock when Paul got back to the office with his notes for the Memorial Day feature. The hot office, littered with crumpled copy paper, ticker tape, and shredded newspapers, was almost deserted. The lights burned on over empty desks. Crosby, the make-up man, dashed in and out on errands to the composing room, making up the final peach edition. The city editor and all the reporters had gone, but Mr. Lytle was still there. He was pacing the floor, champing his dead cigar. He ignored Paul. Paul could see that he was in a rage.

Paul sat down at a typewriter. He felt pretty tired. He picked up the city edition and looked through it, but he couldn't find any mention of Steve Fowler's bribery yarn. He had written five or six practice leads for his Decoration Day story, ripping out and crumpling copy paper with great prodigality, when Fowler came hurrying in. Fowler nodded toward him and sat down at his own mill. He slapped down a pad of notes and began typing rapidly.

The moment he had heard the elevator stop at the floor, Mr. Lytle, heavy man though he was, had moved quickly and stealthily back to his corner office. Soon he slipped out again, bearing a pasted length of typed copy paper, several pages long. Paul, his mind intent on composing an exceptional lead for his Decoration Day feature, watched the managing editor without really seeing him.

Mr. Lytle crossed the room silently. He tiptoed up to the long table where Steve Fowler sat typing. He tossed the length of copy paper down in front of Fowler. Steve glanced up sharply.

"Fowler," Mr. Lytle said in a hoarse voice, "this story is libel. I should think that by this time you'd have learned something about libel law, even if your common sense didn't tell you that this story's libel. We can't print this story. If you had slipped this story past on me, we'd have been in a libel suit with the Moffat Oil Company, our biggest advertising account, tomorrow morning."

"You knew what the story was," Steve Fowler said, his high-pitched voice rising to a scream. "Why didn't you admit in the first place that you didn't have the guts to print it, instead of yammering around now about libeling some little two-bit oil company? That story'll break before the week's out, and it'll carry a Washington date line. Then where'll you be with your God-damn' little holy cows?"

Mr. Lytle's round pudgy face was throbbing with blood. "I've told you and told you that you'd better watch your step!" he bawled, ignoring the questions. "Look at that story you turned in on that rape case last Summer. Started the race riot. Burned out twelve city blocks. Cost the lives of God knows how many people, white and black. White mobs standing shooting down nigger women and children as they ran from flaming homes. And the blood is—"

Mr. Lytle's furious words trailed off. He stood there with his plump lips slightly parted, flicking at them with his tongue tip. The silence in the large room was so absolute that the roar of the presses in the basement came seeping up like far-off Summer thunder. Paul looked on in stark horror.

In the midst of this ghostly silence, intensified by street noises drifting in through the open windows, Steve Fowler had risen slowly from his chair. With a pair of long office shears clutched dagger-wise, he began creeping around to the other side of the long table, where Lytle stood. His face was as colorless as a water blister. He slid slowly along the table, guiding himself with his free hand. His lips were skinned back so tightly that they seemed to have been cut away from his stained teeth. His hot eyes did not leave the managing editor's face for an instant. He pulled himself along the table edge as slowly and horribly as a legless man.

When Mr. Lytle began quavering faintly, it was as if someone had shouted in the silent room. His great bald face looked like something that had been under a board. Sweat drops popped out on it like a drunkard's tears. He whimpered, "I take that back, Steve. I didn't mean what I said, Steve. I apologize."

Fowler did not stop moving. He came on relentlessly with the long scissors gripped dagger-wise in his right hand. "Go on back and finish your story, Steve," Mr. Lytle pleaded. "I lost my temper for a minute there and I didn't know what I was saying. I'm a God-damn' liar, Steve. I admit I lied and I apologize."

Fowler had reached the end of the table. Lytle cried out from the depths of his great stomach, "I know it was my fault about that rape story. I confess it! It was the play I gave it in the final peach that started the trouble. I made the streamers too wild. All my fault, Steve. I lied when I placed any particle of blame on you, Steve!" He wrung his fat, stubby hands in a frenzy of fear.

Steve Fowler stopped abruptly. He was about a foot away. He straightened up and snorted briefly. He studied the scissors for a moment and then tossed them down on the table. "Oh, what a dirty, lying traitor I work for," he said in a sad voice. "I turn in the biggest scoop I ever made in my life, and he trots out to quote me a last year's *Enterprise* editorial."

Mr. Lytle began waggling his head vigorously, "I certainly am a dirty liar, Steve. I had no right to say what I did. You're the best man we've ever had on the staff, Steve, and I can't quarrel with you. Let's shake hands and let bygones be bygones. How can we get out a paper, sore at each other like this?"

Fowler turned his back on Lytle's outstretched hand. "O.K., Lytle," he said.

Mr. Lytle went into his office and came out with his hat and coat. He walked toward the swinging doors. As he went out he called pleasantly, "Good night, Steve!" Fowler grunted without looking up from his typewriter. Paul, his mouth still gaping, noticed that Mr. Lytle left a glistening line of wet tracks across the linoleum.

X

Long after Steve Fowler had finished and had gone for the night, Paul sat alone in the office poring over the typewriter, trying to concentrate on his Decoration Day feature. The early Summer sun reached the level of the third-floor windows. Hot, ruddy light floated in on a stream of dust motes. It was not long until sunset.

Suddenly Paul remembered the glorious feeling that he had had on coming to work that morning. He tried to put it out of his mind, but the memory would not go away.

"Success stuff!" he snorted. His voice sounded melodramatic, mocking him in the empty room. He jerked his head and stared at his notes on his interview with the United Daughters of the Confederacy president.

He got up and went over to the water cooler, and drew himself a drink. As he stood drinking, feeling the cold thin blade of water sink into his hungry stomach, the insidious, taunting memory of his brief day dream about making a scoop and getting a raise, the one that he had had on the street car early in the day, returned to him. His lip curled up.

"God!" he breathed, "God, what a sap I was at that age."

17

FAMILY TWIG

THE DINNER conversation had dealt briefly with Soviet Russia through the soup. It came around to eugenics with the meat. Mr. Mims sat forward in his chair eagerly and kept his lips parted, because this, he felt, was a subject really worth talking about. Mr. Mims, a small man with pale eyes and a shadowy mustache, enjoyed few subjects more than family trees and sterilization statutes and breeding for brains. He had some carefully-thought-out comments of his own to make if he were ever given half a chance.

Mr. Mims, to tell the truth, had managed to bring up the eugenics topic himself. He had more guile than innocence when he wondered out loud, but mildly, how the Soviet government stood on breeding up the race. Then that sturdy fellow up near the host had pounced on the subject, and snatched it away from him, leaving Mr. Mims back in the röle of listener. Mr. Mims seemed always to find himself listening nervously at the very moment he wanted very much to say something.

He felt particularly secure about this eugenics subject, because his own mother had been a Bradford: traced her lineage straight back to old William Bradford of Plymouth.

"Now, you take me," he was fond of imagining himself interrupting boldly. "My grandfather traced his ancestry straight back to old William Bradford, the second governor of Plymouth Colony, although I bear the name of Mims. My father's name was Mims. Whirlwind courtship and elopement, y'understand."

He often thought that he would break out with *that* some time.

That sturdy fellow who was holding forth up near the head of the table. Mr. Mims almost sneered openly. He called himself Evans, the sturdy fellow did, but he might very easily have been a Kallikak, Mr. Mims thought. He detected degeneracy in the fellow's loose mouth and slanting forehead.

Evans, it appeared, was all in favor of eugenics. He had been reading a book lately: *The Fruit of the Family Tree.* Pretty apt title, eh? Well, by Jove, there were the facts all spread out for you, and it was high time America was waking up to them. The tide of morons was rising steadily while the fine old families were petering out. The sturdy Evans adjured everyone at the table who had not read *The Fruit of the Family Tree* to do so at once. They'd learn for themselves what this country was up against.

Mr. Mims bowed his head and made little passes at his faint mustache with his napkin. In a minute, now just as soon as Evans paused for breath, he would speak out in a ringing voice: "That's all very true, but now you take my own case. I come from *Mayflower* stock, although my name is Mims. . . ." That ought to hold them. Petering out, indeed!

II

Evans slowed down a bit, searching for more emphatic words, and Mr. Mims swallowed and put down his fork in anticipation. He glanced up. Now was his time. Evans had gone back to his food.

"Now, you, uh," Mr. Mims began with a dry mouth. The enthusiastic young man with spectacles across the table from him beat him to the breach, however, the same young fellow who had had so many figures on the Five-Year Plan handy to crush opposition a short while before.

"Personally, I think this eugenics stuff is a lot of applesauce," the young man was saying in a positive voice. "I know that book, *Fruit of the Family Tree*. That fellow Wiggam, who wrote it, has no scientific standing whatsoever!"

Mr. Mims leaned forward, his small gray eyes intent on the young man across the table. He was going to say: "Yes, but I come from *Mayflower* stock, for example," but he had no more than got his mouth open when the young man looked away again and went on, talking in the direction of Evans.

"You simply can't breed human beings for character and intelligence in the same way that you breed race horses for speed," the young man continued. "There's where the fallacy lies. It won't do at all. Human behavior is too much a matter of environment."

"Ah, but environment isn't—" the sturdy man began.

"Now, you take—" said Mr. Mims hoarsely at the same moment.

No one heard him, because the young man took the conversation away from Evans. Mr. Mims was glad, at any rate, that that fellow Evans had met his match.

The enthusiastic young man said: "What these fake eugenicists do is simply take the evidence they want, just what suits their purpose, and let all the rest go. Take that study of the Jukes family; that's all been exploded. For that matter, what were some of the first families of America? Convicts! And what does a *Mayflower* ancestry signify, when you come right down to it?"

The young man blinked in rhetorical pause. Mr. Mims pursed his lips and frowned. Now, now; was this any way to talk? This was going a bit too far. He began: "Yes, but take me—"

The plump girl on his left smirked and exclaimed roguishly: "I guess the *Mayflower* must've been as big as the *Aquitania* if it *did* bring across all the ancestors people claim it did!"

"Not at all! Not at all!" said the young man loudly. "There's just my point exactly. Do you realize that if only one couple who came over on the *Mayflower* had had three offspring grow to maturity, and each of these three offspring had borne three offspring—and that's just being conservative for the sake of the argument, because they sure enough had *families* in those days—and if each succeeding generation had continued to do the same, the number of direct—*direct*, mind you—*Mayflower* descendants in this country would be, roughly, four million seven hundred thousand and some odd. Now, all those would be from only *one*

Mayflower couple. Never did stop to think of that, did you? But you can figure it out for yourself. It's just a mere matter of arithmetical progression."

III

Mr. Mims got it all right. He saw the point. All those people! Strange, he never had had that brought to his attention before. Why, nearly everyone in the country must have *Mayflower* ancestors by this time. Surely that couldn't be right. Still, figures don't lie. All those people spread out over the country like so many germs. Doctors and thugs, artists and shoplifters, Congressmen and movie stars, plumbers and professors. Nearly five million of them, just from *one Mayflower* couple. Mr. Mims closed his eyes for a moment, feeling very dizzy.

When he opened them, the plump girl on his left had turned to him and was asking with a condescending smile: "What's your opinion about it, Mr. Uh?"

He started and said: "I beg pardon?" His opinion? Everyone was silent, waiting for his opinion. Even Evans twiddled his glass morosely. Everyone turned eyes on him. Now was the moment for him to sweep them off their feet: Take me. I'm a good example. My mother was a Bradford, direct descendant of William Bradford, *Mayflower* stock, although she married a Mims.

"I said, what do you think about this eugenics idea?" the plump girl repeated, raising her voice slightly.

"What do I think?" said Mr. Mims weakly. "Why, the whole thing is staggering, isn't it? Goodness, yes; simply staggering! I'm simply staggered by it all."

18

NO MORE TRUMPETS

HIS PARENTS were waiting for him in the warden's office when he came in. His mother kissed him damply and started weeping again when he put his arms around her and patted her.

"Oh, Claude, son," she sobbed, "I prayed to God for this day, and now He's answered my prayer."

"Yeow, on the same day my parole come due—ain't it funny it happened like that?" said Claude, turning to take his father's stumpy hand. The old man hadn't found a place to spit yet, and as he shook hands his face was set and very solemn with his mouth full of tobacco juice.

Claude said, "Where's Jim?"

His father spied the warden's spittoon and stooped low over it to discharge his spattering burden.

"Jim's waiting outside in the car," his mother said, wiping her eyes.

"Couldn't get him to 'light," said the old man. He drew the back of his hand across the amber dew on his chin.

"Alice didn't come," his mother began again. "She didn't feel like she ought to in her condition." She looked down modestly. "I guess I wrote and told you Alice was expecting the stork, though."

The warden came in briskly and took Claude by the hand and clapped him on the shoulder. "Well, Mr. and Mrs. Parsons," he said in a jovial tone, "we're certainly going to miss Claude here, we certainly are."

"Thank you, Warden Hintz," said Mrs. Parsons with as much diffidence as if she were the one taking leave.

"He's made a mighty good record here, he certainly has," the warden went on, "and we're all mighty proud of him, we certainly are. His radio program has directed much attention to the work we're doing here with the boys. As I guess you know already, Claude's been assistant director of the band for the past year, and I think he plays the trumpet just as good as Professor Wetstein, the director. Oh, I don't mind saying it at all, Mr. and Mrs. Parsons, your boy's got to be a person of importance here at the reformatory. Yes, sir-ee! Right up there among 'em. Claude's a regular kind of a genius along music lines, he certainly is, and it's going to be a big loss to us to have him leave, it certainly is."

Claude wondered how long the warden was going to keep on talking, and he began to wish that he'd let loose his hand. The warden's hand was sweaty, and it was sticking to his.

Mr. Parsons mistrusted this unstinted praise of his wayward son, and he said uneasily, "Well, Warden Hintz, that's mighty fine. I guess we'd better be gettin' started, though. We're in a car, see, and we got 152 mile to go before night."

Mrs. Parsons, however, had been enjoying the warden's speech, and she bobbled her head. "Yes, Warden

Hintz, Claudie's a good boy at heart. And we certainly appreciate all you done for him here."

Warden Hintz, thus encouraged, talked a while longer, bestowing advice and praise. Claude was glad when he let go his hand, now soggy, and they moved out of the office.

Jim was sitting in the car outside the reformatory gates. He had one leg thrown up over the steering wheel.

"Hi, there, Claude!" he called.

"Hello, Jim," said Claude, shaking his brother's hand stiffly. "Hod-a-mighty! I never would 'a' known you, grown like a weed." Jim was eighteen.

Claude stepped back and looked at the automobile. He said, "You-all have bought you a new Ford, ain't you?"

"I wrote and told you we did, Claudie," Mrs. Parsons said reproachfully. "Don't you recollect I wrote and told you? Sometimes, son, I think you never did read my letters. You never did say nothing about what was in them when you wrote back."

"Yeow, I read them," Claude said, climbing into the front seat with Jim, "but I got so much other mail from them radio bugs."

The car passed through the small town at the foot of the reformatory hill, and out into the open country. It was April. Claude pulled in his belly and filled his lungs with sweet air.

"It's a great life!" he shouted to Jim, feeling the wind in his teeth.

"If you don't weaken," Jim yelled back. And they

both laughed and Jim took one hand off the wheel to slap Claude on the thigh.

His mother kept leaning forward from the back seat, wanting to talk to him. She kept putting her hands on him. He wished she wouldn't do that. It spoiled the feeling he had.

"Don't it feel grand, son, to be out in God's open air again? Just think, five years and fourteen days you've been cooped up in there!"

"Ah, Mamma, you know good and well that I've been going out on concert tours with the band ever' Summer for the last three years," Claude said.

She leaned back in her seat, but after a few moments she was at him again. "Son, don't you ever think no more about going down to the University and taking up an electrical engineering course? You know that Robertson boy, that was in your class at high school with you, finishes this year down at the University. I was just talking to Mrs. Robertson yesterday, and I was just thinking how nice it would be if you could go on to college like you was going to. You're just twenty-two. You're still young."

"Naw," said Claude shortly, "I'm going to be a musician."

"Oh, son, they ain't no living in that no more. The talkies has just took everything. Those Hibberts, I don't guess you knew the Hibberts, but they located in town, and Mr. Hibbert had such a good job playing the drum in the orchestra at the Ritz Theatre. Well, the Ritz put in talkies a year ago last Fall, and now Mr. Hibbert has been out of work for almost a year, and from all I hear they're just on the verge of starvation."

"Sure, I know, but there's always a place for a good trumpet player."

"Well, anyhow, that Warden Hintz certainly did speak high of you, didn't he, son?"

"He ought to, the old gabbo. I've just about been running the band around there. They can't do nothing with the boys in the band without me."

II

It was sundown when Jim threw the gear into second and Claude recognized the grade north of Humphrey's farm. He felt a touch of nausea as familiar places began appearing along the road.

When the car was passing Rose Hill Burial Park, his father, who had been silent most of the trip, leaned forward and pointed. "Now, Claude, if you'll look right through that clump of cottonwoods there," he said, "you can see the marble shaft they put up over that Coker boy's grave. They ought to of put him up a marble shaft, they didn't have to pay no lawyers."

"Spare us the gory details, pop!" Jim shouted.

Stewy Coker was the boy with whom Claude had robbed the filling-station that night, six years ago in June. The filling-station owner had caught Stewy between the shoulder blades with a charge of buckshot. Claude had said on the witness stand that all he was sorry for was having missed when he fired back at the man who killed Stewy.

The old man was imperturbable. He kept on talking.

"Now you can see our new skyline, Claude," he said. "Just look'e. What do you think of that? That buildin' you see goin' up acrost over yonder is the new six-story hotel they're buildin'. Now that tall white one there with the little hen coop affair at the top is the new Fidelity National Bank Buildin'. They claim they're goin' to have a moorin' mast for Zepp'lins on top of that little hen coop business you see. And all this pavement has been put in new since you was here. Oh, you wouldn't know the old town. Quite a city. Quite a city."

Jim drove the car around to the hardware store in Second Street to let the old man out. It was almost dark, and the clerk would be wanting to close up for the night. Mr. Parsons got out and went inside to check up on the cash register. Charlie Rice, the clerk, came out to shake hands with Claude.

Alice and Walter came over after supper that night. Claude had wanted to go out with Jim, but he heard the car back out of the driveway, and he knew that he was stuck. Alice was going to have a baby. My God, she was as big as a tub. He was shame-faced before her.

He had never seen his sister's husband, Walter, before. He disliked his brother-in-law immediately. He didn't like the way he shook hands, straight out from the elbow. Walter was a sleek young man with black hair pasted down so flat that it seemed to be enameled on his skull. He wore spectacles with white gold rims and he laughed unnecessarily and without humor.

After Alice had kissed Claude and had sunk down

into one of the overstuffed rockers in the parlor, Walter came forward and stiff-armed Claude's hand.

"So you're Claude, huh-huh-huh," he said, chuckling in a monotone. "Heard a lot about you. Feel like I know you a'ready, huh-huh-huh."

"Oh, yeah?" said Claude, sourly.

There was a moment's startled pause, but Mrs. Parsons, fussing around the two, filled the breech brightly with, "I wrote you all about Walter, Claudie. Walter's manager of the Great Western grocery stores here. They have five stores in town. They have stores all over the country. Walter got his place five years ago, when he was twenty-two, just your age now."

After the conversation had been drawn around to it, Walter said, "Well, Claude, what're your plans, huh-huh-huh?"

"I don't know as I got any plans," said Claude.

"Didn't think you'd have, huh-huh, but I been talking it over with Alice, I mean, Alice talked it over with me, huh-huh-huh. I often say I'm the head of the family, but Alice is the neck, and the neck turns the head whichever way it wants it to go, huh-huh-huh." Walter demonstrated this by twisting his head stiffly.

"Well, the fact is, we're letting old Krause, our meat-cutter, go at the end of the month. All our meat comes out ready-cut, anyhow, and no use us paying a expert meatcutter, huh-huh-huh. So we thought maybe you would like to take a job clerkin' in the downtown store's meat department. The job won't be open until the first, and that would give you a little time to cat around and enjoy your freedom some, huh-huh-huh. This job won't pay so much, but you could work there until you had a chanct to look around and get into something where you can follow your trade."

"Trade? What d'ya mean, *trade?*" said Claude.

"Why, didn't they learn you no trade?" said Walter, "I thought they always learned you a trade in places like that."

"Well, you've just got another think a-comin', then," said Claude. "I'm a trumpet-player and a bandmaster, and the warden will tell you I'm just as good as any in the State."

Walter said, "Oh! Ah! Well! Huh-huh-huh."

Claude stood up abruptly. "Well, I'm all wore out," he said, yawning. "I think I'll hit the hay."

Mrs. Parsons jumped up and said anxiously, "Yes, you do, son. You just go up to bed and get a good night's rest. You've had an awful hard day. I fixed your bed in Jim's room, and you just go up there and go to bed."

He climbed the stairs, unbuttoning his shirt as he went. He turned on the light in Jim's room, the room that had been his six years ago, and closed the door. He heard his mother come bustling up the steps.

She called to him, "Claudie, don't you want to take a nice warm bath tonight? They's plenty of hot water for you, and you would sleep so much better, son."

"No, mom," he said, opening the door only a crack because he was in his underwear. "I don't guess I do. I'll just turn in like I am."

"You're sure you don't want to take a nice, hot bath,

son? The heater's been on ever since we got home and they's plenty of hot water if you want it."

"No, I guess not." Why, in the Name of God, didn't she stay back downstairs? He shut the door.

"Oh, son, I forgot to put out your sleeping garments. You can wear some of Jim's. Let me get some for you." She rapped softly on the door.

"Wait! Wait till I get my pants back on!" he yelled. He scrambled into his trousers and opened the door. She laid out a pair of Jim's pajamas and went out.

He put on the pajamas and got into bed. He had been asleep hours it seemed when he was awakened by the light going on. It was Jim, come back from his date.

He blinked his eyes and Jim laughed. Claude swore softly. "Where the hell have you been?" he said finally.

"Oh, just out horsing around," Jim said.

Claude sat up in bed. "Well, I was looking for you right after supper. Jim, you know what I want you to do for me?"

"I'll bite," Jim said, peeling out of his coat, shirt, and undershirt with one motion and standing, as white and glistening as an onion, under the light.

"I want you to date me a girl for tomorrow night."

"Just any girl do?" Jim screwed up his left eye into an elaborate wink.

"Sure, any girl. Oh, I want a nice one. You know."

"Yeah, I know. Nice for what?" Jim whinnied under his breath. "All set?" he said, and snapped off the light.

He got into bed and settled himself. Then he said, seriously, "Why, yes, Claude, I think I can fix it up. Maxine, that's the gal I was out with tonight, Maxine

Davis, has got a dumb cousin visiting her, and I think she'll party all right. I'll see Maxine about it, and you-all can ride in the back seat. 'Course we don't have to say nothing about where you been the last few years."

Claude felt his blood surging up in the dark. He knew that he was getting mad. This feeble-minded brother of his was ashamed of where he'd been. The crummy little rat. " 'Course we don't have to say nothing." Why, he ought to be proud to claim kin to a man whose trumpet solos had brought praise from radio fans all over the country. Ashamed to be brother to the assistant director of the reformatory band! The little louse!

Claude waited a moment. He didn't want to blow off and crum everything. But he'd let him know. His voice quavered a little when he began talking.

He said, "You know, Jim, I just been laying here thinking about a little girl I met over to Sunset Park last Summer. See, the reformatory band went on a concert tour ever' Summer. We played over there at that amusement park for a week. We played ever' night. They was pretty strict with us, but one night we had intermission and I slipped off and went to one of these here fun houses, all kinds of trick slides and falls and ever'thing. I was all dressed up in my band uniform. We had keen uniforms. I met this little girl, Lona, her first name was. She had got separated from the party that had brought her, and I didn't have no trouble making a pick-up. We went out on the lake in a boat, and I took her over on the other side. Kur-rist, but that was one hot little mamma. I wisht I had got her to give me her last name. When we got back they was all out looking for me. They thought sure I'd went over the hill. But old Wetstein, he was in charge, he couldn't say much, because he couldn't do nothing with the band without me, and he let me get away with more'n he would the others."

There was silence for a few moments, and then Jim said drowsily, "Yeah, I guess it must of give you a big kick to get out like that once in a while."

Claude could tell that his brother was almost asleep. He said, "Yeah," and lay there in the dark, wide awake, thinking. He thought of the rustic bandstand in Sunset Park, the dreary beat of the merry-go-round's competing music, the swirling garlands of lights on the rides, the cool paths beneath the trees. He thought of the girl, the dark, rush-fringed lake, and how they had soaked their feet getting out on the other side. He remembered how his new band uniform, gold braid and scarlet, had excited her. He tried to bring to mind an image of her face, but it eluded him. He went to sleep and dreamed.

III

The next morning he woke up early, at the habitual time. He remembered where he was, and he stretched out between the cool, smooth sheets to reassure himself. Jim was still sleeping.

"This is something like it," Claude murmured to himself. Then he turned over and went back to sleep again.

When he woke up the next time Jim was out and gone. He got up and dressed slowly. The alarm clock on the dresser said 10 o'clock. He went into the bathroom and shaved with Jim's safety razor, discarding the blade, although it was scarcely dull, and putting in a new one. While he was shaving his mother called up the stairs.

"Claudie, you up?"

"Yes," he called back.

"Well, then I'll put your breakfast on for you."

"Don't bother," he said.

"Oh, yes, I set it back for you, son. It's all warm. All I have to do is put it on the table for you."

He came downstairs and picked up the morning paper as he came through the front room. It was rumpled and scattered, and he stood in the dining-room door straightening it. His mother hurried in with a platter of bacon and fried eggs, the eggs hard from waiting. There was a bowl of corn flakes and a pitcher of cream at the place set for him. He folded the paper over and propped it up, reading as he ate.

His mother hovered about. "I reckon it must feel pretty nice to get some good old home cooking, don't it, son?"

"Oh, not bad," Claude said, "but I used to feed pretty good anyhow. The band played all during meals, and we never did have to eat the regular mess. And after I started broadcasting over KRJR people sent me more stuff than I could eat. What's the matter with you-all? You-all just can't get it through your heads that I had got to be somebody in there, can you?"

When he had finished, he wiped the egg from his lips with a corner of the tablecloth, and called, "Mom!"

Mrs. Parsons appeared in the kitchen doorway.

"Mom," he said, "is my old sax still around here?"

"Why, no, Claudie, don't you recollect, I wrote to you about that saxophone. That little Spurlock boy down the street was taking lessons, and your papa got a chance to get out of it what we paid for it wholesale, so we sold it. It was just laying around here, tarnishing, and we didn't know if you'd care about it, as you wrote that you was playing a horn over there."

"Sold it!" he whined. "Well, I'll be goddam! So you went and and sold my sax, did you?"

"Claudie!" She clicked her tongue. "Don't use swear words, son!"

"Well, what am I going to use to practice on? I guess you think I'm going to set around in there twiddling with that radio?"

"Well, I don't know, son. Didn't they say nothing about letting you bring your horn home with you?"

"Naw, of course they didn't."

"Well, it looks like they might of. You know, the papers all had that big write-up about you last year. They practically just as much as said that if it hadn't been for the way you played that solo of 'My Wild Irish Rose' over the radio for the St. Patrick's Day program, that millionaire never would of bought the reformatory band them new uniforms. So they might of at least let you brought your horn home."

"Ah, how d'ya mean, bring it home? That trumpet was the property of the band. How could I take it?"

"Well, Claudie, after the crops comes in this Fall, money won't be so scarce, and maybe you can get your papa to order you a new horn then. You know, I hate to say anything about it, son, but your pa just never has got back to where we was since we finished paying off the lawyers we had for you."

"Yeow, I know how that goes."

Claude got up and went over to the blue ginger jar on the golden oak buffet, where the milk and ice money was kept. He took out a dollar in small change and went out the front door. He walked to town slowly, cutting through Burbank Park, sauntering in the shade. As he came out on the business street on the other side he noticed that the Pigeon Pool Parlor had a new electric sign. He walked past there. It was cool and dark inside, and the place was deserted.

Claude wondered how long it would be before he could get so he could handle a cue again. Old Man Funk, the proprietor, was idly knocking a cue ball about on the front table. Claude knew that he had better not start off by playing with a shark like Old Man Funk. He hesitated, but he walked on past.

At the corner he went into a red-fronted drug store and bought a seventy-five cent harmonica. He went past the open magazine rack and swiped a *Gangland Stories* magazine. When he came out he started walking toward home quickly.

That afternoon he sat out on the front porch playing the harmonica. He perfected an imitation of a railroad train going through a cut, whistling and chugging.

At four o'clock the school kids began coming past. He whistled through his teeth at some high-school girls. They looked back and giggled among themselves, and Claude called, "Uh-oh! Uh-oh! Uh-oh!" but they went on.

Then he got up and went into the house and shined his shoes and took a bath. He was sprinkling toilet water on his hair when Jim came upstairs.

"Well, ever'thing's set for tonight, big boy," Jim said. "Maxine's got this dumb cousin of hers for you. Now if the old man just don't stop us from taking out the car."

"Ever'thing's all set then?"

"All but about taking the car out tonight. I've already had it out ever' night this week. It's gettin' about time for him to howl."

"That'll be all right. Leave it to me. I'll just tell the old man we're taking it, and that'll take care of that," Claude said.

IV

It was growing dark when Jim stopped the car in front of a small house over on Okmulgee Avenue. Jim tootled the horn, and a girl, dressed in white, came bounding out across the lawn. Another girl came down the front porch steps and strolled along after her.

When the first girl came up to the side of the car, Jim said, "Maxine, I want to make you acquainted with my brother, Claude."

Maxine screamed, "Oh, how do you do," and started giggling.

Claude said gravely, "Pleased to meet you."

He got out of the front seat and came around on the other side to open the back seat door. Maxine ran around and climbed in the front seat.

The other girl came up. She had hair the color of corn tassel, her eyes were round and bulging, and her lips were painted into a pucker. She got into the back seat and Claude got in after her, slamming the door.

Jim turned around from the wheel and said, "Miss —ah, Miss—say, I never can remember your name!"

"Oh, *par*-don *me!*" shrieked Maxine. "Irene, this is Mr. Claude Parsons. Mr. Parsons, I want you to know my cousin, Irene Withers."

"Oh, she does, does she?" said Jim roguishly. "Just that hot, I betcha!"

Everyone laughed at that. Then Claude said, "Well, now we know each other, so we won't get out here and get one another mixed up," and they all laughed more than ever at that. Jim stepped on the starter and the car lurched away. Claude took advantage of the hilarity to slip his arm around the blonde.

"Baby, where have you been all my life?" he said, snuggling down beside her.

"Na-o-ow!" she drawled, glancing at him and moving away.

"What's the matter, girlie?" Claude said solicitously.

She pooched her lips. "Not while we're in town. People can see."

It was quite dark when Jim stopped the car on a side road. He shut off the engine and sighed. They sat there in the dark. Jim and Maxine exchanged casual kisses. Finally Jim said, "Well, I guess Maxine and me will get out and pick some flowers."

They scrambled out of the car and started walking off. They had gone only a short distance when they heard the girl in the back seat start saying, "You quit now! Aw, stop now, Claude!"

And then they heard her screech, "You keep your filthy hands off'n me, you goddam jailbird!"

They stopped, listening. They heard a loud groan.

"Oh, God! he's choking her!" Maxine exclaimed, running back toward the car. Jim followed her.

When they reached the car they found Claude slouched down in the bottom, moaning.

"What's the matter, Claude?" Jim said.

"Ah, the little devil kicked me in the nuts," Claude breathed.

"Why, Irene, what do you mean, acting like that?" Maxine said. "If I'd of knew you was going to act this a-way, I never would of asked you to go with us."

"Well, I don't care," said the blonde. "I'm plenty broad-minded, I guess, but I ain't a-going to let no dirty convict paw me. I got too much respect for that."

Jim turned to Maxine. "So you went and told her, did you?" he said contemptuously.

"No, I didn't, Jim! Honest to God, I didn't, Jim! I never told her nothing. Did I tell you, Irene?"

"Sure you told me, and you don't need to try and lie out of it, Maxine Davis. And I ain't a-going to let no lowdown crook try and maul me, or I'll have him throwed back in the pen where he belongs if he's not careful." She began sobbing heavily.

Claude was beginning to recover. He sat back up in the seat. "Jailbird, hunh?" he asked indignantly. "Why, listen here, girlie, you don't know nothing about me. You don't even know who I am. I'm a band director.

I play over the radio. I'm the best trumpet-player in this State. You didn't know that, did you?"

"Yah, trumpet-player!" said the girl. She quit weeping. Her scorn dried her tears. She took out her compact and began fixing her face in the dark. "I'll trumpet-player you if ever you lay hand on *me* again."

"Well, what do you want to do, Claude?" Jim said, impatiently.

"Do? Do? Why, take this little floozy back to town and dump her, of course."

They drove back in silence. Jim stopped the car in front of the bungalow on Okmulgee Avenue, and the two girls got out. Maxine stepped back up on the running board and whispered to Jim. Claude crawled over into the front seat with his brother.

He kept cursing, "Why, the dirty little tart! Why, the dizzy little slut! Calling me a jailbird! Why, she don't even know who I am. She must not of ever heard me play over the radio. I just wisht I could of had on my band uniform tonight! The goddam lousy little broad!"

Jim didn't say a word. When they reached home, Claude got out, but Jim didn't move away from the steering wheel.

"Going to drive the car back into the garage?" Claude asked.

"Nope. I'm going back around and get Maxine again," said Jim.

Claude stood watching the red midge of the tail light disappear. When it had gone, he murmured, still staring blankly, "If she'd ever seen me in my band uniform, it would of been different. She just didn't know who I was."

He sat down on the brick terrace and took out his harmonica. He began to imitate the sound of a freight train going through a cut, very softly, making the long-drawn wail of the locomotive whistle distant and mournful.

After a while his mother called out from the downstairs bedroom window, "Claudie, is that you?"

"Yeow!"

"Was that you making that noise on a French harp?"

"Yeow!"

"Come on in and go to bed, son. It's 'way past ten o'clock."

He got up and knocked the spit out of his harmonica and went into the house.